ACT OF PASSION

MANDY M. ROTH

Act of Passion (PSI-Ops / Immortal Ops) © Copyright 2017, Mandy M. Roth

ALL RIGHTS RESERVED.

All books are copyrighted to the author and may not be resold or given away without written permission from the author, Mandy M. Roth.

This novel is a work of fiction and intended for mature audiences only. Any and all characters, names, events, places and incidents are used under the umbrella of fiction and are of the author's imagination and should not be confused with fact. Any resemblance to persons, living or dead, or events or places or locales is merely coincidence.

Published by Raven Happy Hour LLC
Oxford, MS USA
Raven Happy Hour LLC and all affiliate sites and projects are © Copyrighted 2004-2018

Suggested Reading Order of Books Released to Date in the Immortal Ops Series World

Immortal Ops
Critical Intelligence
Radar Deception
Strategic Vulnerability
Tactical Magik
Act of Mercy
Administrative Control
Act of Surrender
Broken Communication
Separation Zone
Act of Submission
Damage Report
Act of Command
Wolf's Surrender
The Dragon Shifter's Duty

Midnight Echoes
Isolated Maneuver
Expecting Darkness
Area of Influence
Act of Passion

This list is NOT up to date. Please check MandyRoth.com for the most current release list.

More to come (check www.mandyroth.com for new releases)

Books in each series within the Immortal Ops World.
This list is NOT up to date. To see an updated list of the books within each series under the umbrella of the Immortal Ops World please visit MandyRoth.com. Mandy is always releasing new books within the series world. Sign up for her newsletter at MandyRoth.com to never miss a new release.

You can read each individual series within the world, in whatever order you want…

PSI-Ops:

Act of Mercy
Act of Surrender
Act of Submission
Act of Command
Act of Passion
And more…
And more (see Mandy's website & sign up for her newsletter for notification of releases)

Immortal Ops:

Immortal Op
Critical Intelligence
Radar Deception
Strategic Vulnerability
Tactical Magik
Administrative Control
Separation Zone
Area of Influence
And more…
(see Mandy's website & sign up for her newsletter for notification of releases)

Immortal Outcasts:

Broken Communication
Damage Report
Isolated Maneuver
Wrecked Intel
And more…
(see Mandy's website & sign up for her newsletter for notification of releases)

Shadow Agents:

Wolf's Surrender
The Dragon Shifter's Duty
And more…
(see Mandy's website & sign up for her newsletter for notification of releases)

Crimson Ops Series:

Midnight Echoes
Expecting Darkness
And more…

(see Mandy's website & sign up for her newsletter for notification of releases)

Paranormal Regulators Series and Clear Sight Division Operatives (Part of the Immortal Ops World) Coming Soon!

Praise for Mandy M. Roth's Immortal Ops World

Silver Star Award—I feel Immortal Ops deserves a Silver Star Award as this book was so flawlessly written with elements of intrigue, suspense and some scorching hot scenes—Aggie Tsirikas—Just Erotic Romance Reviews

5 Stars—Immortal Ops is a fascinating short story. The characters just seem to jump out at you. Ms. Roth wrote the main and secondary characters with such depth of emotions and heartfelt compassion I found myself really caring for them—Susan Holly—Just Erotic Romance Reviews

Immortal Ops packs the action of a Hollywood thriller with the smoldering heat that readers can expect from Ms. Roth. Put it on your hot list…and keep it there! —The Road to Romance

5 Stars—*Her characters are so realistic, I find myself wondering about the fine line between fact and fiction… This was one captivating tale that I did not want to end. Just the right touch of humor endeared these characters to me even more*—eCataRomance Reviews

5 Steamy Cups of Coffee—*Combining the world of secret government operations with mythical creatures as if they were an everyday thing, she (Ms. Roth) then has the audacity to make you actually believe it and wonder if there could be some truth to it. I know I did. Nora Roberts once told me that there are some people who are good writers and some who are good storytellers, but the best is a combination of both and I believe Ms. Roth is just that. Mandy Roth never fails to surpass herself* —coffeetimeromance

Mandy Roth kicks ass in this story —inthelibraryreview

Immortal Ops Series Helper

Immortal Ops (I-Ops) Team Members

Lukian Vlakhusha: Alpha-Dog-One. Team captain, werewolf, King of the Lycans. Book: Immortal Ops (Immortal Ops)

Geoffroi (Roi) Majors: Alpha-Dog-Two. Second-in-command, werewolf, blood-bound brother to Lukian. Book: Critical Intelligence (Immortal Ops)

Doctor Thaddeus Green: Bravo-Dog-One. Scientist, tech guru, werepanther. Book: Radar Deception (Immortal Ops)

Jonathon (Jon) Reynell: Bravo-Dog-Two. Sniper, weretiger. Book: Separation Zone (Immortal Ops)

Wilson Rousseau: Bravo-Dog-Three. Resident smart-ass, wererat. Book: Strategic Vulnerability (Immortal Ops)

Eadan Daly: Alpha-Dog-Three. PSI-Op and handler on loan to the I-Ops to round out the team, Fae. Book: Tactical Magik (Immortal Ops)

Lance Toov: Werepanther and vampire hybrid. Book: Area of Influence (Immortal Ops)

Colonel Asher Brooks: Chief of Operations and point person for the Immortal Ops Team. Book: Administrative Control (Immortal Ops)

Paranormal Security and Intelligence (PSI) Operatives

General Jack C. Newman: Director of Operations for PSI North American Division, werelion. Adoptive father of Missy Carter-Majors

Duke Marlow: PSI-Operative, werewolf. Book: Act of Mercy (PSI-Ops)

Doctor James (Jimmy) Hagen: PSI-Operative, werewolf. Took a ten-year hiatus from PSI. Book: Act of Surrender (PSI-Ops)

Striker (Dougal) McCracken: PSI-Operative, werewolf

Miles (Boomer) Walsh: PSI-Operative,

werepanther. Book: Act of Submission (PSI-Ops)

Captain Corbin Jones: Operations coordinator and captain for PSI-Ops Team Five, werelion. Book: Act of Command (PSI-Ops)

Malik (Tut) Nasser: PSI-Operative, werelion. Book: Act of Passion (PSI-Ops)

Colonel Ulric Lovett: Director of Operations, PSI-London Division

Dr. Sambora: PSI-Operative, (PSI-Ops)

Garth Ingersson: PSI-Operative

Rurik Romanov: PSI-Operative, werebear

Immortal Outcasts

Casey Black: I-Ops test subject, werewolf. Book: Broken Communication

Weston Carol: I-Ops test subject, werebear. Book: Damage Report

Bane Antonov: I-Ops test subject, weregorilla. Book: Isolated Maneuver

Cody: I-Ops test subject, wereshark.

Shadow Agents

Bradley Durant: PSI-Ops: Shadow Agent Division, werewolf. Book: Wolf's Surrender

Ezra: PSI-Ops: Shadow Agent Division, dragon-shifter

Caesar: PSI-Ops: Shadow Agent Division, werewolf

Gram Campbell: Shadow Agent Division, werewolf and magik

Armand: Shadow Agent Division, vampire

Crimson Sentinel Ops Division

Bhaltair: Crimson-Ops: Fang Gang, vampire. Book: Midnight Echoes

Labrainn: Crimson-Ops: Fang Gang, vampire

Auberi Bouchard: Crimson-Ops: Fang Gang, vampire

Searc Macleod: Crimson-Ops: Fang Gang, vampire. Book: Expecting Darkness

Daniel Townsend: Crimson-Ops: Fang Gang, vampire

Blaise Regnier: Crimson-Ops: Fang Gang, vampire

Paranormal Regulators

Stamatis Emathia: Paranormal Regulator, vampire

Whitney: Paranormal Regulator, werewolf

Cormag Buchanan: Paranormal Regulator, master vampire

Erik: Paranormal Regulator, shifter

Shane: Paranormal Regulator, shifter

Miscellaneous

Culann of the Council: Father to Kimberly; Badass Fae

Pierre Molyneux: Master vampire bent on creating a race of super soldiers

Gisbert Krauss: Mad scientist who wants to create a master race of supernaturals

Walter Helmuth: Head of Seattle's paranormal underground. In league with Molyneux and Krauss

Dr. Lakeland Matthews: Scientist, vital role in the creation of a successful Immortal Ops Team. Father to Peren Matthews

Dr. Bertrand: Mad scientist with Donavon Dynamics Corporation (The Corporation)

Dedication

To my readers. Thanks for all of your support. And to Mr. Mandy who read over each chapter while trying to calm my nerves (there was a lot of chocolate involved).

Blurb

Act of Passion

Paranormal Shifter Military Special Ops Romance. Book five in the bestselling series PSI-Ops!

Paranormal Security and Intelligence operative and lion-shifter Malik "Tut" Nasser's past is about to catch up to the ancient Egyptian.

When he agreed to help test a drug that could help supernaturals with control issues, he never thought it would have the opposite effect on him. So when he finds himself fighting the urge to lay claim to a human woman, he's far from prepared for what happens next.

Winning an all-expenses-paid trip to Egypt felt like a dream come true for Brooke Larner.

Everything in her life is lining up perfectly—even the handsome new man she's found herself attracted to. Before long she's handing over more than just her heart, thinking it just might be for keeps. When it doesn't go as planned, Brooke finds herself running right into the hands of madmen bent on creating super soldiers. And she soon realizes that creatures from stories and nightmares are altogether too real.

After five years of searching for Brooke, Malik has finally reached his breaking point. Already the obsession to find her left him shifting into a lion in a very public place before being forced on mandatory leave. Still, he can't get her out his mind. The suppression drugs have been out of his system for years. The burning desire for Brooke should have gone with them.

It didn't.

So when chance leaves their paths crossing once more, he realizes destiny is at play. The only problem is, she doesn't trust him and she has a secret she's willing to die to protect.

As demons from their past resurface, they find themselves in a battle to save everything they hold dear.

Chapter One

EGYPT, FIVE YEARS AGO...

MALIK NASSER STOOD in the center of a giant warehouse that he and his teammates had taken control of nearly an hour back. The lighting was low, the number of rats in the facility was high, and the smell of urine was present, as if the bad guys who owned it really wanted to commit to the evil villain aspect of it all. To top it all off, the warehouse lacked anything beyond large cooling fans, which were currently off, so it was a lot like standing in an oven. He was hotter than hell, tired of the smell, and annoyed with the entire mission thus far.

It didn't help that he'd foolishly agreed to undergo voluntary testing at PSI (Paranormal Security and Intelligence) headquarters Division

B back in the States before he'd deployed. The test was simple: try out a new drug that was supposed to help supernaturals with control issues better manage their condition. It was given to a set number with control issues and an equal number without. Since Malik never before had issues with his lion side, he figured it was a no-brainer to possibly help others who suffered.

The suppression drugs would be in his system another month or so and then he could report the effects and feel as if he'd done his part to help out.

But something felt off.

The warehouse belonged to an arms dealer who was rumored to be in possession of new weapons that could cause serious damage to supernaturals. The paranormal underground had been abuzz about it all for some time, and PSI had been chasing down leads for months. Somehow, the bad guys always managed to be at least two steps ahead.

Like now.

Crates full of weapons were packed into the warehouse. Huge, floor-to-ceiling metal shelving units filled one end, each stuffed full of crates, while the other end of the warehouse looked more like a hangar, with vehicles and free-standing crates. While everything housed in the warehouse could be deadly in the wrong hands and needed to be removed from the streets, there was nothing specific to supernaturals that had been discovered.

From all the information they'd gotten before the mission, there should have been a buttload of supernatural-threatening weapons.

So far, none had been uncovered.

They'd also encountered little in the way of security at the facility, which was extremely odd considering the number of weapons they'd found. All of which would fetch a pretty penny on the black market. It was rare that a big player in the arms game left a cache of weapons this large to be guarded by a small number of relatively inexperienced men.

Captain Garth Ingersson (head of Team Eight) came around the corner with his teammate Rurik Romanov. Garth, a six-and-half-foot-tall shifter male who hailed from the Viking Age of Scandinavia, was armed to the teeth. It looked as if the man had acquired additional guns and explosives since their arrival. Knowing the Viking as well as he did, Malik assumed Garth had probably lifted whatever he wanted from the reserve of weapons upstairs. The longer they stayed in the warehouse, the more likely Garth was to start loading their vehicles with whatever he could fit to take it home with him.

The man loved guns and weapons of any kind. He'd once spent the greater part of a day showing Malik his sword collection that dated back centuries. There was a high likelihood that the Viking liked weapons more than people.

Malik seriously worried about the man's state of mental health.

Garth was lethal unto himself. The weapons added another layer to it all. He motioned to the upper level that he and his teammate had just finished going through. "Nothing up there that should raise an eyebrow for us. Just your average, everyday asshole arms dealer bullshit."

It didn't matter that Garth had lived in the United States for centuries; he still had a Scandinavian accent that only increased when he was worked up or angered. Often, Malik found he couldn't understand the man. Garth's twin brother, Grid, had been far worse. It would have taken less time to learn the man's native language than to try to understand his English. Malik hadn't seen Grid since the brothers had a falling-out over a century ago.

Malik nodded to Garth's new toys. "But cool enough to keep a few."

"Hell yes," said Garth proudly, his grin saying he knew something everyone else didn't. "One doesn't walk away from neat toys. Find anything down here?"

Malik glanced around. "Nothing above the norm. This whole thing smells fishy to me."

"Smells like dead rats and piss to me," said Rurik, his Russian accent thick. He moved closer to Garth.

The pair began double-checking the open crates as if Malik and the other members of Team Five were incapable of telling the difference between a normal weapon and one made to harm a supernatural in a big way.

Garth pulled out an AK-47. "Oh, look. Favored by black markets everywhere."

Rurik scowled. "Do not make fun of it. It is a work of art that my country is proud of. And what I prefer to take on most missions. Reliable. Trustworthy. All you need."

"If he breaks out in song in honor of Mikhail Kalashnikov I'm going to think he's as nutty as you are," said Malik to Garth.

"Mikhail Kalashnikov was ahead of his time," supplied Rurik, standing tall as he stroked an AK-47 lovingly. "The AKM, the AK-74." A dreamy look came over him.

Malik snorted. "You need us to turn around a moment to give you some alone time with that?"

Garth moved to another crate and pulled out an MTAR. As he withdrew the 9mm suppressor made for it, he looked to Malik. "So many weapons, but so few guards."

"Agree," added Malik, surveying the endless rows of crates

"Trap?" asked Garth.

"Probably," returned Malik. "I really hate it when they try to lure us to our deaths. You'd think it would get old for them after a while."

"I've found the enemy often lacks originality," said Garth, still looking the MTAR over.

Rurik paused in his admiration of the crate of AK-47s. "Should we go?"

Malik shook his head. "And leave all this here to possibly end up on the streets and in the hands of drug dealers and criminals? Or to be used to help launch a war? No. We need to stay until a clean-up crew arrives."

"And if it is a trap?" asked Garth.

Malik grunted. "Then we do what we

always do—survive and kick the shit out of them."

While Garth technically outranked Malik, they'd been friends far longer than they'd been with PSI. There was an unshakable level of trust between them. And Garth was nearly as old as Malik, which was saying something, considering Malik was old as dirt. The men had worked together too many times to count over the years and trusted one another fully.

The same could not be said for Garth's former second-in-command, Gram Campbell. Gram was a stubborn Scotsman with a huge chip on his shoulder who fancied himself a cut above the rest of the shifters in PSI because he was part wolf-shifter and part Fae.

He was also one hundred percent asshole.

Rurik wasn't winning any personality competitions, but the man was far better to deal with than Gram had been. Malik was happy Gram had gone over to the Shadow Agents side of PSI nearly twenty years ago. It made being around Garth and his unit so much easier. Before Gram's transfer, things always ended in a fight between Malik and the outspoken male. And it wasn't as if Malik lacked patience with Scotsmen. He'd worked with Striker, who was as

Scottish as they came, for over a century now and hadn't wanted to actually kill him—yet.

Rurik pried open the crate nearest him with nothing more than his hand. He lifted a rocket launcher. "They aren't playing around," said the Russian bear-shifter, sounding like he was fresh out of the Kremlin. "I hate arms dealers. They always go for the easy money. They are probably American."

Malik hid his laugh under a cough.

Rurik had a lot in common with Malik's teammate Duke Marlow. The two pretty much hated everything and everyone. Though, Duke was an all-American man. Born and bred in the States, the man bled red, white, and blue. Rurik still missed the Cold War and the "glory days" of the U.S.S.R, reminiscing about it often. Each still viewed the other as a possible threat, and neither would admit they were just alike.

Duke came up behind Malik holding a large rocket launcher of his own. A passing glance was all he gave Rurik. "Mine is bigger."

Rurik's lips pressed together in a white slash. "Americans. And for the record, yours is not bigger. You just think it is."

Duke used his free hand to grab his belt. "One way to settle this."

Rurik faced Duke and began to undo his black cargo pants, still holding a launcher as well, a line of Russian falling free from him in the process. While Malik's Russian was rusty, he was fairly sure the man had just called Duke a dickhead before insinuating that Duke's dick was the size of a pencil.

"I hear you talking there, Ivan Drago, but the proof is in the pants. There is nothing pencil-like about my wood," returned Duke, undoing his belt fully while he still held the launcher over his right shoulder.

Rurik appeared baffled. "My name is not Ivan Drago."

Miles "Boomer" Walsh came around a set of stacked crates. While he was technically dressed in ops gear, he somehow managed to look as if he was headed to a rave, not raiding a warehouse owned by a big-time arms dealer. "Dude, it's from the movie *Rocky*. Man, even Duke has seen it and he's a damn Luddite. You should have seen how long it took me to teach him to use a DVD player."

Confusion covered Rurik's face.

Boomer shook his head, his long blue-black hair hanging to his mid-back. He narrowed his catlike violet eyes on Rurik. "We've had this talk,

Romanov. You can't understand pop culture references if you don't bother to learn about pop culture. I sent you DVDs talking about the last few decades and popular references from each. Let me guess, you didn't watch them."

"I hate DVD players," returned Rurik, undoing his pants more. "They're unnecessarily complicated. The last time I tried to watch one, strange voices played over the movie the entire time, telling me about the scene."

Duke stiffened. "That happened to me too."

Boomer pressed a fist to his mouth. "Seriously? You two realize you were watching them with the director commentary turned on, right?"

Duke growled. "Fuck you. And no, I didn't know that was what it was. I hate technology. Pointless. Plus, you're a shit teacher."

Boomer paused and glanced between the men. "Why are you guys undressing?"

Malik folded his arms over his chest. "They're about to whip out their dicks. Apparently, there is some debate on which country produces the biggest one. And how much, if anything, Duke and a pencil have in common."

Pursing his lips, Boomer put his hands up

and stepped back. "Sounds like they need a private moment here. I don't want it coming out later that I was alone in a dark warehouse with a bunch of guys who had their dicks hanging out."

"Asshole," Rurik and Duke said together, both glaring at Boomer.

"Yeah, you two are *nothing* alike." Malik stared at them.

"This is going nowhere fast," added Boomer, drawing more of their ire. He flashed a mocking smile. "And besides, you're both wrong. I'm the biggest."

"Fucking cats," snapped Duke, gaining him a nod of approval from the Russian.

"You guys are a lot like taking preschoolers on a field trip," said Malik, feeling like he was turning into his team's captain—Corbin Jones. Corbin often referenced how dealing with them all was like handling small children. He was starting to see the guy's point, and considered issuing a nap time mandate before writing a lengthy apology letter to Corbin for having ever judged him before.

Garth shrugged, seemingly unconcerned with the possibility that pants were close to dropping around him. "I say we allow them to see who is bigger. Maybe then it will shut them up."

"What a fine role model you are," returned Malik, reaching out and touching a grenade fastened to Garth's vest that wasn't PSI issued. It was obviously an item he'd acquired since their arrival at the warehouse. "Tell me again who thought you should head your own team?"

"Somebody whose dick was actually pencil-sized," supplied the Viking with a smile.

Malik looked up, silently willing himself to another location. Unfortunately, he was stuck with a bunch of testosterone-driven alpha males. If Corbin wouldn't have split off and gone to a secondary location with the other portion of Garth's team, *he* could have dealt with the giant man-children.

"Och, if I knew we were taking a break I'd have stopped going through boxes that smell like they were soaked in rat piss and shite thirty minutes ago," said Dougal "Striker" McCracken. The exceedingly tall Scotsman had given up shaving not long back and had a face full of scruff. His long hair was pulled up and he had thankfully left his kilt behind for the mission. It was hard enough for the man to blend in with his height (not that any of the PSI-

Act of Passion

Ops were considered short); adding a kilt was like adding a blinking sign. Not that Striker would have minded a blinking sign above his head. He was something of an attention whore.

He strolled up and leaned against a crate full of C-4, crossing one ankle over the other. He reached into the front pocket of his vest and withdrew a cigar.

"Bad idea," said Duke, pointing to the crates near Striker.

The Scot shrugged. "Och, I've had worse ideas. And there is no blasting cap so where is the harm?"

Boomer motioned to the barrel behind the crate. "My Arabic is so-so but I'm pretty sure that one says gunpowder."

Duke nodded. "It does, which is why I told him the cigar was a bad idea. Let's leave him here to smoke it and blow himself up. Serves him right."

"We are taking a break then?" asked Striker, biting the end of the cigar off and spitting it onto the floor.

"It's not a break so much as a dick-measuring contest," said Boomer, taking the cigar from Striker.

"I'm in!" Striker had his pants undone and

down before anyone could comment. He stood there with all his manly glory hanging out for the men to see. He put his hands on his hips, puffed out his chest, and jutted out his stubble-covered chin. "Och, there is no competition. I win."

"For fuck's sake, put that away!" shouted Duke, covering his eyes with one hand while supporting the launcher over his shoulder with the other. "My brain needs bleaching now to get that image out of my head."

"I agree with the American," said Rurik, curling his lip as if he might be sick at the sight of Striker's full-frontal.

Garth ignored Striker's antics and began to remove weapons from the crate nearest him. He lifted out a Stuart Mitchell survival knife and ran his fingers over it gently. "Oh, I don't have one of these."

Boomer laughed. "Is it me or is Garth handling that like it's a woman? He might need a private moment too."

Garth's eyes crinkled with mirth. "Gentle strokes bring out the best in everything."

Malik reconsidered the nap mandate. Not that it would do any good. They'd all ignore him anyway. They obeyed orders when they felt like it. He missed the good old days when he'd issue a mandate and thousands obeyed.

His comm unit made a light noise before Corbin's voice came through.

"Anything of interest discovered there yet?" asked the Brit.

"Not unless you count seeing Striker's junk as interesting," said Malik as he gave Striker a stern look.

"Do I want to know?" asked Corbin, sounding as English as ever. "Wait. I am quite positive I do not want to know."

The Scotsman finally pulled up his pants, looking as if he didn't have a care in the world. He then reached into a pouch in his tactical gear meant for additional ammunition and pulled out a flask.

Malik rubbed his temple, a low-grade headache setting in. At least the flask was better than smoking a cigar while standing near explosives. "Captain, how is it you haven't killed Striker yet?"

"Pretty much a daily challenge," replied Corbin.

"Och, I heard that," said Striker before taking a swig from his flask.

He then handed the flask to Duke, who took a sip too.

"There is a hell of a lot of firepower here, but nothing noteworthy. The clean-up team hasn't arrived yet so we're just holding down the fort until they get here, all the while waiting for it to come out that this is a trap. Find anything where you are?"

Corbin sighed over the line. "No. But we did find a large quantity of peculiar medical supplies. They're all stamped with Donavon Dynamics. We're finding more and more here, but nothing that sticks out as what we were searching for. I put a call into a contact I have on the human side of things. He said no reports of missing shipments have come in from the company."

"Maybe they don't realize it's missing yet," said Malik.

"Possibly," replied Corbin before going silent for a bit. "We'll be here for a couple of hours yet and then we can meet to discuss our findings. Be sure there isn't any threat there before leaving the clean-up team. They may be trained operatives but let's be honest, the majority of them aren't really fighters."

"Will do," he said, having long since given

up on proper radio communication. He was too old to bother.

The flask was now with Rurik, who handed it back to Striker with a nod.

"Corbin wants us to hang here a bit and be sure the clean-up team doesn't require a clean-up team," said Malik.

Striker groaned. "I'm sweating my balls off in here. Can we wait outside?"

"Your balls were just aired out. You'll be fine for a bit." Malik was about to sit on a crate when he heard the sound of approaching vehicles. His shifter senses homed in and a feeling of unease came over him.

"Sounds like the clean-up team is here," said Striker, capping his flask.

Malik gave the hand signal for silence and Duke grunted.

"I really don't like your hinky vibes, Tut. They never lead to anything good," said Duke.

Garth went to a side window and peered out. He then chambered a round in the weapon he was holding. "Want the good news or the bad news?"

Boomer laughed, finding humor in odd situations. "The bad."

"We're standing in the equivalent of a giant

powder keg and that isn't the clean-up crew out there, armed and ready to start shooting in here," said Garth evenly.

Duke eyed the man. "There is a good side to this somewhere?"

"Yes. We have more firepower," said Garth, motioning to the crates. "If we don't blow up first. Anyone here able to survive being blown to bits?"

They all looked at Malik as if awaiting his answer to the question.

"What?" he demanded.

"Well, can you survive that?" asked Boomer. "Inquiring minds want to know. When you're as old as time, does it give you extra superpowers?"

With a roll of his eyes, Malik joined Garth near the window to survey the situation. When he saw eight vehicles forming a barricade of sorts with men standing behind them, aiming at the building with more than just guns, he rubbed his temple again. "Sure. Why not? Garth?"

Garth flashed a wide smile, clearly loving the fact they were going to get into a firefight. "Rurik and I will take the east corner."

"Och, I'm ready to be done with this shite and find a bonnie lass to bed up with for the night," said Striker, taking the rocket launcher from Duke. He then stood behind a crate full of explosives and lined up to take a shot at the side of the building. His intention clearly was to shoot through the thin metal wall of the warehouse and out at the men.

Boomer tackled him and rolled, taking the launcher with him. Since Boomer's nickname had been born out of his love of blowing things up, he rarely was the voice of reason when it came to anything that went boom. "Dude, no. Just no."

Striker grumbled. "Kitty, you suck all the fun out of everything."

"Guys, try to act like trained professionals here," said Malik as the sound of a rocket being launched *at* them came from outside. The men shared a look and then ran in the direction of the exit, each one knowing they needed to get out of the area with the explosives.

They only just made it out of the building when there was a loud noise followed quickly by a series of explosions. The force of them blew Malik up into the air as flames licked past him. He struck something massive and it moved with him. He and the object tumbled, taking turns skidding against the ground before finally coming to a stop. Disoriented, Malik tried to figure out why he didn't feel ground beneath him and what the smell was that now surrounded him.

Garth was suddenly there, beating out the flames on Malik with his shirt, his vest, and gear discarded. Someone was yelling at him but he couldn't make out what they were saying. It took him a second to realize that someone was Duke, who was under him and pissed.

"Get the fuck off me, Tut," snapped the surly wolf-shifter, using a nickname Malik barely tolerated. He was born in ancient Egypt and had been alive for thousands of years. The men enjoyed teasing him because of it. They didn't know the half of it. If they did, they'd never let him live it down.

He wouldn't have minded the nickname so much but he'd never really cared for Tutankhamun. He'd found the boy king to be spoiled. But it could have been worse. The guys could have decided to call him Amenhotep, or Akhenaten, as the pharaoh later referred to himself. That pharaoh had been so full of himself that one would have thought him an actual god.

He wasn't.

Not by a long shot.

Malik would know.

Malik rolled off Duke and groaned, the smell of burning flesh filling his nose. Lifting his arm, he saw just how much of his flesh was burnt. He lifted his head partially and spotted Striker meandering over to them. The man still had a rocket launcher over his shoulder, which meant the Scot had delayed escaping the warehouse to grab the thing.

"I wish I had a camera. That compromising position you were both in was Asshole of the Week worthy," said Striker, his Scottish accent thicker than normal, indicating he was worked up.

The Asshole of the Week Award was one no one really wanted to be the recipient of. While it wasn't official, it was an award all the men had won at least once. It basically commemorated anything exceedingly stupid or funny that the operatives did. Often the men tried to find creative ways to set up situations in hopes they could catch another operative in a situation that was award worthy. Not that anyone needed help doing something stupid.

"Son of a bitch!" shouted Duke as he came off the ground with a huge snarl. "That hurt!"

"You smell like a roasted pig," said Rurik with a grin before turning and firing at the row of vehicles as well.

Malik sprang to his feet and did the same, ignoring the bite of pain in his arm. He didn't need to look to be told the flesh was burnt away and pieces of his shirt were stuck to him. It wasn't his first brush with fire. It wouldn't be his last. The arm would heal within an hour. The shirt was pretty much toast.

He shot at the bad guys, taking three out in succession.

Boomer lifted his weapon and doubled-tapped it in the direction of the vehicles. Another bad guy fell to the ground.

Rurik sprayed gunfire in the direction of the dicks who had nearly blown them all to bits.

Boomer snorted. "Romanov, you missed one."

"My count has to be like fifty," said Striker proudly. "To your one, kitty."

"I took out that guard team at the point of entrance when we first got here," returned Boomer.

The two then launched into an argument over who had killed more enemy combatants.

Malik glanced at Duke and shook his head. "They make me tired."

"Join the fucking club, Tut," said Duke.

Striker fired a rocket at the vehicles, blowing up one and starting a chain reaction. He flashed a smile. "I win, yet again."

Duke watched as the last bad guy fell. "Corbin is going to be pissed. He says we need to learn to be more low-key."

Malik noticed the giant plume of black smoke rolling high into the air from the burning warehouse. It would more than likely be seen from miles and miles away. "Oh, this is totally low-key."

Boomer grinned. "Yeah, I'm sure this is no way signaling to more asshole dick arms dealers to head this way."

"At this rate, we'll be here all night," snarled Duke. "I fucking hate arms dealers. Also, I do smell like barbeque. Dammit!"

Chapter Two

BROOKE LARNER STARED out the window of the white limo that had picked up her and her best friend at the airport. The limo had a full bar in it and snacks even. As if riding in a limo wasn't enough of a treat all by itself. She'd never been in one before. There had been a lot of firsts for her as of late.

The last three weeks had been something of a whirlwind. The two women had obtained master's degrees and were now on the trip of their lifetimes.

It was as if she were living a fairy tale.

She turned and touched her best friend's leg as the resort they were set to stay at appeared on the horizon. "Look. That's it."

Edee slid up alongside Brooke and peered out the window as well. "It's like its own city. It's huge!"

It was, and it was beautiful.

Brooke smiled. "I really don't understand how we got this lucky."

The girls had won an all-expenses-paid trip to Egypt yet neither one could remember entering to win said trip. Despite explaining as much to the travel agency that had sent them all the information, they were still awarded the trip. Since it coincided with them finishing grad school, the women had given in and decided to make the trip a celebration. It wasn't as if they could afford something so lavish any other time.

No.

The two had busted their butts working odd jobs while going to school full time in order to get their master's degrees. They had big plans and good jobs lined up. Of course, they'd just be starting out in their chosen fields but still, it was the path they'd always talked about. They'd made it a reality and it looked as if the universe was rewarding them for their efforts.

The limo pulled under the giant fully lit sign for the resort, and Brooke and Edee shared a look before bursting into an excited fit of giggles. They hugged each other and then squealed some more. It didn't matter how silly it was. They'd been best friends for years and were on the adventure of their lifetimes.

Brooke twisted in the seat. "I'm having a hard time wrapping my mind around this all being real."

"You and me both, sista," said Edee, pushing her long dark red hair behind her ears, her white dress was short, barely covering everything she had. "If we're dreaming, do me a favor and don't wake me up."

"Deal. Do the same for me, okay?" Brooke sat back in the seat and smoothed down her royal-blue dress. "Operation Have a Good Time has officially commenced."

Edee winked, her blue gaze holding a glimmer of mischief. "Funny, I could have sworn it was a mission to get you laid."

"Stop," said Brooke, pushing her friend lightly.

Edee liked to joke about Brooke's missing sex life. Brooke had spent so much time focused on studying and working various odd jobs that men just hadn't been something she'd been able to schedule in—and she loved her schedules.

Edee was far more of a free spirit. She

wasn't exactly extremely experienced in the ways of men either, but came off as being worldly on the matter. The woman just naturally oozed sex appeal. All Brooke oozed was awkwardness around the opposite sex. And she always went from fine one second to two left feet the next.

Brooke found comfort in computers and anything technology related. Human interactions tended to be something she avoided. Thankfully, Edee had become something of a spokesperson for Brooke. How they'd become friends was still a mystery. They were almost total opposites when it came to their personalities. Though, under all the siren qualities, Edee was a giant science nerd. It surprised everyone who met her.

Looks-wise, the woman didn't have a lot in common except for their height. They were nearly matched in height, with Edee standing just a smidge taller at five-ten. Edee had skin that at times Brooke could swear was translucent, it was so pale. And Brooke's skin was sun-kissed with a natural glow. Edee's eyes were a deep blue and Brooke's were olive green. Both had long hair, though Brooke's was brown and had slight curl on the ends, where Edee's was dark red and straight.

When they'd met their freshman year of high school, they'd just hit it off from the word go. Edee had taken Brooke under her wing socially and Brooke had appreciated it. Edee loved to get lost in music and dancing, and Brooke always found comfort in cross-country and swimming.

Edee eyed her. "Are you ready for this?"

"I am," she said and then bit her lower lip. "At least I'm pretty sure I am. I'm ready for us to have fun. We've done nothing but study and work for years. We've earned this, right?"

Edee put an arm around her. "You worked your butt off. I was not as dedicated to it all as you. And I was fired from different jobs too many times to count. You worked the same three jobs for six years."

"In your defense, how many of your bosses were total douchebags who thought hiring you meant you'd be offering them special favors?"

She groaned. "Too many to count. That's it. I'm going to find a super-rich Egyptian guy and use him as my sex slave before he buys me a palace or something and makes me his wife."

Brooke laughed hard as the limo pulled to a stop in front of the luxury resort.

Edee snorted. "Was it the bit about making him my sex slave that was so hard to believe or the part about a palace?"

"Neither. The you being married was the hysterical part," said Brooke. It was true, Edee always talked about how she hated the idea of ever getting married. And the woman never committed to any level of a relationship with a man. She dated and that was it. No boyfriends, no special someone.

Edee grinned. "Yeah, I threw that in to make you worry less about my actions for the next two weeks."

"Good luck with that," said Brooke as the limo driver opened the back door. He put his hand out to her and she took it—instantaneously feeling cold and empty inside. She'd felt the same thing when he'd helped her into the limo at the airport. She hadn't thought much of it at the time, but now that it was happening again, she jerked her hand from his.

He reached for Edee. Brooke nearly knocked his hand away from her friend but didn't. She was being ridiculous. The man had been nothing but professional and nice to them since greeting them at the airport. He'd even had a sign with their names on it that looked professionally done. Not handwritten.

Edee took his hand and her gaze narrowed slightly before she pressed a smile to her face. She eased close to Brooke and they stepped back as men from the resort appeared and spoke with their driver. Neither of the women spoke Arabic despite their best efforts to study a guidebook with helpful phrases and tips. Turns out there were different forms of Arabic spoken in different regions—as if learning the basics from one wasn't hard enough.

The men from the resort took their bags and smiled at her. All were pleasant to look at, yet there was something that felt…off. She couldn't put her finger on it, but it was there.

"Oh, look at those hotties," said Edee, pointing to a group of men in designer suits. They were each tall and built and most of them had short hair that was styled with ample amounts of gel. They all seemed a bit too flashy for Brooke's tastes. And all of them were staring at Brooke and Edee.

The men looked away quickly.

Edee began talking about all the things she wanted to do after they got to their suite. Brooke didn't pay attention; her focus was still on the men in the suits. One of them touched his ear, and it was then she noticed an earpiece like something a Secret Service agent would wear.

Were the men the resort's security detail?

That would make sense.

The brochure said the place catered to the rich and famous. It stood to reason security would be important. That being said, she couldn't seem to look away from them. Like the limo driver and the men who had grabbed their bags, the men in suits felt off to her. She couldn't explain why, but kept her eye on them.

Get a grip. You had a long flight.

Edee hooked her arm through Brooke's and the two walked towards the resort's entrance, their heels clicking as they went. Edee had insisted they dress up for travel when all Brooke had wanted to wear was a pair of yoga pants and a T-shirt. Edee wouldn't hear of it, citing the fact they were headed to a luxury resort.

There was a giant fountain that had water shooting at least twenty feet in the air while colored lights shined on it. The colors changed from gold to white and back to gold.

"Awesome!" Edee pulled away. "I'm going to

get some pictures really quickly. Can you check in for us?"

"Sure thing," said Brooke.

Something caught her attention from her left, and she looked over to see a different large group of males walking in the direction of the resort. Unlike the men in suits, these men were in black from head to toe. Their hair wasn't gelled in any way. In fact, most of them had long hair. Longer than she saw on most men. Then there was the fact that they somehow managed to make the men in suits seem short and ugly, when in truth, they were anything but.

One man in particular held Brooke's interest. His long dark hair was pulled up in a messy way off his neck. He had short stubble on his face and down his neck, though it looked to be groomed to be that way, making her instantly think he was into fashion and his appearance, despite the fact the black long-sleeved shirt he had on looked as if someone had set the arm of it on fire. The skin showing under the scorched shirt was smooth and unblemished, but covered in a variety of black tattoos. His pants and belt reminded her of something men from military movies wore. He was as built as the men around him and walked in a way that screamed suave with an undertone of badass.

A taller redhead was near him, talking and using his hands in an animated fashion. The man who had caught Brooke's eye rubbed his temple as if the other male was making him tired.

When Brooke realized she was standing in front of the resort staring at a stranger, she blinked and then hurried into the resort, happy the man hadn't noticed her.

As she entered the lobby, her breath caught at just how ornate it was. No expense had been spared in its creation. Not to mention, the place was massive. She knew it had more than one nightclub, numerous bars and restaurants, not to mention a spa that had rave reviews.

Edee was right. It really was like a small city.

And it was where they'd be hanging their hats for the next two weeks. She had to resist putting her arms out wide and spinning as if she were in a scene from *The Sound of Music*. Since Edee would never let her live it down, she held back.

It was harder than it should have been.

Brooke turned and bumped into a man dressed in an all-white suit that looked to be custom-made to fit him. He wore a black dress shirt under it. Instantly it felt as if spiders were crawling all over her skin. The man was handsome but there was something in his eyes that said he was ugly on the inside. He had expensive-looking rings on every finger and was surrounded by men who reminded her of the group out front—the ones with earpieces.

Mr. Rings said something to her but she didn't catch any of it as she didn't speak the language.

"Excuse me," said Brooke, pressing a smile to her face, attempting to walk around him.

Mr. Rings invaded her personal space in a big way, setting off all her inner alarms. He leaned in, putting his face close to hers. "I see no point in this charade. You will come with me."

"W-what?" she asked, barely able to think.

"Come," he said.

She shook her head and took the smallest of steps back. He grabbed her arm, squeezing to the point it hurt. Her jaw dropped as a gasp came from her.

Chapter Three
―――――――――

SUDDENLY, the very guy Brooke had thought was hot in front of the resort was there, planting himself between Brooke and Mr. Rings. The sexy newcomer thrust Mr. Rings's hand away, puffing out his chest as he did. He made Mr. Rings look small. He glared at Mr. Rings and said something she didn't understand.

Words were exchanged, sounding heated. The guys who looked like hired muscle moved in, putting their hands inside their expensive sports jackets. She half thought they'd pull out weapons and the entire event would turn into a shootout.

Brooke wasn't sure how everything had gotten so out of control so quickly.

The hot guy put his hand out to her and she felt compelled to take it. As she placed her hand in his, heat flared between them. His breath caught and he jerked her behind his powerful frame, making her feel small. At five feet nine and a half inches, she rarely felt dainty. But the man was well over six feet tall and had a muscular frame that was just this side of being too much. The way he carried himself said he was no stranger to a fight.

"Malik, everything all right there?" asked a man who was dressed in the same type of clothes, though his weren't ripped and burnt. The man's long black hair looked as if it had bits of blue in it and, if she wasn't mistaken, the guy was wearing eyeliner. Not to mention he had a number of silver piercings on his face.

The hot guy shielding her body with his replied, "Everything is fine now, Boomer, but if this asshat thinks of touching her again, I'll rip his head off and spit down his neck."

The man had an accent that was slight but she couldn't place it even though it was sexy as could be. His voice was deep and the timbre of it licked at her insides. Automatically, she pressed against his back, confirming that he was indeed very muscular.

Boomer strolled over to them and glanced at her, his eyes a bright violet and shaped in a way that made Brooke think of an exotic cat. "Malik, didn't you just lecture us on the way back to the resort on being low-key? I think Corbin would frown on us starting a fight in the lobby of the resort. It's enough we skipped changing and came straight here. I don't think a brawl is going to help any."

Malik rotated his shoulders, somehow looking even bigger than he had before. He kept his body in front of hers in a protective way. He said something to Mr. Rings, and whatever he said caused two of the hired muscle guys to converge on him.

"They have no idea who they're dealing with. Dumbasses," Boomer snorted.

Brooke gasped as she realized a fight was about to happen. She reached for Boomer, making contact with his forearm. "Stop this. I don't want anyone to get hurt. Not because of me."

"American?" asked Boomer, moving his arm away from her touch as if she'd burned him.

She nodded.

"Yeah, well, Malik doesn't look like he's about to back down and those assholes are pretty much begging to get a world of hurt put on them," said Boomer with a shrug. "I could help Malik but there are only six of them. It's hardly fair to them."

Six against one? Wasn't fair to *them*?

Brooke boldly touched Malik's shoulder. "Please don't do this. Not for me. I'm fine. I don't want you hurt because of me."

Mr. Rings said something to Malik in a snide tone.

Malik laughed, but it didn't sound friendly. It sounded cold and threatening.

Whistling, Boomer shook his head. "Now he went and stepped in it."

"What did he say?" asked Brooke, looking at Boomer, desperately wanting everything to settle down.

Boomer bit his lower lip before responding. "Asshat there might have mentioned that you were nothing more than a high-priced, erm, woman by the hour, and Malik seems less than pleased with that comment."

As Brooke realized the ring guy had called her a whore, her temper flared. She darted around Malik and stood before the guy with the rings. "How dare you! You arrogant, flashy—"

"Oh dear, what did I miss?" asked Edee as

she came into the lobby. "Wow, it's like a hunk fest is going on in here. Someone should have told me. I'd have been in here much faster then and I could have been taking pictures of the yummy male specimens instead of the front of the resort."

Malik put his hands on Brooke's hips, causing more heat to flare through her. Much to her shock, he lifted her as if she were a feather. He set her aside, near Boomer, and stepped forward, cracking his knuckles as he did.

One of the hired musclemen went at him. Malik caught the man's fist and squeezed, making the man go to one knee and cry out in pain. The other men made a move to attack.

The next thing Brooke knew, a big guy with dark red hair came in from the side, standing next to Malik. And another large man, this one with brown hair, moved to Malik's other side. The men formed a wall of sexy muscle.

"It would be unwise to make another move," said the redhead, leaving no doubt he was Scottish.

The guy with the brown hair snorted. "Come on. Make my day, boys."

"Och, Duke, you were the one bitching about wanting a shower on the way here. Something about washing Malik off you. Now you want to take time out to get in a fight?" asked the Scotsman.

The brown-haired one smiled wide. "I'm always in the mood for a fight, Striker."

Striker grinned. "Aye. Me too."

Boomer eased Brooke back from the wall of muscle. "Malik will rip my nuts off if I let a hair on your head be hurt."

"What? Why? I don't even know him," said Brooke.

Edee raced over to Brooke and cast an approving look at Boomer. "Mmm, you wear black very well."

He grinned. "Thanks."

She pointed to the men. "What is going on with the A-Team of hotness there?"

"Asshat in the white pimp suit called your friend a whore. My friend is about to tear his throat out," replied Boomer as if that sort of thing happened daily.

Edee's jaw set. "Someone called you a whore? Ohmygod, you've never *been* with a guy. You're a friggin' virgin! That is about as far from a whore as you can get."

Brooke's cheeks heated. "You didn't need to

announce that to the entire lobby full of people."

Edee grinned. "I know, but I think that one there, with the great ass, liked hearing it." She motioned to Malik, who was staring over his shoulder at Brooke with a hunger in his dark eyes that made her belly feel as if hundreds of butterflies were fluttering about in it.

Brooke's cheeks heated more.

Edee laughed. "Oh honey, if I beg, will you please take that man to bed for a night of hot, crazy, unapologetic sex? This trip is supposed to be life changing. I'd say that would completely qualify."

Boomer coughed in an attempt to hide the choking sound that had come from him.

Edee looked at him. "You're not bad. Keep standing this close to me and I'll be taking *you* to bed. Then we could trade eyeliner tips. And you should know, I have a thing for men in leather."

His eyes widened and he took a giant step back from her. "I think you might be too much woman for me there, Red."

Edee shrugged. "Not the first guy to say that."

Striker turned partially. "Och, there is no such thing as too much woman for *me*. I'll gladly spend the night rocking yer world, lass. And I think my arse is way better than Malik's. I love to bed redheads, though I'm nae much into wearing leather. Chafes my balls."

Brooke cringed. That was way more information than she needed to know.

Her friend licked her lower lip. "There are creams for that you know."

Striker raked his gaze over her slowly. "Aye. You offering to rub yer cream on my balls?"

Brooke groaned.

Edee did not need any encouragement, and from what Brooke could tell, Striker might be Edee's male counterpart.

Edee shook her head. "You're sexy, but you know it. Pass. Besides, I did not come all the way to Egypt for a Scottish guy. I came for a prince or something. They have princes here, don't they? Regardless, I'm guessing you're all talk and no game."

Striker waggled his brows. "I sense a challenge there, lass."

"Uh, not to interrupt the talk of creaming chafed balls," said Duke, sounding gruff. "But Malik is about to rip a guy's arm off. Maybe we should pull our focus here?"

Brooke gasped as she realized the man

was right.

Malik still had one of the men's fists in his hand while his other hand was on the man's throat. The man was still on his knees in front of Malik.

Malik spoke to Mr. Rings in what she strongly suspected was Arabic.

All of Malik's friends shared a look that said they more than understood the exchange.

Duke ran a hand through his shoulder-length hair. "Did Malik just warn the man to avoid even looking at *his* woman?"

His woman?

"Aye," Striker said with a curt nod. "Cannae fault him. The lass is bonnie indeed. So is the redhead. Think they'll want to get naked and in a Jacuzzi with me? I'm all in for a hot-chick layered dessert."

Malik snarled and set his sights on his friend.

Duke grabbed Malik. "No killing him. It would make Corbin way too happy, so how about we take a nice deep breath and calm down. That, or we can beat the snot out of these pretty boys."

Edee clapped. "Oh, I vote for the fight. I really want to see all of your muscles flexing and you guys being all manly. Yummy and a major turn-on. It would really help that cream thing."

Boomer choke-coughed again.

Striker flashed a wicked smile. "Redheads are always worth the trouble."

Brooke rushed forward and did what felt right—she slipped her arms around Malik's waist and tugged. There was no way she was moving him unless he wanted to move.

He released the guy and twisted, wrapping an arm around Brooke's waist protectively.

It was then she got a good dose of his smell. The man smelled good enough to eat. She inhaled again, the smell of him making her body respond. Her nipples hardened and her pulse sped.

Malik's gaze snapped to hers and he took in a deep breath as well, tightening his hold on her waist. "Honey and lotuses."

"W-what?" she asked.

"You smell like honey and lotuses," he returned, still looking hungry for her.

Duke cleared his throat. "Try not to fuck her in the middle of the lobby."

Brooke yelped and jerked out of Malik's grasp.

Mr. Rings snorted before speaking in

English. "Take your whore for now."

"Oh boy, now you went and did it," said Duke, shaking his head.

Malik released Brooke and went at Mr. Rings. One second Mr. Rings was standing and the next he was flat on his back, knocked out cold with one hit from Malik. Mr. Rings's men converged on him, all looking lost as to what to do. None of them appeared to want to take on Malik.

Brooke stood there, too stunned to comment or move.

Edee squealed in delight. "That was so hot! Do it again."

"Edee!" Brooke glanced at her friend. "This is not okay."

"Honey, it was hot as hell and you know it. Now, thank him by taking him to our room and having your way with him. Look at him, that is a body you don't pass up on."

Boomer coughed again. "Christ, she might actually be *worse* than Striker."

"Och, no one is worse than me," said Striker before touching his chin. "Wait, I mean…hell… I said what I meant. No one is worse than me unless we're talking about my cousins. They make me look tame."

Edee perked. "Oh, cousins? So I could have a reverse harem of hot guys? I might make an exception about the Scottish-non-prince thing if that's the case."

Striker looked hopeful. "Redheads are dynamite."

He'd know. He was one.

Hotel security finally arrived and Boomer went to them, speaking with them and pulling out some form of identification. Within seconds, the security team backed up, taking Mr. Rings and his men with them.

Malik turned slowly. His gaze snapped to Brooke's arm. The one Mr. Rings had grabbed and squeezed. "Your arm, it has the start of bruising on it. That is it. He dies."

Duke and Striker grabbed Malik, lifting him up and off his feet and walking him towards the elevator. The men appeared to be exuding a lot of energy to keep Malik from getting free.

Boomer laughed and ran to catch up, stopping briefly in front of Brooke and Edee. "We're going to wash dead arms dealers off us and then we were planning on grabbing something to eat before hitting the clubs. You two want to meet us for dinner? I think Malik would be very happy if you said yes, miss."

"Dead arms dealers?" asked Brooke, feeling faint.

Edee waved a hand dismissively. "He's kidding. Right?"

Boomer pursed his lips. "Yeah. Kidding. So is that a yes to meeting us for dinner and then clubbing? We can meet you in the lobby here if you want."

Brooke shook her head no, only to find Edee stepping forward. "Oh, we'll be there. What time?"

"Give us an hour. We'll need thirty minutes of that to convince Malik not to kill us for taking him from your friend."

"Me?" Brooke asked, her eyes wide. "But he doesn't even *know* me."

"Doesn't change that he wants you safe, and he wants to inflict a lot of pain on the guy who hurt and threatened you," said Boomer, heading for the elevator. "You should know, we'll all step in and kill the asshat if he dares to hurt either of you."

Malik snarled and struggled to get free from his friends' grasp.

Brooke didn't like seeing him behave that way. It did something to her that she couldn't explain. Before she thought better of it, she hurried over and reached for him, touching his scruffy jawline. "Stop. Please. I don't want this."

His nostrils flared. "He hurt you."

Duke and Striker looked concerned.

Brooke kept her hand on Malik's cheek. "And you hurt him right back. Thank you. But if you can't control your temper, then how are you any different from the other guy?"

That did it. Malik stopped struggling against his friends and went still. "I'd *never* hurt you."

"I know," she said, feeling deep in her gut that he was telling the truth. He'd never harm her. "I just, well, I don't like seeing you like this. I can't explain it. Can you stop?"

"Malik, she's meeting us for dinner in an hour. You'll see her again," said Boomer.

"You will be at dinner," Malik said in a way that was a declaration, not a question.

Brooke lifted a brow.

"Corbin once told me the lasses do nae like to be ordered about in today's day and age," said Striker with a huff. "The sex clubs I go to are full of lasses wanting me to take control. I do nae know if the Brit has a clue about women but the look on yer woman's face says Corbin might have been on to something. She's nae British too, is she? If she is, run!"

Malik cleared his throat. "Please meet me in an hour."

She nodded and drew her hand off his cheek slowly, liking touching him more than she should. "Try not to maim anyone on the way to your room."

His lips quirked. "No promises."

He backed into the open elevator and his friends all seemed relieved. Malik caught the door before it could close. "Wait. What is your name?"

"Brooke," she replied, smiling wide. He'd done all he had for her all while never knowing her name.

He let the door close, his dark gaze never leaving her as it did.

Edee eased up alongside her. "Honey, I have no idea what happened, but that man has it bad for you. Tell me you're going to entertain making him your first."

Brooke glanced at her best friend in all the world and took a deep breath. "Oh yeah, I'm entertaining it all right. More than entertaining it."

Edee laughed long and loud. "That's my girl. I knew I had to rub off on you at some point."

Chapter Four
———————

EDEE PEEKED her head into the bathroom as Brooke finished applying mascara. "Oh, you look hot."

Brooke frowned. "Is it too much?"

Edee snorted. "Honey, if you'd have let me dress you, I'd have put you in a mini skirt that barely covered your ass. You're in a dress that hangs to your ankles. It's not too much. It's you. It's just right."

She stepped back from the mirror. "Edee, that was weird tonight, right? I mean, the way Malik reacted on my behalf?"

Shrugging, Edee headed back into the main area of the suite. "He didn't like seeing you manhandled and he really didn't like that douchebag calling you a whore."

"Right, but why?" asked Brooke, trying to make sense of the way Malik had made her feel. "He doesn't know me."

"Because real men don't hurt women or call them whores. And he'll get to know you," said Edee. She slipped on her heels. "Stop over-thinking it, Brooke. You always do that."

Her friend was right. She did tend to over-think everything. She slipped on her knee-high, heeled brown boots, much to Edee's dismay. Edee hated Brooke's choices in fashion.

Edee groaned. "All right. We're nearly thirty minutes late. They probably think we stood them up."

Brooke snorted. "They probably forgot they even asked us to join them. I bet they've already all found other women to keep them company. None of them look as if they're hurting in the way of attracting the ladies."

Edee stuffed money into her bra and smiled as she headed for the door. She opened and then turned, staring at Brooke. "I don't think they forgot they asked us to join them."

Snorting, Brooke finished zipping her boots and then looked around the room for her small backpack that doubled as a purse. "Have you seen my bag?"

Edee glanced out into the hall and then back at Brooke. "I really hate that bag. And it's not needed."

"Of course I need it. I never go anywhere without it," argued Brooke. "You can never be too prepared. What if I need a flashlight, or tissues, paper and a pen?"

"Brooke, I love you but you are so weird," said Edee with a snort. "Let's go."

Brooke bent, looking under the coffee table. "We're already late because of my mini freak out about everything. And I think you're wrong. Those guys looked like they have lines of women at the ready. They won't notice we aren't there yet."

"Oh, I wouldn't be too sure of that," said Edee, sounding amused. "In fact, I can guarantee they didn't start the party without us. Okay, most of them didn't. Get a move on or I'm going to start throwing stuff at you just to watch your freakish reflexes work."

"I don't have freakish reflexes," Brooke said, bending more.

"Brooke, I think your reflexes need to be studied, because trust me, they're freakish," said

Edee. Something in her voice told Brooke her friend was about to prove a point.

Out of the corner of her eye, she saw the TV remote coming at her. Calmly, she snatched it out of the air and kept looking for her bag.

Edee laughed. "Freak."

"Diva," Brooke shot back.

"Thank you," replied Edee.

"Found it," said Brooke as she spotted her bag tucked partially under the sofa. She wiggled to reach it and her backside felt hot all of a sudden. Like it was getting stared at. She reached farther and grabbed the bag.

"Dear Lord, woman, you really need to stop shaking that rump or you're going to have a super-hot dude trying to mount you," Edee said, laughing.

Brooke came up too fast and bumped the back of her head on the coffee table. "Ouch!"

Edee laughed more. "The idea of getting mounted wigged you out that much?"

Sensing something coming at her, Brooke put her hand out without looking behind her and caught a small figurine that had been near the entrance to the suite. She set it down on the coffee table. "Stop throwing stuff at me."

Getting off the floor, Brooke turned to find

Malik standing just inside the door to the suite. He was dressed in an off-white dress shirt that looked expensive. The shirt was partially undone, showing off some of his chest and tattoos. The black leather pants he wore fit him like a glove. He wore a gold watch and a gold bracelet. His hair was down and hung to his mid-back.

She'd thought he was sexy when he was in a shirt that looked like it had survived a fire. The man was downright delicious cleaned up. She blinked as her throat went dry. "How did you figure out our room number?"

"He paid the desk clerk an obscene amount of money," said Striker from the hall.

Edee cackled with laughter. "See, doesn't look like he found another woman to keep him company. He brought the Scottish jerk though. Win some. Lose some."

"Yer full of piss and vinegar, lass," said Striker with a growl. "Want to do it?"

Edee rolled her eyes. "Come on, big guy. Let's head down to the restaurant and let these two have a moment together. You okay with that, Brooke?"

She stared at Malik, unable to think clearly. "Am I okay with that?"

He flashed a large white smile that nearly made her melt. "I'm fine with that, but if being alone with me makes you uncomfortable, I'll understand. I don't want you nervous around me, Brooke."

"Then you should probably button your shirt more," she blurted, her gaze locking on his chest again.

Edee laughed more. "Bye, Brooke. See you in a bit. Don't do anything I wouldn't do."

"Gee, that really limits it," returned Brooke before wringing her hands in front of her.

Malik entered the room more and the door closed behind him.

Brooke tensed.

He sighed. "I'll wait in the hall. I don't want you scared of me. That is the last thing in the world I want."

She moved forward fast, needing to make contact with him for some unknown reason. She tripped and fell into him. His large arms encased her and warmth shot through her entire body.

Looking up, she found his lips so close to hers that she did the only thing that made sense—she kissed him. His lips parted and his tongue darted into her mouth. A low growl started deep in his chest, only serving to excite her more. She swirled her tongue around his, her hands finding his chest. His hands made their way to the small of her back. He jerked her against him fully, taking the kiss to another level.

He eased a hand up her back slowly and then slipped it into her hair, tugging lightly. She tipped her head back, granting him better access to her mouth. He took it and she found herself cupping his scruffy face.

He walked her backwards and she went willingly, never feeling this wanton before. She felt as if she might burst into flames if he didn't touch her more. The next thing she knew, she was being eased onto the sofa. Malik moved up and over her, never breaking their kiss.

She barely knew the man and she was making out with him in a serious way. This was so out of character for her that it jarred her back into reality. She stopped kissing him and froze under him.

He withdrew his tongue from her mouth but remained on top of her. He stared down at her, his dark gaze smoldering. She nearly kissed him again but knew it was all moving too fast. She needed a moment to adjust to this wild side. To him.

"I should get off you, shouldn't I?" he asked as if he wasn't sure of the answer.

Brooke couldn't help but smile up at him. "Probably, since I'm on the verge of another panic attack here."

He eased off her, his movements stiff. When she realized why, her eyes widened. He extended a hand to her, helping her off the sofa. "I'm sorry about that."

"I kissed *you*. You didn't kiss me first," she said softly, surprised by the truth of it.

She was not sexually aggressive—at all.

Well, she hadn't been until Malik. Now she just wanted to throw him down and jump his bones. That caused panic to well in her more.

He touched her cheek tenderly. "How about we eat and get to know one another?"

A shaky breath left her as she retrieved her bag. "Yes. I'd like that."

Malik took her hand in his and led her from the suite. They walked hand in hand down the hall, as if they'd been a couple for ages. It felt right. Like this was how life was supposed to be.

"Where are you from?" she blurted, wanting to fill the silence.

"Here, but I've not lived here for a *very* long time, and it didn't look anything like this when I did live here," he said, slowing their pace as if he didn't want to get to the restaurant too soon. "What about you? Where are you from?"

"When I was little I lived with my parents in South Carolina," she answered. "Then when I was five, I went to live with my maternal grandmother in Ohio."

"Why is that?" he asked, seeming to actually be interested.

She drew to a stop. "My parents died. My grandmother raised me after that. She passed away right after I graduated from high school. So, I just really have Edee that I count as family."

He reached up with his free hand and smoothed her long brown hair over her shoulder. "I'm sorry. I didn't mean to pry."

"Normally, I go to great lengths to avoid talking about it all, but I feel like I have to tell you all of it. I don't know why. Weird, huh?"

"I'm struggling with the same thing," he confessed. "I want to tell you things that I don't normally get into with women. Things humans shouldn't know about."

"Humans?" she asked, laughing softly at his word usage. "You're really an alien from outer space, aren't you? It would explain the accent that I can't place, yet it's kind of familiar too. Weird."

"You have found out my secret," he said, his lips twitching. He raked his gaze over her. "How old are you?"

"I'll be twenty-four in a week. How about you?"

"Older than twenty-four," he replied.

"Twenty-seven? Twenty-eight?"

Malik appeared uncomfortable with the question. "Are you hungry?"

"I am," she said, moving as he started to walk again.

He pressed the button for the elevator and then eased closer to her. She liked knowing he wanted to be near her as much as she wanted to be close to him. It made her feel less needy.

They entered the elevator and Malik slipped his other arm around her waist. As the doors closed, he looked down at her. "What brings you to Egypt?"

"Believe it or not, Edee and I won a trip that neither of us remember signing up for," she said, squeezing his hand slightly. "We just got our master's degrees and when this offer came up, we took it. Seemed like perfect timing—a way to celebrate. It's my first time outside of the States."

"How long have you been here for and how long before you leave?" he asked, and for a second she could have sworn his dark brown eyes had hints of amber in them. When she didn't see it again, she chalked it up to a play of the lights.

"We arrived today. We'd just gotten to the hotel when you saw us in the lobby. We're here for two weeks."

His gaze hardened. "If that asshat comes near you again—"

She snorted. "Thanks. I think. What about you? When did you get here and when are you leaving?"

He closed his eyes slightly. "I don't want to lie to you, Brooke."

"What does that mean?" she asked before realizing what he was saying. She thought back to his military-like clothing earlier. Had there been something to it all? "You can't tell me, is that it?"

A nod was his only response.

"Can you tell me how long you're here for?" She didn't want to look clingy but she honestly felt like she needed to hold tight to him for fear he'd be gone.

His gaze darted away. "No."

Brooke thought harder on what she was doing. She was holding hands with a man she barely knew. She'd made out with him, which was totally not her norm. To top it off, he could be gone at any moment and she'd never see him again. It wasn't as if she knew anything about him that would help her locate him later. They were basically two strangers passing in the night.

Two strangers with a lot of chemistry.

Too much chemistry.

She wasn't sure she'd bounce back after spending a night with him, only to never see him again.

She worked her hand from his and hugged herself to keep from touching him once more. It was all she wanted to do, but the pull to him was unnatural. Too intense. And she certainly didn't make a habit of bedding men one night and never seeing them again the next. Hell, she didn't make a habit of bedding anyone.

Malik reached for her but then stopped. "You're upset with me."

"I'm not a one-night-stand kind of girl.

Thank you for your help in the lobby, but we should part ways now. This is too much."

The elevator doors opened and Brooke stepped out. She intended to find Edee, make sure her friend was behaving herself, and then head back to the room to think about the way Malik made her head spin.

Malik stepped out of the elevator behind her and pressed his body to hers. He slinked his arms around her waist and drew her back against him. He pressed his mouth to her ear. "I arrived here almost a week ago. If my team is called away, then I'll need to go. If I can, I'll try to stay, but there are things at work I can't tell you about. It's not that I don't want to tell you. Please know that. And I know you're not the type for a one-night stand. You should know *I'm* not the type to be there come morning—but I want to be there come morning with you, Brooke. Let's spend time together to see where this might go. Please."

She couldn't move. The feel of his long, hard erection was pressed to her back. Her entire body lit with need. Brooke knew she should cut her losses and steer clear of him. He'd just admitted to being a womanizer, and the odds that he'd fed her a line about wanting to be there come morning were great. That being said, she wanted him. She wanted all of him.

Risks be damned.

As Edee always reminded her, you only live once.

"Okay, let's go to dinner," she said softly.

He put his mouth to her ear. "Thank you."

Chapter Five

MALIK ENTERED the restaurant to find his teammates and Rurik and Garth there as well. The restaurant leaned heavily on modern styling and had floor-to-ceiling shelves behind the bar that were backlit, creating the perfect lighting level and ambiance.

Several long, dark tables had been put together to accommodate their group size, not to mention the size of the men. Supernatural males tended to run on the large size.

Duke and Rurik sat across from one another, each glaring at the other. Boomer was next to Duke, talking with Brooke's friend Edee. The two seemed engrossed in conversation. Garth was next to Corbin, who appeared to be keeping Striker sitting as far from Edee as could be.

Malik hid his laugh, wondering what the Scot had done to earn him a timeout. Knowing Striker, the sky was the limit.

Corbin looked up and his blue gaze locked on Malik.

The next Malik knew, his team captain's voice was in his head.

I heard you made quite the scene for the woman, said Corbin.

Malik inclined his head. *Yes. And I'd do it again.*

That's what I thought you'd say, Corbin returned as he stood and buttoned the suit jacket he was wearing. The man cleaned up well and preferred to be dressed nicely, as did Malik.

Corbin came around from the other side of the table and put his hands out to Brooke, taking hers in return.

Malik's lion pushed up, wanting to warn the fellow lion-shifter away from what was his.

Mine?

He swallowed hard. The damn suppression medicine was really doing a number on him. If he wasn't careful, he'd do something stupid.

"You must be Brooke," said Corbin, his

English accent showing through with ease. He'd made no attempt to ever try to rid himself of it. "I've heard so much about you already. Your friend tells me you just graduated university with exceptional pass marks."

Brooke's cheeks heated, and Malik realized she didn't like attention on herself. He couldn't understand why. She was stunning. Other women he'd seen who paled compared to her loved attention. But not Brooke.

"Yes. This trip is to celebrate graduating," she said.

Corbin's lips twitched. "I see. Then it's not to, how did your friend put it? To find you a hot hunk to rock your world for a night?"

Brooke squeaked and leaned forward, looking past Malik at Edee.

Edee lifted her glass of wine and blew Brooke a kiss.

Brooke yanked her hands from Corbin's and went ramrod stiff. "No. Not at all. No. Did I mention no?"

Corbin chuckled. "You did. Though I'm sure Malik was hoping for a different response."

Brooke's attention swung to Malik. She raked her gaze over him slowly, making his dick harden again. If she kept it up, his cock would be permanently erect. He'd been struggling with it from the second he'd caught her scent in the lobby—honey and lotuses. She licked her lower lip and the act made him think of what her mouth would look like wrapped around his cock.

"Well, I'd be willing to make an exception for him," said Brooke quietly, surprising Malik with her humor.

Corbin laughed long and loud, something he tended to avoid doing. The guy was so repressed. "Note the glimmer of hope returning to Malik's eyes."

Malik grunted. "That will be enough from you. Go sit by Striker before he does something else to get himself in trouble."

Corbin groaned. "Boomer told me about the, uh, measuring incident earlier, and Edee asked more about it. Striker offered to take her upstairs and show her what a real Highlander came built with. She in turn offered to remove anything he showed her with a butter knife."

Brooke snorted. "Sounds like Edee."

Corbin grinned. "She's refreshing and seems more than capable of dealing with Striker. Never thought those words would fall from my lips. I'm considering hiring her just to babysit him."

"So why does he look like he's being punished?" asked Malik.

"Oh, he's by me because he and Duke wanted to team up and see if they could bring Russia to his knees," said Corbin, sounding exhausted. "Garth and I grew tired of putting out that fire so we thought it best the main instigator be separated from the other two. Hence, Striker is being punished."

Malik took Brooke's arm gently and led her to a chair at the table. He held the chair out for her and then made sure she was seated and comfortable before taking the chair next to her, leaving Duke seated to his left.

Corbin returned to his side of the table and sat across from Malik. "Edee didn't mention what you studied while at university."

Brooke smiled and smoothed her long brown hair behind her ears. "Computer science engineering with a focus on cyber security."

"Interesting," said Corbin. "Have you started your job search yet?"

She nodded. "I have four great offers that I'm thinking about while here. One is with the

DOD and the others are with the private sector."

"I hate computers," said Duke before he lifted his glass of wine and gulped it down. "And if you're smart, you'll avoid the DOD like the plague."

"I love computers," said Brooke, her eyes lighting. "I love everything to do with technology. I hope to one day own my own cyber security firm. Edee just laughs. Though, I don't know why. She's a total science nerd. Molecular science. No thanks."

"I laugh because you're a social leper. Instead of meeting men, you spent your time hacking. Brooke, how are you going to get laid if you hide away all the time? You're young and hot, you only live once," said Edee loudly from the other side of Duke.

Brooke rolled her eyes. "Can we not discuss my lack of a social and sex life in front of people we just met?"

Rurik lifted a dark brow. "You are very attractive, for an American."

Brooke eased her chair closer to Malik, looking nervous. "Um, thanks."

He put an arm around her. "He's harmless. Just loud and very proud to be Russian."

"Russians are arseholes," said Striker, earning him a nod from Duke.

Garth touched Rurik's shoulder, keeping his second-in-command in his seat for the time being. "What did we talk about, Rurik?"

Rurik grunted. "My temper is warranted around them. Let me kill one of them and then I'll promise to behave. Just one. You pick the one. Doesn't matter to me."

Brooke's giggle eased the tension at the table. She lifted a glass of water that was in front of her. "How long have all of you been friends?"

Malik cleared his throat. "Some days it feels like forever."

"Because you're ancient, old man," said Boomer under his breath. "Old as fucking time."

"Dick," returned Malik, partially under his.

Brooke laughed again and sipped her water, her hand finding his thigh.

Instantly Malik's throat went dry. He grabbed his water goblet and downed it before taking Duke's and doing the same.

Duke stared over at him and grunted. "What is with you tonight? Normally you're the picture of suaveness, saying all the right things to the ladies, making us all look like Neanderthals. You're acting like you're about to get laid for the first time. Not like the six thousandth."

Brooke's hand moved quickly off his thigh and she eased away from him slightly.

Malik turned a hard gaze on his longtime friend. *Do not ruin this for me.*

What the hell has gotten into you? You're picking fights in public. You're nervous as shit at dinner. Seriously, what's with this piece of ass? asked Duke.

Malik was up and out of his chair in the blink of an eye. He had Duke by the throat and was more than willing to kill the man. *Speak of her in such a manner again and I will be your end.*

"Whoa!" said Striker, moving suddenly around the table and touching Malik's shoulders. "No killing Grumpy. He comes in handy every once in a while."

Malik, control your anger. That is an order, said Corbin mentally.

Malik did his best to rein in his temper. It was hard. He didn't like hearing Brooke referred to as a piece of ass.

Brooke slid her chair out and stood. "Edee, let's go."

"What? Wait. Why?" asked Malik, spinning to catch her by the elbows lightly. "Don't go."

"Don't be a jerk and I'll stay," she said, her lips pressing in a thin line.

Striker laughed and then stared past Malik, his face paling. "Do nae be thinking of using that on me, lass."

Malik looked back to find Edee eying a butter knife on the table. "Gelding him would be so much fun and so easy."

Striker backed up and cupped himself before hurrying around the table and taking a seat, as if he was the most well-behaved operative to ever live.

Yeah, right.

Malik kept hold of Brooke. "I didn't like what he said about you."

"He didn't say anything," she snapped back.

He remembered then that she couldn't hear their mental communications. "Right. I just, um, I'll sit down and not be a jerk anymore."

Duke huffed at the same time as Rurik before they both said, "Good luck."

"How cute," said Boomer, leaning back in his chair, appearing entirely too amused by the events. "The pissy doppelgangers now share a brain cell."

Malik fought to keep from laughing but failed.

Brooke stared up at him. "Is everything all right now? Are you done with the violence?"

He averted his gaze.

"Malik, violence isn't the answer. It should be the last resort, not the go-to response. I would have thought your parents would have taught you as much."

"My mother was Roman and put my brothers and I in an arena when we were little and demanded we fight to see who would be the next to take over the pride. And then the winner had to face off against the winner out of my cousins. She cared little for us if we were weak in any way. There was no place for the weak in my world. Violence is what I grew up knowing."

As the words left his mouth, he wanted them back.

All the men around him jerked in their seats, obviously catching on to the fact he'd just slipped up about being a shifter. He'd also never told any of them about his upbringing. Very few operatives knew the truth of it all.

Malik tensed. "Metaphorically speaking."

Brooke's expression was pained as she cupped his face. Her gaze searched him.

Whatever she saw made her eyes grow moist. "I'm sorry she didn't nurture you the way you should have been nurtured." She went to her tiptoes and wrapped her arms around his neck. Her lips went to his ear. "Don't think with your fists. Think with your head and your heart."

"My heart tells me to never let you go," he said before thinking about the fact that every male at the table was a supernatural and could easily hear his whispers.

Is she your mate? asked Corbin via their mental path.

She's human, said Malik, though he had to admit she had damn fast reflexes for one.

That didn't answer the question, replied Corbin.

Does she smell like a supernatural to you? he asked of Corbin.

No, returned the Brit.

She can't be my mate. Humans aren't mate material, returned Malik, his body tense. *The suppression drug is having adverse effects on me.*

Then exercise extreme caution around the human, added Corbin.

Malik nodded, wrapping his arms around Brooke's waist.

Edee tapped the table. "I'm hungry. Let's

order. You can listen to your heart and never let her go later. Food now."

She'd heard him whisper to Brooke too? How?

Brooke took his hand and led him back to his seat before taking her own. She then put her hand on his thigh as the waiter came to take their order. Malik couldn't tear his gaze away from her profile as she laughed at Duke and Rurik, who started calling each other various country-specific insults.

The antics continued and the tone at the table lightened. Striker began telling dirty jokes and Corbin looked tired.

"Would that I could fire you," said Corbin.

Edee offered a joke that made Striker's sound tame, making the entire table laugh.

Brooke cringed. "I really can't take her anywhere."

"It's okay. We have Striker. We understand," said Duke with his version of a smile.

Before long the food arrived and everyone ate, having fun, something they'd all been in short supply of as of late.

Edee and Boomer were the first to stand. Boomer ran a hand through his long black hair. "We're going over to the nearest club. We heard they have a DJ and dancing. Our goal is to watch Duke and Rurik try to bust a move."

Edee laughed, and it was good to see Boomer letting loose with someone he clearly clicked with.

Striker stood fast. "I'm in."

"Of course you are," said Edee with a sideways glance at the Scotsman.

Duke shook his head. "No dancing for me. Malik is the one who does that shit. Not me. He also likes that hip-hop crap."

"My taste in music is not crap." Malik finished off the last of his wine. It was true, he did enjoy dancing in clubs. And he did like hip-hop music. Something that got on Duke's last nerve. When Malik broke out the old-school rap, Duke normally hightailed it out of the room.

Rurik stood and pushed his chair out, his shoulders back. "Russians are not afraid to dance."

"I'm not afraid," protested Duke.

Edee laughed. "Dance-off! The bear versus the eagle."

Rurik stared at her. "How is it you know I'm a bear? And he's not an eagle. He's a wolf."

Corbin rubbed his brow, expelling a long

breath. "A bullhorn announcing all our secrets would be easier."

Rurik's brow furrowed. "What? What did she mean by bear versus the eagle?"

Garth touched Corbin's shoulder. "I've got this one."

Malik put his hand over Brooke's. "Up for going to the club?"

She nodded. "But I'm not much of a dancer."

Chapter Six

BROOKE SAT close to Malik in the oversized booth that they'd all claimed as theirs. They'd been at the club for two hours and she couldn't remember a time she'd laughed more in her life. All the men were funny in their own ways, even when they weren't trying to be, and they all seemed to care greatly for one another. Like brothers.

She and Edee had a relationship like that. It transcended friendship boundaries. Brooke glanced out at the dance floor to see Edee and Boomer hamming it up together, taking turns doing '80s dance moves to club music.

Duke and Rurik were at the end of the booth, leaning on one another as they polished off what she was sure was their sixth bottle of vodka. Though, she didn't understand how that could be. No one could drink that much and live to tell the tale. They raised their glasses and then slammed the shots.

Brooke smiled. "Who knew it would just take vodka to bond the eagle and the bear?"

Malik laughed. "Glad we finally got Rurik to understand the meaning of that. You know, Russian versus American."

Brooke touched Malik's hand as she began to people watch. Malik, Corbin, and Garth talked about medical equipment and from the way they kept sharing looks, she knew they were trying to speak in code around her. She didn't mind. She was still having a nice time even if she didn't understand what they were going on about.

She noticed Mr. Rings across the club, seated at a large booth, surrounded by the men in suits. Women were draped all over the men. The resort clearly had a very liberal view on public displays of affection for the Middle East. That, or everyone involved was worth so much money that new rules were made for them.

That was probably more the case.

Mr. Rings locked gazes with her and smiled

in a way that made her shiver. Instinctively, she pressed her side to Malik, who lifted his arm, putting it around her as he continued to talk to the other men. He rubbed her upper arm and she put her palm to his chest.

Mr. Rings whispered something to the man sitting closest to him, and Brooke's inner alarms went off again. Something deep inside said they weren't talking about her, they were talking about Malik. They intended to do him harm. She was sure of it. She'd never thought of herself as a violent person, but the very notion that Malik might be hurt by Mr. Rings and his hired muscle made Brooke want to gouge the man's eyes out.

Boldly, she sat up straight and glared at Mr. Rings. Cowering and shrinking away from violence faded from her mind. It took her a second to realize Malik was talking to her.

"What? Sorry." She glanced at him.

He looked in the direction she'd been glaring in and his nostrils flared. "What the fuck is he doing here? Does he want to die tonight?"

Corbin glanced over his shoulder. "Let me guess, asshat is the guy in the white suit."

"Yes," said Garth. "Hmm, I would have thought he'd have major bruising and a broken nose with as hard as Malik laid him out."

"If he keeps looking over here, a broken nose will be the least of his concerns," said Corbin, shaking his head. "Because I'm not sure I can stop Malik should he go at him fully."

Garth sighed. "Trust me when I say, you do not want to step in the path of that."

Malik took a deep breath and then looked upwards. "Think with my heart, not my fists. Hell, now I just want to think about ripping his heart out with my fists."

Brooke couldn't help but laugh as she realized he was repeating what she'd said to him in an attempt to calm his temper. She touched his cheek and turned his head to face her. Channeling her inner Edee, Brooke pressed her mouth to his, kissing him in a way that left no room for interpretation. She wanted him, and they would be together tonight.

Malik moaned into her mouth and ran his hand into her hair, upping the level of the kiss.

Brooke smiled against his lips. "Did that help?"

Malik kept his lips close to hers. "Help what?"

Corbin laughed.

"Help you with your temper," she said.

"I'm guessing he doesn't even remember what he was mad about," said Garth with a chuckle.

"I was mad?" asked Malik, his gaze on Brooke's lips.

The men laughed.

"Take her upstairs and show her what an ancient Egyptian can do," said Duke, slurring his words slightly. "Question, if a mummy has sex, do pieces of it fall off?"

Corbin groaned.

Garth laughed.

Brooke just looked at Duke, confused. "Aren't you two the same age?"

Duke opened his mouth to speak but Rurik covered it with one hand as he took another shot of vodka with the other. "Americans are shit with secrets."

"Fine one to talk, mister I'm a bear and he's a wolf," said Garth.

"We should probably cut them off," added Corbin. "They've had more than enough."

As the words left his mouth, the song changed from club music to "Eye of the Tiger" by Survivor. It was so grossly out of place that everyone took note. Brooke nudged Malik when she saw Boomer and Edee near the DJ booth.

Boomer looked over and waved. "In honor of Ivan Drago!"

"Why is he honoring the Russian character from the *Rocky* movie?" asked Brooke, making Malik and Garth snort.

Rurik eyed her. "Does everyone know of this Ivan Drago?"

"Is he for real?" asked Brooke.

Malik's lips twitched. "Afraid so."

Duke removed Rurik's hand from his mouth and stunned Brooke by belting out the words to the song.

There was a giant pregnant pause at the table before Garth, Corbin, and Malik whipped out their phones and began recording Duke as he sang to Rurik.

Rurik put his arm around Duke and rocked back and forth with him as he poured them more shots. He began trying to sing along too but didn't know the words so he basically just repeated what Duke said.

Striker walked up to the booth and raised a brow. "What the hell is in that vodka? Also, was anyone else aware Duke could carry a tune?"

"No, and I had no idea he had a thing for '80s soft rock," added Garth.

Striker looked to Malik. "I want a copy of that video later."

"Of course," said Malik, smiling wide.

Duke pointed at Garth, and Brooke was fairly sure that the only reason he and Rurik were still upright was because they were supporting one another. "Shut up, Swedish Chef."

As much as Brooke tried to avoid laughing at the insult, she couldn't help it. Garth's accent did kind of remind her of the Muppet slightly.

Garth kept his phone up, recording Duke and Rurik as they launched back into the song. "Laugh it up, Marlow. I feel an Asshole of the Week two-way tie coming on."

"For sure," said Malik, putting his phone away and taking a sip of his drink. He then focused on Brooke. "Are you having a nice time?"

She beamed. "I am."

Edee hurried over. "Come on, Brooke, let's dance."

Brooke put her hands up. "No way. I have two left feet."

Edee snorted. "Right. I've seen you play all

those sports. And you have crazy-fast reflexes. Like a friggin' cat."

"That doesn't mean I can dance," said Brooke. She didn't want to embarrass herself in front of Malik on the dance floor. "And I do not have fast reflexes. I fell into Malik earlier in the hotel room."

Edee grinned. "Because he makes you nervous. I've seen you, Brooke. And I've seen you dancing while doing that kickboxing workout you love so much."

"Kickboxing?" asked Malik.

"Name a sport and Brooke probably has done it. I swear Sporty Spice is my best friend. It's all I can do to get her out of yoga pants and cross-training sneakers. She makes me tired just watching her work out. I don't see the point, and I've explained that sex done right can give her just as good of a workout if not better."

Striker flashed a wide smile. "Aye! We should test that though. Especially if it will improve our health and all. One can never be too fit."

"In your dreams, big boy," returned Edee.

"Well if I'm nae getting sex, can I least get a dance?" asked Striker as he put his hand out to Edee.

"I'll dance with you if you convince Brooke

to come out and dance too," said Edee, a knowing smile on her face.

Striker set his sights on Brooke.

Brooke didn't want to see what the man would do next. She lifted a hand, stopping him before he opened his mouth and something suggestive fell out. "Go dance with her. I'll be out in a minute. I promise."

"Guid enough for me." Striker turned and picked up Edee, making her laugh as he carried her to the dance floor.

Another '80s song came on and Brooke had to wonder what deal Boomer had worked out with the DJ.

Rurik whistled and she glanced over as he lifted an unopened bottle of vodka. "Liquid courage?"

"No," said Malik sternly.

Brooke ignored him and nodded to Rurik. One second he had the bottle in his hand and the next it was coming at her at a high rate of speed. Without thought, she stood as much as she could in the booth and grabbed it, keeping it from hitting her or anyone else.

A half second later, Malik's hand was over hers, as if he were catching the bottle as well.

A round of gasps surrounded them.

Garth eyed Corbin. "Did she just get to that bottle before Malik did?"

Corbin gaped at her. "Yes."

Malik snarled as he glared down at Rurik, taking the bottle and flinging it at the drunk Russian, who caught it with ease before falling out of the booth, holding the bottle in the air.

Duke hoisted the man up. "Way to save the liquor."

"Yes," said Rurik, taking a seat next to Duke again.

Anger poured off Malik.

Brooke touched his back. "Stop. He was trying to give me the bottle so I could have a drink before I went out on that dance floor and made a fool of myself. He wasn't trying to hurt anyone."

"He's too drunk to know *what* he was doing," snapped Malik.

Corbin stood and stared at Malik. No words were spoken but Malik nodded and calmed somewhat.

Corbin looked to Brooke. "I'm with your friend. You have *very* fast reflexes. So much so that you managed to get the bottle before Malik did. That's saying something, Brooke."

She didn't comment.

Boomer danced his way to the table. He thumbed in the direction of Edee and Striker. "She sent me to retrieve you. She said, *she gave in and danced with the asshole. A deal is a deal.* Just so you know, Striker is the asshole in this story, not me."

Brooke laughed softly as she eased out of the booth, stepping in the direction of Boomer.

Boomer glanced past her cautiously. "Malik, take it easy. I won't let anyone touch her."

Brooke groaned. "He's ridiculous, and I swear if he keeps up the displays of dominance I'm going to show him everything I learned in kickboxing classes."

"Please let me watch," said Boomer, leading Brooke to the dance floor. True to his word, he pushed other men out of the way, getting Brooke to Edee and Striker quickly.

Edee was in the process of forcing Striker to do the robot dance. Much to Brooke's surprise, the guy gave in and did it. Brooke couldn't contain her laughter at seeing the large man dancing in such a way.

Edee yanked Boomer into the mix, leaving him no choice but to join in, which left Brooke cackling. "I have to visit the little girl's room before I wet myself laughing."

Edee gave her a thumbs-up.

Brooke headed in the direction of the restroom and did what needed to be done. She exited the bathroom and was nearly to the dance floor when it suddenly felt as if spiders were crawling all over her again. She knew without looking that Mr. Rings was behind her. His hand fell upon her shoulder.

"We have big plans for you and the other," he said, pressing against her. "Getting you here was so much easier than we ever expected it to be. I was against the farce. No need to waste any time or money. When we can take what we want—you."

She stiffened. What did he mean by that?

He laughed deeply in her ear. "And if you think they can protect you, you're wrong. We have plans for them too."

With that, he released his hold on her shoulder, and Brooke wasted no time running out and towards the dance floor. Strong arms caught her, and she nearly screamed until she realized the person holding her was Boomer.

"Brooke?" he asked, concern on his face.

She glanced behind her to find Mr. Rings and three of his men in suits walking out from the hall that led to the restrooms. He winked at her and adjusted his suit jacket.

Boomer kept hold of her. "What did he do? You're scared. I can smell it."

Smell it?

"I'm fine. He's just a creep who tried to get under my skin," she said, unsure she believed as much.

Boomer released her and locked gazes with her. "Did he threaten you or touch you in any way?"

Biting her lower lip, she looked away; she'd never been good at lying.

"Shit," whispered Boomer. "If Malik finds out, he will kill him—and no, I'm not embellishing. Malik will skin that asshat, probably alive. And then he'll skin me for taking my eyes off you."

"Then we should probably not tell him," she said, staying close to him, still shaken from the ordeal in the hallway.

"Not tell who what?" asked Malik as he walked up behind Boomer.

Boomer's eyes widened.

Brooke pushed past him and caught Malik's arm, turning and tugging him onto the dance floor fully. She pointed up at him. "Laugh at my dancing, I dare you."

Heat flashed through his dark gaze as he drew her closer to him and began to move in sync with the music. Somehow Malik made dancing to '80s music appear erotic. Gulping, Brooke realized just how sexually over her head she was with the man. Yet she still wanted him to be her first.

He lifted her arms, draping them over his shoulders, his hands finding her hips. He grinned but it faded fast as he sniffed near her shoulder—the very one Mr. Rings had grabbed her by. Malik's expression hardened. "He fucking touched you again. His scent is on you."

"His scent?" she asked.

He made a move to go towards Mr. Rings but she cupped his face, forcing him to keep his attention on her. "I'm tired of trying to control your temper. Thank you for a fun evening."

She walked away from him, only to find herself being spun around. He yanked her against him, his face going to the shoulder she'd been grabbed by. He nuzzled his face against her skin and then her neck. As he licked his way up her neck, she shivered and he put his lips to her ear, purring softly.

Instantly her body responded.

He began to grind against her, one hand going into her hair as the other cupped her ass. He licked her ear and then kissed his way to her lips, tugging on her hair lightly.

Brooke thought she might honestly faint if he kept going. It took a second to remember to breathe. She did and felt lightheaded. She was vaguely aware of Malik inching her dress up slowly.

"Malik," said Boomer, sounding close. "Don't do this out here with her, where every man in the club can see. Unless you want Asshat getting a firsthand view of her ass."

Malik broke the kiss and she could have sworn there was amber in his eyes again. He glared at Boomer, snarling, sounding like a large-breed cat.

Boomer put his hands in the air. "I'm not saying it to get you going. I'm saying it so you take the show somewhere private."

He continued to glare at his friend.

Brooke touched his chin. "Malik, I'm ready."

"Ready?" he asked, still looking as if he wanted to rip someone's head off.

She blushed and gave him a knowing look.

His eyes widened. "Really?"

"Really," she said with a smile.

Bending, he lifted her off her feet and carried her over the dance floor, past Edee and Striker.

Edee tossed her hands in the air in a celebratory manner. "Be gentle to start and then fuck her until she loses consciousness!"

Striker laughed. "Och, lass, you may verra well be worse than me."

"Thanks," returned Edee, still smiling at the sight of Brooke being carried out of the club.

Chapter Seven

MALIK POURED himself a drink at the wet bar in his room and used the moment to try to cage his beast. It had been beating at him from the inside out since he'd arrived at the hotel and caught the scent of honey and lotuses.

The scent of Brooke.

Her scent had made its way to him in the lobby and his lion had nearly burst free, and it had taken all his control to stop it. When he'd figured out the source of the smell was a woman, and that a man was hurting her, he'd shut off. He'd wanted to kill the bastard in the most painful of ways, and then he'd wanted to fuck the woman until she knew she was his.

Mine.

He winced, his beast still acting up.

Having her in his room, wanting to be with him, nearly did him in. He needed a drink to take the edge off. He looked at his reflection in the mirror above the wet bar, noting the feral look in his eyes. "She's human. She's not mate material. Pull yourself together," he whispered to himself in hopes it would sink in fully.

"Malik?" she asked, her voice sounding timid.

The last thing he wanted was for her to fear him in any way. He polished off his drink and poured another, unable to face her at the moment.

"Should I take my clothes off now?" she asked, and his cock hardened to the point he thought he'd come in his pants. "That was a stupid question, wasn't it? Of course you'll want my clothes off. Sorry. I'm a bag of nerves."

Dear gods, she was going to kill him.

He set his glass down and turned to face her. He had every intention of slowly undressing her, unwrapping the prize beneath, but his beast had other ideas. Before he realized what he was doing, he had her lifted off the floor, his mouth crashing down on hers.

She returned the kiss, her legs wrapping around his waist, which left her long dress riding high, exposing long bare legs to him. He growled into her mouth as he cupped the back of her thighs. Everything on him was heightened, making his entire body tingle with pleasure.

Brooke began to grind on him, and he lost the last shred of control he had. He reached between them and undid his pants. Much to his delight, Brooke's hands moved over his. She reached in and freed his erection, stroking it with an eagerness that spurred him onward. Jerking, he thought he'd come then and there. He fought with the buttons on his shirt with one hand before ripping it open, sending buttons flying in all directions. To hell with the fact it had cost over five hundred dollars. He wanted to be skin to skin with Brooke.

She pushed his leather pants down more and began jerking him off in a way that was going to make him come in seconds if she continued, and he wasn't a man who came easily that way—or any way for the last few hundred years. She raked her nails over his shaft lightly and Malik's lion roared within.

The next he knew, he was reaching under

her, a claw emerging from his fingertip before he tore through her panties. The claw receded at once.

Malik was about to walk Brooke to the bed so he could spread her out and lick her until she screamed his name and was good and ready to take all of him, when she lifted herself on him, lined up with his cock, and pressed the head of his dick to her soaked, hot core.

"Brooke," he managed between kisses and the urge to fuck her in two. He didn't even have his pants down yet. He couldn't recall a time he'd ever been this eager to be in a woman. This driven to join.

"Yes," she responded. "A thousand times over, yes."

"You're not ready yet."

She bit his lower lip hard enough to draw blood. His inner beast took the lead, wanting what she was offering. Malik thrust into her, tearing through resistance. He couldn't think harder on it because her body gripped his so tight that he nearly came then and there. She cried out in his arms, her legs wrapping tighter around his waist as he rooted in her.

Malik continued to control the movements and the speed with which they made love. And it was making love. It was hard and carnal, but it meant something to him. He wanted to drive like a piston into her, but the threat of breaking her was all too real. As a supernatural male, he could easily harm a human woman. His beast was already acting off—harder to control than normal despite the suppression drugs he'd taken before the mission. If anything, he seemed worse than normal, not better, and he'd never had control problems before.

Brooke dug her nails into his upper chest. "That feels so good."

He smiled against her cheek as he kissed his way to her lush lips. He pounded into her, driving himself deep into her tight, wet channel. He caught the faint whiff of blood and knew he was smelling her innocence that he'd taken.

A swelling of pride rose in him, but he couldn't understand why. She was hardly the first virgin he'd bedded. He'd been with thousands of women in the thousands of years he'd been alive. He'd been with so many they'd all started to blend into the same. But not Brooke. The very thought of other women turned Malik's stomach as he continued to drive himself into Brooke.

The woman was unlike anything he'd ever

felt wrapped around his cock. He wanted to explode deep in her and bathe her womb in his come. That was something he'd never done before. In all his years, he'd never released in a woman. But it was all he wanted to do with Brooke. The carnal need to mark her was nearly maddening.

Afraid he'd do the unthinkable and lose control of his shifter side, Malik took a deep breath and walked Brooke across the room to the wall, using the moment to try to collect himself. He then pressed her body to the wall with his, putting his hands to the surface. When he felt that he had at least a thread of restraint, he began to move in and out of her again.

She wiggled just right, making his ball sac tighten in preparation for release. He was about to pull out of her even though he didn't want to when her pussy fluttered around his cock. A gasp of pleasure came from her as she orgasmed.

Reason left him and he slammed into her, jetting seed into her, his beast roaring from within with victory.

A niggle of fear crept up on Malik, but Brooke's demanding kisses chased it away. He should have been sated at least for a bit, but his cock hardened again, still inside her. There was no stopping him as he found a rhythm that made her squirm in his arms and her channel continued to tighten in bursts around his shaft.

Chapter Eight
———————

MALIK CAME awake to find it was still dark out. He wasn't sure how long he'd slept. He found that he was partially draped over Brooke's naked form, effectively pinning her sleeping body to the bed. Even asleep he'd been afraid of losing contact with her. Whatever the scientists at PSI had given him needed some serious work. If it was supposed to help supernaturals with control issues, it was a failure.

Big time.

He could still feel his lion just below the surface, still wanting to bite Brooke, forever marking her—claiming her. He knew he should go somewhere else, even to one of his teammate's rooms, but the idea of being far from her set his beast even closer to the edge.

He stared at Brooke, committing every tiny detail of her to memory. She was simply breathtaking. Not only that, she was funny and didn't seem to understand just how beautiful she was.

He reached for his cell phone on the side table and took a picture of her, something he'd never bothered doing with any other woman. He didn't want to forget her. Not that he ever could. Still, he wanted something for himself—a token of their time together. He set his phone back on the side table.

The sounds of music filtered up and through the open doors that led out to the balcony. Below, one of the outdoor bars was still in full swing. He realized then that he must have only dozed off for a bit. As his cock stirred to life, he groaned. It should have been more than satisfied for weeks with as many times as he'd been with Brooke before they'd fallen asleep, but it was as if he'd never even taken the edge off his need for sex.

No. My need for Brooke.

His chest tightened with concern. He couldn't keep her. She was human. And his lion side was simply confused from the suppression drugs that had gone sideways. That would work itself out and he'd lose interest, as he did with every woman he'd ever bedded. Though, with the others, he was generally bored by now. And he never slept next to any of them. No. He was the type of man who got what he wanted and left right away. He didn't stay to hold women or have tender moments.

As he looked at the way he was pinning Brooke to the bed with his body, he knew just how much the drugs had messed with his system. They'd turned him into a cuddler. That should have been enough to motivate him to sneak out of the bed and leave Brooke, but it wasn't.

His gaze trailed down the length of her body, settling on her abdomen.

Claim her.

His breath caught at the inner drive to make her his.

Did his lion not understand she wasn't mate material? She was human. That meant she couldn't be his mate. It was impossible. And he'd know if she was a supernatural, right? His senses weren't that out of whack, were they?

He found himself reaching out and skimming his fingers over Brooke's cheek ever so lightly. He didn't want to wake her. She needed her rest, but he did want to caress her.

Her eyelids fluttered open and her olive gaze locked on him. A smile tugged at the edges of her lips.

"Is it morning already?" she asked, her voice husky from sleep.

"No, my sweet," he said, surprising himself with the term of endearment. He wasn't the type of man who used pet names with women. He'd never found the need or desire to, but he wanted to whisper in his native language to her and tell her everything he felt for her. Things he *shouldn't* feel for her, as he'd only just met her, not to mention she was human. But the words were on the tip of his tongue, so much so that they spilled out.

Brooke lifted a brow. "I'm either very tired or that wasn't English."

He stilled, stunned he'd just confessed to being in love with her. That was absurd. Wasn't it?

It didn't feel very crazy at the moment.

Fucking suppression drugs.

"Malik?" she asked, her hand going to his bare chest. "What's wrong?"

Act of Passion

"Nothing, my sweet," he offered softly, wanting to calm her worry.

"Mmm, what did you say before? What language was it? That wasn't Arabic, was it? It's familiar to me."

"It's a language that isn't really spoken anymore. One that I haven't spoken in centuries," he said.

A giggle erupted from her. "Centuries? Being a bit dramatic there, aren't you? You're making yourself out to be an honest-to-God ancient Egyptian like Boomer teased you about."

He found himself nodding partially, unable to outright lie to her.

"Tell me what you said." She bit her lower lip seductively.

He ran his thumb over her lip. "I told you things you are not ready to hear, and I'm not sure I'm ready to translate."

"You didn't tell me that you're married, did you?" she asked, her body stiffening.

He laughed softly. "No. I'm not married."

Yet.

The more he looked at her there in bed with him, the more he wanted to claim her, making her his wife in the eyes of the supernatural community. How he wanted to shout from the rooftops that he'd found the woman for him.

Her olive eyes traced his face and a wicked grin spread over hers. "In case I forget to tell you, thanks for being my first."

He touched her arm, his beast stirring from within. "And I will be your only."

She didn't comment.

As he watched her, soaking in her beauty, the picture he'd taken began to weigh on him. With a sigh, he reached back and grabbed his phone again. He pulled up the picture he took of her and handed her the phone.

"If you don't want me having that, delete it," he said, hoping she wouldn't.

She held the phone and smiled wide at him. "You took a picture of me sleeping?"

"Yes."

"And you're offering me the chance to delete it? Why?" she asked.

He grunted. "Because it's intimate and I should have asked you first. I just wanted something of you, I don't know. It was stupid and I may be an asshole, but even I have my limits."

"Malik, you took a very beautiful picture of me. I'm naked but you can't tell in the picture. Thank you for that. I don't want to delete it."

She bit her lower lip. "Can I have a picture of you?"

He squirmed. He couldn't allow photos of himself to go into the world. He didn't age. He didn't need a digital footprint proving as much. It was one thing for the guys to take photos of each other. They knew better than to release them into the world or to social media. Well, at least most of them did. Striker had issues following that rule. A human wouldn't understand that there even *were* rules.

She lowered her gaze. "Whatever you do that you can't tell me about means you can't let me take a picture of you, doesn't it?"

"Yes, my sweet," he said softly.

She held the phone out for him. "I understand. I won't lie that I wish things could be different, but I knew what I was getting into when I entered the room. You're not the type of guy who calls the next day, or ever. I know I won't ever see you again after this is done. Thank you for giving me a night I'll never forget. I hope it was at least semi-memorable for you too."

He grabbed for her and ran his hand into the back of her hair, pulling her mouth closer to his. He kissed her, wanting to show her how much she meant to him. How much he didn't want their night to end. He eased off the kiss slightly. "Call your cell from mine. My number will be in your phone then, and yours will be in mine."

She raised her brows but took his phone and dialed hers. It rang in her small bag across the room. The smile she cast at him moved him down to his very soul.

"There are things about me, about my life, that I can't talk about with you, Brooke, but if you're open to the idea of seeing where this goes, I'm in." His words shocked him. He'd just told a human woman he wanted a relationship with her. Hell, he'd never told *any* woman that. Human or not.

"What do you mean, exactly?" she asked, watching him carefully.

He kissed the edge of her lips softly. "It means I want something with you that I've never wanted before. I want a future with you. If you'll have me."

Her skepticism was easy to read by her expression. He couldn't exactly blame her.

A thought occurred to him. "What if I was able to find you a job close to where I work? Would you consider it?"

All that did was make her look at him as if she was waiting for the punch line. He wasn't sure how to handle the burning need to never let her go. He'd never asked a woman to commit to a relationship before and was apparently shit at it.

He brushed her hair back from her cheek. "Brooke, I have a lot of connections within the DOD and private organizations where cyber security is a must. I know I can find you something perfect close to my headquarters."

"Headquarters?" she asked.

He cringed. "Uh, ignore that bit. Focus on the idea of taking a job close to me. Not that you have to work."

"I kind of do if I want to live and eat," she said calmly.

"Move in with me," he blurted.

Her eyes widened. "I'm sorry, but what?"

Malik found his face heating as he tried to find the right words to convince her to come back home with him. He knew it was incredibly stupid to ask a human to live with him, but he didn't care. He'd find a way to keep what he was a secret from her. He'd find a way to make it work. "Move in with me and you don't need to worry about a job. Money isn't an issue for me.

I'll give you whatever you want. Name it and it's yours."

Brooke touched his eyebrow and traced her fingers over it, before trailing them down his face slowly. "I'm sure you didn't mean to make that sound like you'd be buying me."

"No, gods no," he said, only to have her press her finger to his lips to silence him.

"Malik, I know you didn't mean it that way, and what you're offering is very generous and very sweet, but we just met. I don't really think you want to have me move in when you've known me less than a day."

"Well, you'd be wrong," he said, even with her finger against his lips. "I want you, Brooke."

"We don't know each other well enough to move in together," she said, tugging lightly on his lower lip.

He drew her finger into his mouth and sucked on it, his gaze locking on hers. "I know I want you with me. I know thinking of not having you near me sets me on edge."

She pushed on his shoulders until he lay flat on his back. Brooke eased up and over him, her naked form pressed to his. She dipped her head and kissed him and his cock responded at once, lengthening under her.

The damn thing didn't seem to ever tire of being in her.

She straddled his waist and sat up. She reached down and took hold of him, guiding him to her wet entrance. She sank down onto his cock slowly and he found himself mesmerized by the sight of her riding him. Her long hair was tousled from sleep, only serving to make her even sexier. And her breasts bounced as she began to move up and down on his shaft.

He took hold of her breasts and realized they didn't quite fit in his large hands. He grinned and kneaded her soft globes as she moved on him. If he lived another thousand years, he'd never forget this moment. Never forget what she looked like there, taking him deep into her, gaining pleasure from his body while gifting him so very much more.

It was on the tip of his tongue to blurt out three little words he'd never said to a woman before. *I love you.*

She bounced on him, increasing her pace, and Malik found he couldn't hold off his orgasm any longer. He released one of her breasts and used his thumb to rub her clit, making her gasp and then toss her head back in ecstasy. She stilled on him as her channel grasped him fully. Malik exploded, his jaw going slack as he moaned in pleasure.

Her body was awash with the afterglow of sex. "You are the sexiest man I have ever seen."

When he spoke, it was in his native tongue. He told her that she was the type of woman who could launch a thousand ships. The type of woman a man worshiped, loved, and cherished. The type of woman a man made his wife.

She pursed her lips. "No idea what you said but let me be the first to say that was hot as hell and oddly familiar."

He laughed.

She stayed on him, her gaze skimming his upper body. She touched one of his many tattoos. "This one means god, right?" she asked as she skimmed her fingers over script from his native tongue that he had on his body.

Surprised that she knew that, he put his hand over hers. "Yes. How did you know?"

She eased off his shaft but stayed on him, her hand still pinned under his. "It was in one of the books I had when I was little…before my parents died. It was a book about ancient Egyptian gods and pharaohs. My dad used to read it to me until I could read myself, when I turned four. Then he'd sit while I read it, and others like it, to him. And he would make up his own stories. He'd say very weird things—like he'd really been in ancient Egypt. I miss him and my mother."

Malik wanted to kiss away her sadness. "Do you remember any of his made-up stories?"

She kissed his chest and then eased up slightly. "Yes. He had a really strong dislike of King Tut."

Malik snorted. "I can sympathize."

"He'd talk about a king who didn't want to be king so he stepped aside," she stated, smiling a touch.

He held her thighs, keeping her on him. "W-what?"

"He would tell me these made-up stories and make me say them back to him over and over," she confessed. "And he'd cry when he told me some of them. Like when he talked about being good friends with the king who didn't want to be king. And that one day I'd know him too." She wrinkled her nose. "But then he'd grumble about wanting to kill the guy because of his appetite for women. I was little then. I thought the king who didn't want to be king actually sat at a table and ate a feast of cooked women. I was scared senseless for a while that he'd show up and gobble me up too."

He ran his thumb over her lower lip, unable to shake what her father had said to her. It hit a little too close to home.

She touched another of his tattoos. "What does this one mean?"

He moved her fingers over his tattoos. "This all means 'son of the god king.'"

Brooked looked stunned—and when she spoke again, it was in perfect ancient Egyptian. She said "son of the god king."

With a sharp intake of breath, he continued to run his thumb over her lips. "Brooke? How did you know how to say 'son of the god king' in ancient Egyptian?"

She laughed hard. "I don't know. It was part of my Dad's stories."

It was anything but made up. Malik tilted her chin upwards. "Brooke, did he teach you anything else?"

"I guess," she said. "But I don't remember much of it anymore. Just certain things he made me repeat endlessly."

"Can you tell me what else you remember him teaching you or about him?" he asked.

"I remember what he looked like. He was tall, like you. Well, honestly, he had a lot in common with you; same color hair, same skin tone, lots of tattoos like you, and your temper," she said softly, tracing circles on his chest. "Oh, and he had an accent similar to yours but thicker. My mom used to laugh when he'd attempt slang. I thought he was perfect. And I thought he hung the moon. I was totally and completely a daddy's girl."

For a split second, Malik wondered if her father was like him, immortal, but Brooke would be as well, and she wasn't. She may have fast reflexes but she was human, nothing more. He'd smell it on her if she wasn't.

Brooke traced the tattoo that had launched the discussion. "Son of the god king. That would make you a prince, right?"

Malik bit his inner cheek, unsure how to respond. There was so much he kept from everyone in his life that lying about his past had just been second nature. But lying to her felt wrong. "Yes."

She snorted and then kissed the tattoo. "Uh-huh. What you're saying is I'm living out Edee's Egyptian fantasy. You know, come here, find a hot prince and make him my sex slave."

Malik really liked the idea of being her sex slave. "Edee's fantasy is that?"

"Yep," said Brooke, kissing his chest again. "She's going to be really jealous when she finds out I did it."

He could tell by her tone that she didn't believe for one moment that he was a prince. But it was true. In what felt like another life, he was heir apparent to the throne. A throne he'd never wanted but had been thrust upon him. A throne he walked away from, allowing another to rule in his place.

He ran his fingers through her hair. "So now that you have a prince at your service, does it make you want to change your mind on moving in with me?"

"No," she said, bending and kissing the tattoos in question once more. She then moved to others. "How many do you have?"

"I have no idea. A lot. They aren't anywhere that people can see when I'm dressed and in a long-sleeved shirt. Do they bother you?" he asked, willing to have them removed. It would involve needing to have his skin peeled fully from the area and then allowing his shifter side to heal the damage. The act of getting tattoos to stay and not heal over was something of an art form for supernaturals, and was painful. He didn't care about the pain. But if Brooke didn't like them, he'd get rid of every last one.

"I like them," she said, lying down on him fully.

He hugged her to him, his chest tightening with a swell of emotions. "Move in with me."

She laughed. "We're back to that again?"

"Yes," he said, running his hand over her ass cheek. "Say yes and I'll stop asking."

She put her cheek to his upper chest. "Can't we just let this be what it is?"

Malik frowned. Was she rejecting him? No woman had ever done such a thing before. He wasn't sure if he should be offended or not. He did know that her answer wasn't acceptable. "I bet Edee would tell you to move in with me."

Brooke laughed. "No. She's commitment phobic. She'd run with me as quick as she could to save me from a life with just one man. That freaks her out big time. And should you somehow manage to sway her to your side, you'll find I'm not so easy to convince. I'll live with someone, someday, probably. If I ever get married or something like that. I never really gave it a lot of thought."

"So you're saying you'd live with me if we were married?" he asked.

"You are so weird." She took a deep breath. "I'm excited to start the next chapter of my life. And while I very much want to see you again, I'm not expecting you to commit to me or have me move in with you."

His lion tried to push up, wanting to dominate the situation and make her understand she was his. The damn suppression drugs were making him think irrationally. What was he doing asking her to move in with him? And why the hell was he entertaining marrying her?

She was human.

It would never work or last.

At some point, she'd notice he wasn't aging.

The idea was insane. When he opened his mouth to say as much, something altogether different came out of him. "Marry me. Move in with me. We're meant to be together. My house has plenty of room."

Brooke snorted and rolled off him, going to her stomach next to him on the bed. "For a guy who claims he's not much into hanging around for the next morning, you're going out of your way to dispel that theory," she said, gifting him a smile. "I should say yes and then force you to hold up your end of it all. Somehow I think you'll run in the other direction the minute this goes from pillow talk to a reality."

He rolled onto his side and began to rub her back lightly. "One way to find out. Say yes."

She grinned more. "Okay, yes. Let's get married and move in together. Hurry up, if we get dressed now we can try to find somewhere to marry us. Ooo, can it be on camel back?"

"Yes," Malik said, excitement racing through him. He made a move to get out of the bed to get dressed but she caught his wrist.

"What are you doing?" she asked.

"Getting ready to take you and marry you on the back of a camel," he said, as if it was self-explanatory.

Brooke lost it, laughing so hard that she stopped making noise.

His ego deflated. The woman thought he was joking? He did not joke about marriage or commitment. In fact, the topics were as far from funny as one could get in his mind. The very idea of such things used to sicken him. He only slept with as many women as he did because he required it. And with Brooke, he'd only be with her. He wouldn't need another woman.

"If you're not careful, you'll find yourself

claimed," he said, before stiffening at his own words.

A mocking laugh came from her. "Oh yeah. Shaking here. Claimed? Like baggage at an airport?"

"Like mine for eternity," he said, reaching down and stroking himself, the fierce need to mount her sweeping over him. He leaned and kissed her shoulder, his gums burning with the need to shift and allow his lion teeth to emerge.

Brooke glanced down the length of him. "Do you ever get enough?"

"Of you? No," he said, kissing her shoulder once more. "Have you had enough of me?"

"This is going to sound really weird, and I don't want to freak you out or anything, but I'm not sure I could ever have enough of you," she confessed. "Is this normal? I think we've already established that I don't have anything to compare this to, but it seems intense. Really friggin' intense."

It was.

"That being said, I'm not agreeing to move in with you or marry you," she said with a snort.

Malik slid up and over her, the entire length of his body covering hers. He used a knee to spread her legs and Brooke lifted her backside, as if sensing what he and his animal needed. He needed to dominate. He needed to know she wasn't really rejecting him. He needed to mount her. He needed to taste her flesh while he did.

He kissed her back, trailing a line down it to her backside. Malik nibbled playfully at her ass cheeks, wanting to be buried between them, but he knew she wasn't ready for that yet. He continued planting kisses down the back of her thighs, to her calves and then to her feet.

She giggled as he kissed the bottom of her foot. "That tickles."

He licked it, making her jerk and laugh more. Her light energy and happiness was infectious. She made him feel young again. He nibbled his way back up her, biting her ass cheek slightly harder than before, causing her to gasp. He kissed the spot he'd bitten and then took hold of her hips, lifting her off the bed more. He went to his knees and gripped his cock, stroking it, lining up with her wet core.

Seeing her bent before him was exactly what the lion and the man wanted. He wasted no time driving home, feeling complete once she was wrapped around his cock once more.

He gritted his teeth, sure he'd explode if he dared to move. She had that effect on him.

When he felt as if he could move, he did, easing in and out of her slowly at first before increasing his pace. He focused on her upper back, just beneath her shoulder. He felt his teeth beginning to lengthen, but he didn't stop fucking Brooke. He couldn't. She felt too good. The moment felt too right.

Her tiny intakes of breath as he pounded into her only served to drive him onward in a frenzy. Brooke clutched the sheets, her body spasming around his. He thrust in, going balls deep, bending over her as he did. She cried out, coming hard, and for a split second he could have sworn he felt Fae power around them. As quickly as it had arrived, it vanished.

"Mine," Malik ground out.

He opened his mouth and bit the tender flesh near her shoulder. Seed burst free from him as nothing short of what could be described as nirvana washed over him, making his lion roar with victory as his cock twitched more, pulsing more seed into her.

The taste of her coppery blood eased over his tongue, and reason began to set in. He opened his mouth and stared at the bite mark on her flesh. Blood oozed from it and the lion in him pushed up faster, forcing him to lick the wound. He did, and the healing agents in his saliva went to work closing the bite mark over.

Malik's mind swam with worry as he realized he'd not only bitten her during sex. He'd done it while coming in her. As his lion continued to try to fully take over, he knew he wasn't safe to be around.

He'd hurt her if she remained close to him. He couldn't have that. He couldn't let his beast hurt the woman who stole his heart.

Malik hurried off the bed, horrified at what he'd done. He'd bitten her during the height of passion. He'd claimed her. Thankfully, she was human, which meant the claim wouldn't stand. It was a by-product of the suppression drugs.

His arms heated and he felt fur starting to spring forth. He was losing control and about to shift forms fully.

Brooke wrapped the sheet around herself and slid off the bed. "Malik? What's wrong? You look pale. Are you okay?"

"I can't," he managed, his teeth lengthening. "Get out."

"You're kicking me out? You just got done trying to convince me to move in with you and consider marrying you. Now you're throwing me out of your hotel room?" Her expression fell. "You regret this, don't you?"

"Yes," he said, meaning that he regretted losing control. He did not regret being with her. Being with her had been the best night of his life—right up until he fucking lost his damn mind and bit her while releasing his seed in her.

Hurt flashed in her eyes. "Oh, okay. Wow. You weren't kidding about being gone by morning. Guess I should feel flattered you bothered to feed me the lines about wanting more. You know what, you *are* an asshole."

"No," he said, trying to get across that he hadn't fed her a line. He didn't want to be away from her. He didn't have a choice. If his lion broke free with her there, it could kill her. "Go!"

Malik wanted to explain in detail that it wasn't her, it was a drug meant to help give his kind more control—and failing—but he couldn't even speak with his mouth shifting forms, let alone explain that things that went bump in the night were real and he was one of them.

Brooke found her dress and yanked it on, leaving her ripped panties on the floor. She grabbed her boots and her bag, refusing to meet his gaze as tears streaked her cheeks. "Malik…"

He held on by a thread, unable to respond to her.

"I'm sorry that I started to believe there was more to this than just sex. I'm sorry that I already started to let my guard down with you. Mostly, I'm sorry I ever met you. I'll go. Do me a favor and lose my number. I don't want to ever see or speak to you again."

That wasn't what he wanted in the least. Telling her wasn't even an option. His lion was too far gone.

She ran for the door and he fell to his knees, trying to stop a full shift from coming. As Brooke shut the door behind her, his body contorted and he lost the battle against his beast.

The last clear thought he had before fully becoming an animal was that he'd just ruined the most perfect thing that had ever happened to him.

Chapter Nine
―――――――

STRIKER MCCRACKEN STROLLED down the hall of the hotel, whistling a song that was an ode to the lycan legend William Wallace. So far Egypt had been a great mission. He'd wanted to get laid last night, but he'd ended up closing the bar with Edee and Boomer. He had to admit he'd had fun, even without having sex.

That was rare.

He was partway down the hall, nearing his room when he saw Brooke running out of Malik's room. She slammed the door behind her and twisted, tears running down her face.

Unsure what was going on, Striker put his arms out and caught Brooke just as she tripped. "Careful, lass."

She sobbed and righted herself, pushing out of his hold.

His wolf stirred, scenting Malik all over her, in more than just a sexual way. It was almost as if Malik had marked her. But that was ridiculous. The Egyptian would never claim a human. None of the men he knew would. Hell, he didn't even think they could claim one. From his limited understanding of mating, it was instinctual and only happened with one's chosen mate. Not randomly. And only with another supernatural.

Still, he could have sworn the woman was marked by his friend.

She wiped her cheeks, dropping her boots in the process.

Striker retrieved them for her and stayed close to her, concern for her state of distress filling him. He didn't want to think the worst happened, but he'd be remiss if he didn't ask. "Lass, Malik dinnae hurt you, did he?"

Shaking her head, she continued to cry. "Not physically. I was so stupid. I'd heard all about men like him. I thought I knew what I was getting into, but then he said he wanted more. He brought up moving in together and getting married. And then he freaked out and threw me out of the room. Why did I let him be my first?"

Striker pursed his lips, at a loss for what to say to smooth the situation over for his friend. "As far as firsts, it could have been worse. It could have been an English guy. I do nae think they're verra guid lovers. Erm, not that I'd know or anything. I do nae bed them myself, but they do nae look as if they'd be worth much in bed. Never mind. Ignore me. So, about that rat-bastard Egyptian?"

The look she cast him said he wasn't helping in any way.

Striker shrugged. "Can I help you find Edee? She has nae threatened to unman me in hours. She's overdue."

Duke stepped out into the hall from his room, looking like hammered shit. He drank enough to cause one hell of a hangover. When he spotted Brooke in tears, he arched his brows in question. His gaze snapped to Striker. "What did you do?"

Offended one of his best friends would think so low of him, he huffed. "Och, I dinnae cause this. Malik did."

Surprise coated Duke's face. "Malik caused this? I'd have laid money on it being you."

"The show of support is amazing. Do you nae have some 'Eye of the Tiger' you could be singing?" asked Striker.

Duke looked puzzled. "'Eye of the Tiger'? Singing? What the hell are you going on about?"

"I'll show you the video later," said Striker.

Duke opened his mouth to say something else when a huge roar sounded from Malik's hotel room. From the volume level, it could mean only one thing. Malik was fully shifted into a lion.

"What was that?" asked Brooke, her eyes wide.

"Oh shit!" yelled Duke. "Get her out of here! Now!"

Nodding, Striker took one look at Brooke and did the only thing he could think to do in an emergency. He lifted her and tossed her over his shoulder, making her yelp and drop her boots again. If Malik broke loose and ran through the resort, it would be very bad.

Striker ran in the other direction with the woman over his shoulder, swatting at his back to be let down. The last thing he wanted was to have Malik eat the woman or maul her. He ran in the direction of the elevator and heard something large crashing from the other end of the hall.

Duke's curses sounded next. "Fucking Egyptian! I fucking hate cats!"

"The stairs it is," said Striker as he pivoted and headed to the stairs. He struck the door with so much force that he knocked it completely off. With the woman still over his shoulder, he hurried down the stairs, wanting to get her to safety and then get back to help Duke corral Malik.

In all the years he'd known Malik, the man had never lost control or had anything close to an issue with his shifter side. Often Striker was envious of Tut. Something had gone seriously wrong for the man to lose his shit to that point.

When Striker got the woman to the lobby, he set her on her feet gently and tried to smooth down her dress.

"Striker!"

He blushed as he realized he'd run his hands over her backside, trying to be sure she was covered fully. "Sorry. I, um, have to go now. You should get as far away from here as you can. Do nae look back. Forget you ever met him. Run."

More tears appeared and he knew then he'd said the wrong thing. But it was the truth. For her own safety, she needed to be far away. Malik would never forgive himself if he hurt an innocent.

She turned and ran in the direction of the hotel exit. Striker started back for the stairs but realized he should probably make sure the woman got back to her own room safely. He spun around and went after her.

She was nowhere to be seen.

Had she gotten out of the hotel that fast?

He jogged to the exit and the doors slid open automatically. He stepped out but found no sign of her. Her scent lingered, mixed with something else, but she wasn't anywhere he could see. Out of the corner of his eye, he spotted several large black SUVs. The assholes were driving way too fast out of the parking lot. If they weren't careful, they'd kill someone.

"Humans," he said, heading back into the resort quickly. "Here's hoping the cat can get back in the bag."

Chapter Ten

MALIK BLINKED AND FOUND DUKE, Striker, and Corbin on him, pinning him to the floor of his hotel room. Garth was close and partially shifted, and Rurik was next to him, holding a weapon on Malik.

"W-what the fuck?" Malik demanded, realizing he was naked and under a pile of his teammates. "Get off me."

Corbin locked gazes with him. "Are you finished acting like a fool?"

Unsure what Corbin was talking about, Malik lay perfectly still, thinking of the last thing he could remember. As his thoughts went to biting Brooke during sex, he gasped. "Brooke! Where is Brooke? Did I hurt her?"

Striker grunted. "Och, the wee lass ran out of here crying, thinking you did nae want her and that you used her. When I last saw her, she was leaving the resort to get far from you."

"Asshole," said Duke, easing off Malik. "Shifting into a fucking lion? Cat-shifters are dicks."

Corbin cleared his throat and stood, righting his shirt sleeves, looking as if Malik had given him a hard go of it.

Striker was the last to move off Malik. The Scotsman boldly looked down at Malik's groin. "I dinnae think you were packing something like that. Impressive. Glad you dinnae participate in the dick-measuring contest."

Ignoring him, Malik pushed to his feet and looked around for his pants. "Clothes. I need clothes and to find Brooke."

Duke thrust him backwards. "The last damn thing you need is to find her. She messes with your head."

Corbin nodded in agreement.

Rurik lowered the weapon. "Is the female your mate?"

"Why does everyone keep asking me that?" demanded Malik, shoving Duke out of his way. "Where are my pants?"

Garth, now back in human form, tossed a pair of pants at him from the closet. "Dress, but I agree with Duke. The woman ties you in knots. It's for the best you let her go. Nothing can come of it all, Malik. You know it, and so does every other male standing here."

Malik shook his head. "You're wrong. I have to find her. How long was I shifted for?"

Garth checked his watch. "About two hours. Took all of us to hold you down for a while there."

Two hours? He'd been out of control for two entire hours?

Boomer came into the room with a tranq gun. "Oh, he's back to normal. Guess this won't be needed."

"Do nae be too sure," said Striker. "Tut wants to find the female again."

Boomer's brows went up. "Not that I think you should be around her, but I saw the cleaning crew in the room she and Edee were sharing. I heard them mention something about the girls who had been staying there had checked out early and instructed that their luggage be shipped to them."

The air left Malik's lungs as he wrapped his

mind around what Boomer was saying. "She's gone?"

"Can you blame her?" asked Boomer, stepping closer. "From what Striker told us, you were a total douchebag to her."

Striker gave a curt nod. "Aye. And I dinnae know the two lasses had checked out."

Malik yanked his pants on and ran for the door, only to be stopped by Striker. The wolf-shifter shocked him by lifting him into the air and then body slamming him to the floor. The force it took to do such a thing to Malik of all people was staggering. He never knew Striker possessed it.

Striker stood above him and pointed down at him. "You do nae deserve her. Leave her be. She's better off without you. You've lived a charmed life, Tut, and wouldnae know a guid thing if it bit you in the arse. Find a woman who does nae care that you bed anything that moves. Brooke isnae it."

Boomer put a finger in the air, opened his mouth and then closed it again before facing Corbin. "Did my ears deceive me or did Striker just lecture Malik about being a manwhore?"

"Your ears are fine," said Rurik, crossing his

arms over his chest. "I'm with the wolf. The American girls were okay, you know, for Americans and all."

Duke rolled his eyes and pointed to Striker. "That shit they gave you two back in the labs is messing with your heads and your personalities. Malik, the man who makes sleeping with a different woman nightly an art form, wants a human woman for keeps. And the Scot is offended for the woman."

Malik eyed Striker from his spot on the floor. "You took the suppression drugs too?"

"Aye." Striker put a hand out to him, helping him up. "They're nae stopping me from wanting to do you great harm."

Garth snorted. "He had hopes for bedding the redhead. We tried to tell him that was never going to happen. He saw it as a challenge. You've gone and ruined that for him now."

"Aye."

Malik's jaw tightened and he desperately fought to keep from showing his raw emotions. "I know I don't deserve her but I'm asking for your help here. I need to find her. I need to know she's okay. I need her to understand that I chased her away because I claimed her, not because I didn't want her. She's *all* I fucking want!"

The room fell silent.

Garth spoke next. "You claimed a human?"

Malik rubbed his eye, fighting pending tears. "Yes and no. I mean, I couldn't stop myself from biting her during sex and saying *mine*, but she's human so it doesn't count. That doesn't mean I want her out of my life. I want her more than I've ever wanted anything and I have to know she's okay."

Seconds ticked by before Corbin took out his cell phone. "This is Captain Jones. I need some information on the following two humans." He lowered the phone. "Malik, what is Brooke's full name?"

Malik gasped. "I don't know. I didn't ask. Why didn't I ask? I asked her to marry me and move in with me but I didn't stop and think to ask her name?"

"Fuck me sideways. Tut asked a woman for something serious?" Duke shook his head. "They're ice skating in hell."

The men shared a look and Corbin hung up the phone. Corbin looked around at the men. "Fan out and ask the staff if they know where the women went. We'll assure they are safe and well and then we'll get Malik as far from the woman as possible."

Malik tensed. "W-what?"

"The suppression drugs are messing with your mind, dude," said Boomer. "You claimed a human. That's seriously whacked."

Rurik nodded. "Yeah, whacked."

Garth tossed Malik a pair of shoes and a shirt before walking towards the door. "We'll check with the front desk for any leads. Malik, why don't you ask the valet service if they know the women's destination?"

He nodded, put a shirt on, not bothering with the buttons, and slipped on his shoes before rushing over and grabbing his cell. He hurried out of the room. Striker was right behind him. They took the stairs and were in the lobby before Garth and Rurik exited the elevator. Malik ran out of the resort and looked around out front, catching the faintest hint of honey and lotuses.

He called Brooke's phone from his. It rang and rang but she didn't answer. Her voicemail picked up. "Brooke, my sweet, I'm so sorry. Please call me the second you get this."

Striker was staring off in the other direction, his gaze narrowed as Malik disconnected the call.

Malik tensed. "What is it?"

"Maybe nothing," said Striker. "Call the lass again."

Malik did as requested, and Striker ran over to the landscaping near the front door. He stepped into it and came out with Brooke's bag. It was ringing.

Malik's stomach dropped as he remembered Brooke telling Edee that she never went anywhere without the bag.

Garth came out front, his face long. "Malik," said Garth somberly. "Rurik has the front desk man in the back, pressing him for answers."

Striker put his hand on Malik's shoulder but looked at Garth. "What is it? What did he say?"

Garth sighed. "That they were paid handsomely to look the other way while men in large vehicles took the women against their will."

Nothing else was heard by Malik as his lion thrust upwards. He caught sight of Boomer walking out and Garth motioning to him. Boomer ran at Malik fast, a tranq dart in hand.

Try as he might, Malik couldn't contain

himself, and knew his friends would do what they thought was best to protect him, even from himself, but that didn't change the fact that someone had Brooke.

Someone had his woman.

Chapter Eleven

PRESENT DAY...

MALIK SAT at his desk in what he and his coworkers called the bullpen and worked on the last of his reports. Paperwork had piled up during his recent forced leave of absence. He hadn't had a chance to catch up on it since his return because there had been one mission after another. All were important and none could be missed. If he wasn't going on missions with his current team, he was being loaned out to others. Such was the way of things with PSI.

And when he finally had a moment off from

work, he tried to get a lead on where Brooke was. It had been five years since their night together. Five years since he'd asked her to move in with him and to be his wife, and five years since he'd lost his shit and nearly shifted fully in front of her.

And five years since he'd learned that she'd been abducted.

In all that time, there hadn't been a single clue as to where she'd been taken or who the men worked for. For the first few months, his PSI teammates had all assisted when they could in his search for Brooke and Edee, but after a while they began to look at him with pity in their eyes. As if they knew the women would never be found alive.

Only Striker brought possible leads about the women to Malik anymore. Even those were few and far between, and they never went anywhere. There wasn't a day that went by that Malik didn't think of Brooke. He suffered in silence, never letting his teammates or co-workers know just how much the human still meant to him.

He knew deep down that she wasn't dead, though he couldn't explain how or why he thought as much. But he did know the odds of him ever seeing her again were nearly zero.

Malik had to force himself to focus on finishing up his reports. He had enough pull and time in with the organization to be a division head with PSI, but that held little appeal to him. He'd been offered advances too many times to count. Somewhere around sixty or so years ago his superiors had stopped bothering to ask, knowing what his response would be. No. He didn't want to be one of the men in charge. Had he wanted a position of authority, he'd have taken his father's throne long ago. He hadn't. He liked being able to walk away from the job when need be. At least he used to like the idea of walking away from work.

Being forced away was an altogether different matter.

It had left him with far too much time to think. Time to dwell on the past and the future. Time to think about how much he'd screwed up everything with Brooke and time to obsess over why it was he couldn't get the human out of his head. Time to wonder where she might be and if she was hurt or, worse yet, dead.

He liked working to avoid facing his

personal issues. He liked helping others and taking evil bastards off the street. There had been a time in his life when he'd walked the line between good and evil. And there were days he felt as if he'd step over the line, never able to return again. It had been that way since his last trip to Egypt.

Since Brooke.

As of late, he worried nonstop that he'd give in to the darkness that he'd lost so many friends and loved ones to. That he'd become what PSI dealt with all the time. Already PSI had to step in to clean up the mess Malik had made in a crowded plaza recently.

The beast within him stirred as he thought about it again. As a lion-shifter who was thousands of years old, he'd had a long time to learn to be one with the animal inside him. To learn to control it with ease, and it had learned to submit to his demands. He could count on one hand the number of times he'd ever struggled with his beast. Oddly, they had all happened within the last five years. The first being in the resort in Egypt the night he'd been with Brooke. The most recent incident had been the worst—as there had ended up being countless human witnesses. The

Act of Passion

fact that he'd lost his shit—and shifted in front of humans nonetheless—hit him hard. It shook his faith and trust in his control and his beast.

And he didn't know why it had happened. He'd been fine one second and the next, he'd caught the scent of honey and lotuses—the scent of Brooke—and his body had contorted in the most painful of ways. Shifting had never hurt before but what he'd done that day had been excruciating. His body ached just thinking about it.

All the rules had gone out the window.

What they left behind was a man who was a shell of his former self, and Malik wasn't sure he liked the new version. Of course, he hadn't exactly been the man he used to be for nearly five years now.

Malik glanced around the open bullpen area of division headquarters. For as late into the night as it was, the place was full of operatives. All seemed to be in a mad dash to get their required reports done.

Entering the last of the required data for his reports, Malik hit submit and waited for confirmation of receipt to show before closing his laptop. He wasn't one who liked to leave anything to accumulate. And he was about as far from a procrastinator as one could get.

Though, as of late he'd been off his game.

Yeah, really off my fucking game, he thought as a snort broke free from him.

Duke sat at the desk next to Malik's. Duke's dark brown hair was pulled up in a haphazard way that spoke volumes to how much the man didn't care about fashion. Since Duke had mated and found a wife, his clothes always matched and he no longer came in wrinkled, looking as if he'd slept in his attire. Which was ironic considering Duke's wife, Mercy, was absentminded on her best days and often wore mismatched shoes. Malik strongly suspected that Duke had simply started to care more about his appearance now that he had a wife—someone to spend the rest of his immortally long life with.

Something Malik knew he'd never have. Hell, he couldn't even have sex any longer. Finding a mate was simply out of the question. His lion unfurled and began to make itself known. It's interest in mating was hard to dismiss. Malik clenched his hands behind his head and fought the beast back into submission, refusing to permit it even a taste of freedom since its outburst in the plaza.

Normally, he made a point to shift shapes at least once a week and run through the acres of land that surrounded Division B headquarters. The woods were stocked with game, all there for the alpha males to hunt. It helped to take the edge off. But Malik had refused to do so since his return to work.

He didn't trust that he'd be able to return to human form. Throughout the ages, he'd known far too many shifter males who had gotten locked in animal form due to a loss of control. Each and every one had needed to be put down in the end as they became too feral to be permitted to live.

He'd even been charged with dispatching some. He didn't like thinking about it, but it was hard not to considering he was now showing all the signs of mentally breaking down. It was merely a matter of time before he became the mission—before he became the hunted. The shifter in need of a mercy kill.

"I fucking hate reports," growled Duke.

Duke was considered something of a luddite around the office. He tended to break the technology first and tried to figure it out later. He was well on his way to killing yet another laptop.

Corbin had already gone rounds with Duke over breaking two in the past four weeks. Victim three would be headed to IT soon from the looks of it. At the rate Duke was going, IT would make him send smoke signals in place of reports.

They'd probably get the information faster that way as well.

Malik leaned back in his computer chair, eyeing Duke's screen as the man continued to delete everything he'd spent so longing using two fingers to type. Malik had caught up on several months' worth of paperwork in the same time it had taken Duke to do one report. With the wolf-shifter's refusal to learn to type, that wasn't too surprising.

Duke hit the delete key repeatedly; each time muttering yet another curse at the machine, as if *it* were the problem.

"What, exactly, are you trying to do?" asked Malik, amused with Duke's irritation. The man tended to hate just about everything, except his mate. He was head over heels in love with the woman. Truth be told, Mercy, Duke's mate, had grown on Malik as well. As much as he couldn't see himself ever mated, a part of him envied what the young wolf-shifter had with his woman.

Slowly, Duke turned his head, his onyx gaze raking over Malik as if murder was on the man's mind. "I'm trying to submit my reports. Corbin has been on my ass for a week to get these done."

Malik laced his hands behind his head and put his feet on his desk, his loafers looking newly shined. "And you're actually listening to him? Don't you normally take months to get reports in?"

"Ha, he's hiding from his woman," said Garth as he entered the room. The Viking stood just shy of seven feet tall, making all the other men present look short when they were anything but. "I heard pregnancy hormones have made her downright terrifying."

Duke cast his murderous gaze to Garth. "Fuck off, Swede."

Malik couldn't hide his laugh at the dig Duke took at the Viking.

Duke grunted. "Don't laugh, King Tut. Don't you have a stone tablet you should be chiseling or a pyramid you should be building?"

As much as Malik disliked the nickname his

teammates had given him, he knew they'd done so out of a sense of brotherhood. The men on his team were like family to him and because he'd been born in Ancient Egypt, they had a lot of fun at his expense. He returned the favor as often as possible. It was simply another way in which the men bonded. "Stop trying to get me to tell you how the pyramids were really built."

Garth grinned, his long white-blond hair falling forward. Tiny braids were done through it, looking as if they had no rhyme or reason. Malik suspected they held more meaning than that. "Boomer and Striker still think it was aliens?"

Malik nodded as he thought about Boomer and Striker. The pair tended to act like overgrown children as often as possible. Sometimes, they managed to get other operatives to join in. "Yep. Striker is positive little green men used ray guns to build them and Boomer is convinced they used their spaceships to do the heavy lifting."

"They're idiots," mumbled Duke.

Malik and Garth nodded in agreement. Both Boomer and Striker could certainly be idiots.

"Everyone is an idiot," snapped Duke, glaring holes into his laptop screen.

"Sounds as if he's bitter that his people are boring," said Garth, sitting on the edge of Duke's desk. "Americans are so quick to show pride in their country but really, let's take a look at their crowning achievements throughout history."

Malik grinned. "I have clothing older than this country."

"Ditto," said Garth as he glanced at Duke, who was still hitting the delete key. "If you're trying to submit the report, why are you hitting delete?"

"I'm not. I'm hitting the Del key. Striker told me that's how I send stuff," grumbled Duke, hitting the key again. "All it does is eat what I typed. Stupid thing. These are about as pointless as carrier pigeons."

Garth slid the laptop away from Duke and glanced up at Malik. "He's thousands of years younger than us. Shouldn't he be teaching *us* how to use technology?"

Malik wagged a foot, still leaning in his chair. "Have you seen him try to work a cell phone? Trust me when I say, he won't be instructing any classes on technology anytime soon. It's all the man can do to send a text."

Garth laughed and then handed the laptop back to Duke. "Click on the blue button on the screen when you want to submit a report. Striker told you wrong. My guess is for his own amusement."

Duke stood and rotated his neck. "When I get my hands on the Scot, I'm going to kill him."

Garth grinned. "Mercy still not putting out?"

Duke growled. "Do not talk about my wife like that." He then slumped his shoulders. "And no. She's not. She's making me sleep in one of the extra rooms. She says I smell funny to her all of a sudden."

Garth lost it, laughing so hard he bent, nearly falling off the edge of the desk. "Your wife thinks you stink."

Duke reached out, pushed the Viking hard, making the man tumble to the floor.

Garth kept laughing as he stood. "Wait until Rurik hears."

Malik did his best to hide his amusement. "It's not so unusual for a woman who is expecting to have problems with smells."

"I'm her mate!" shouted Duke, looking lost rather than outraged. "She's not supposed to have a problem with *my* smell."

Dr. James Hagen entered from the side hall that led to the medical wing of PSI Headquarters. It was good to have him back after being gone from PSI for a decade. "Are you still moaning and groaning about your mate making you sleep in the extra room?"

"Yes," said Duke, his bottom lip jutting out in a pout, making him appear about as far from alpha as one could get.

James grinned. "I told you before. This will pass. And whatever you changed recently does have a different scent to it. I'm guessing she's sensitive to it. So is baby."

"I haven't changed anything," said Duke, his brows meeting.

Malik continued to lean in his chair. "That's not exactly true. You ran out of deodorant about a week ago. Striker had an extra one in his gym bag. He gave it to you and you put it on. I'm pretty sure you tossed it in your bag and have kept using it each day since."

Duke's eyes widened. "Holy fuck, my woman has banned me from our bedroom because I smell like Striker!" He headed for the door so fast that he nearly knocked over James.

James caught him and held him in place. "What are you doing?"

"Going to shower and throwing away that damn deodorant. My balls are practically blue and I want to feel my mate under me."

Garth slapped his knee. "This is too much."

Duke pointed at him. "You wait until you're mated. I'll be having the last laugh then."

Garth's eyes widened and he sobered quickly, his laugh fading. "Don't go cursing me with your American tongue."

Duke flipped him off.

James closed his eyes, appearing tired of all their antics.

Malik remained in place as Duke stormed out of the bullpen, clearly a man on a mission to get laid.

Garth righted himself as Auberi Bouchard entered the room.

The Viking and the vampire had a long-standing history of not liking one another. Auberi curled his nose at Garth. "I thought I smelled something."

Garth eyed the man. "I heard there was a Jerry Lewis movie on television. I figured you and your other French friends would be glued to it."

Auberi leaned against Malik's desk, sitting partially on it. "Tell me again why you permit such trash to be part of your organization?"

"We work for the same place," reminded Garth, standing slowly, a challenge in his eyes.

Malik eased his feet from his desk, preparing to break up the two alpha males should the need arise. To this day, Malik wasn't even sure what had caused the animosity between the men, but time had only caused it to grow worse.

Auberi licked his lower lip, his posture saying he was more than prepared for an attack. "Is there not a village in need of pillaging?"

Garth made a move to go at Auberi and Malik leapt up, putting himself between the men. The shifter growled and the vampire snarled.

Malik groaned. "Guys, really?"

James moved in quickly to lend an assist. He touched Garth's shoulder. "He baits you because he knows you'll take it."

Garth narrowed his gaze on Auberi. "Vampires have no business here. Go back to your division."

Malik pressed closer to his longtime friend,

knowing the vampire well enough to know he'd rise to a challenge. Malik caught Auberi's gaze with his own and shook his head. "Enough."

"Cool. A fight," said Boomer as he came in from the direction of the training rooms. He had a towel around his neck and was only wearing a pair of workout pants. "Did I miss any good stuff?"

James grunted. "No, Garth was heading out for the night."

"I was?" asked Garth, sounding unhappy that he was being forced to go.

Boomer shrugged and towel dried his long hair. "I miss all the action. Hey, James, did you have that file on that girl you wanted me to look for?"

All men present turned their attention to the doctor.

James stepped back and grunted. "Stop looking at me like I'm cheating on my mate. I'm not. That isn't even possible and you all know it. And beyond that, I would never do that to Laney. You know me better than that."

Boomer raised his hand. "Erm, Doc, only I know it. I'm the only other guy standing here who's mated. They don't get that their dick will have one desire and one desire only when they meet the woman meant for them."

Garth shuddered, as did Auberi. The pair shared a look and seemed surprised to be of equal opinion on the act of mating.

Malik instantly thought of Brooke and had to force her from his mind. He turned his attention to James. "Is this something I can help with?"

"Sure." James walked to Malik's desk and pointed to the laptop on it. "May I?"

Malik waved a hand, granting permission for the man to do as he pleased with the laptop. Had it been Duke, Malik would have grabbed the laptop and ran, for the laptop's safety of course.

James turned the laptop in a way that Malik couldn't see it. He went to work on something and then pointed to the screen as Boomer leaned near him. "I just got a call from Laney telling me that she thinks this should be looked into. I don't want to sleep on the sofa, so how about we make sure this isn't something important."

Boomer's face paled. He glanced behind him at Garth, and the Viking went over to stand near him. He too paled, his gaze flickering to

Malik before he lurched forward, grabbing the laptop and flinging it.

The laptop hit the wall and broke in several pieces.

Malik stood fast. "What the hell, Garth? I'd have let Duke use it if I wanted that result."

Boomer pressed a fake smile to his face. "Hey, Auberi, didn't you mention you had something cooked up for Malik's upcoming birthday?"

Auberi licked his lips. "I do."

"You two should get going then," said Boomer, shaking his head at James as James started to speak.

Garth eyed Auberi. "*Now* would be the perfect time to take him to celebrate."

"You are all so fucking weird," said Malik, walking over and picking up the pieces of his laptop. "IT is so going to think I let Duke touch this. Want to tell me why you went postal on my computer?"

Garth shook his head. "Nope. Go enjoy your birthday."

"It's not my birthday. It's not even close to my birthday," said Malik. "Auberi just picks a day of the year each year and decides that's when I should celebrate."

"Because you won't tell us your actual birthday," said Auberi. "Let's go, Tut."

"I'm going to lend James a hand with something Laney wants us to look into," said Malik.

Boomer lifted his hands. "Garth and I have it. Rurik can help. And Striker will lend a hand if we call him. You go. Have fun. You're just coming off leave and we don't want you pushing too hard or anything."

Malik stared at his friends. "What's going on?"

Garth shook his head. "Nothing. Go. We've got this."

"Yeah, this will bore you," said Boomer, clearing his throat. "Have fun. We'll call if we need anything."

Giving in, Malik shrugged and put the broken pieces of his laptop on the desk nearest him. "Fine, but Garth, you take your ass down to IT and explain what happened. Get me a new computer."

"Sure thing," said the Viking. "Go. Have fun, Malik."

"I will make sure he has nothing but fun," said Auberi with a laugh.

"This is going to end with a lot of naked

women, isn't it?" asked Malik, already knowing his friend's idea of a good time.

"And maybe some naked men," supplied Auberi with a wink.

With a groan, Malik followed behind Auberi, thinking of ways he could bow out early on whatever it was he had cooked up.

"Let's go find you the perfect woman or women to spend the night with," said Auberi.

Chapter Twelve

MALIK MADE his way onto the dance floor, a drink in hand, moving to the beat of the music at the club Auberi had taken him to. The music was hard thumping hip-hop. Finding the perfect woman to have a night of amazing sex with wouldn't happen. He'd not had sex in five years. Not since he'd spent a night under the influence of the experimental drugs in Egypt. Since he'd lost control and nearly shifted form fully while buried deep in the most beautiful woman he'd ever seen.

Brooke.

That had been it for him.

His dick simply refused to work unless he

was alone, stroking himself to Brooke's photo that he'd taken with his phone. Even achieving orgasm by that means was getting harder and harder. Soon that option would be gone and he knew what would happen then. He'd succumb to the pull of the lion inside him. He'd seen it happen to others—men who tried to deny their animal instincts and the need for sex.

He'd gone to great lengths to hide the truth of it all from his friends, knowing they'd have seen it as a sign that he didn't have control of his beast. He was on borrowed time before he'd need to confess it all to his friends. After all, they'd be the ones who would have to hunt him and put him down when he lost control. The least they deserved was the truth.

The famed ladies' man had fallen from grace.

He took a sip of his vodka on the rocks. Suddenly, two beautiful women were there, in slinky dresses that only just covered their asses. One was in a red dress and the other wore gold. They pressed up against him, moving with the music as well, grinding their bodies against his.

He caught sight of Auberi not far from the dance floor, a drink in hand as well. The man lifted his drink and nodded to Malik, clearly pleased to see him starting to loosen up again. If he only knew the truth. That Malik hadn't bedded any woman in years.

Auberi would be horrified.

The man lived for sex.

He was French. It was expected.

Auberi sipped his drink as he grinned. The two had spent centuries romancing women. Sometimes they even romanced the same woman at the same time. Auberi's tastes ran both ways. Malik's did not. That hadn't stopped them from sharing women in the past.

More than once.

The woman in red slipped her hand into the open portion of Malik's shirt, running the palm of her hand over his chest. This was the point when his cock of five years ago would have been all in for sex.

Nothing.

PSI's scientists had effectively neutered him.

Frustrated, but not deterred, Malik continued to dance, his free hand finding the hip of the woman in the gold dress. He felt as if he were going through the motions. Nothing more. He'd had countless women in his immortally long life. He'd taken women in every way possible and some not so possible. Though he'd only spent his seed in one, having been told at an early age of the dangers of doing so. And he'd not meant to do so ever, but the fucking medication had messed with his judgment as well as his dick.

He had a long history of infamous incidents with women throughout the ages. More than once he'd leaned on his fellow PSI operatives and friends to get him out of a hairy situation, all revolving around him bedding women.

Auberi appeared next to Malik, minus his drink. He drew the woman in red to him and touched her chin, forcing her gaze to meet his. The woman licked her lips and the smell of her arousal filled the air, doing nothing to ignite Malik's sex drive.

Auberi spun the woman, putting her back to his front, and turned his head, his gaze colliding with Malik's. "Just what the doctor ordered."

Malik barely managed to contain a groan. Auberi was a doctor. He'd studied some form of medicine at least once a century since he'd been alive.

We could share these beauties, said Auberi down the mental path they shared.

Malik shook his head. *Nah. I'm not really feeling it with them. They're not my type.*

Auberi snorted. *I find that hard to believe.*

I think I'm going to call it a night, returned Malik, giving up the farce.

Auberi caught his arm. "I've arranged a surprise for you tonight, to help you out of your recent funk."

Malik fought a groan. Knowing Auberi, he'd hired a harem to come and try to get Malik off. It would be a very Auberi thing to do.

Auberi drew the two women closer to him and stared down at them, his gaze going to jet black quickly. "Go. Find others to occupy you for the evening."

The women obeyed. It's what humans did when a powerful vampire mesmerized them.

Auberi motioned for Malik to follow him as he made his way deeper into the club. He went up the stairs to a roped-off darker section. They passed by several bouncers who all seemed as if they knew Auberi well. They probably did. The man was more than likely a regular.

Instantly, he was hit with the scent of honey and lotuses, making him stumble slightly, his beast surging up. Malik stopped and took several deep breaths, hoping to stave off a full shift. He inhaled again and was hit with the smell of Brooke once more.

"Tut?" asked Auberi, touching Malik's shoulder and chasing away the scent of the woman who haunted Malik to this day.

Auberi led Malik to a large back room that offered a view of the dance floor below but that was so dimly lit, none could see up and into it. There was a table, a booth, a bed of all things, and several oversized comfy chairs. The table had two gold-colored masks on it. When Malik saw the theme of the masks—ancient Egyptian—he shot Auberi a hard look.

"Sit. Put this on," the vampire said, handing Malik a mask that looked a great deal like a rendition of Tutankhamen.

Malik eyed the mask and his friend. "No. I'm going home."

Auberi grinned. "Indulge me. I think you'll enjoy it. This surprise is one of my better ones. Let's give you a birthday to remember."

Malik stared at the mask. "It's not my birthday."

"Tut," said Auberi, knowing Malik disliked the nickname. "You're being very boring. You didn't used to be boring."

Malik tensed and took the mask. He put it on as Auberi put on a similar one and then took a seat in one of the oversized chairs. This was going to end poorly. Anything Auberi thought was fun normally did.

Chapter Thirteen

"BROOKE," said Joe, the bartender for the VIP section, as he stood behind the bar.

Brooke made her way over to the man and sighed when he pulled out a half-mask. This one was different from anything she'd been asked to wear before. The thing looked to be plucked from an Egyptian museum. "You have got to be kidding me."

"Nope. Some big spender set this up. Wait until you see the outfits he had sent over for you and Stacey to wear," said Joe, looking less than amused. He was a middle-aged man who had tended bar for over twenty years. He was protective of the women who worked there and wasn't like some of the men there who tried to be touchy-feely. He also didn't look happy with the client for the night.

"They didn't tell me *you* were on tonight," said a shrill voice from behind Brooke.

With a groan, Brooke turned partially to see a buxom fake redhead there, chomping on her gum. The woman raked her gaze over Brooke and sneered. "You always make bigger tips than me and you don't even let the men touch you or anything. I don't get it! I strip all the way down and give them anything they want, yet you make more."

"Stacey," warned Joe. "You know the rules. No full nudity and no touching. I don't care how big the tips might be."

She rolled her eyes and took a second mask from the bar top before heading to the back changing room.

Reluctantly, Brooke followed. Neither woman said another word as they changed into the skimpy outfits. There was a skirt that barely qualified as one. Most of the material was sheer white. The waist portion reminded her of something from an Egyptian museum, like the mask. She couldn't help but think of her limited time in Egypt. It had been amazing and terrible all in one. She'd gotten the most precious gift ever, yet had endured something no one should ever have to go through.

She adjusted the thin material of the top and then put her mask on, waiting for Stacey to harness her giant breasts into the top. They barely fit.

Glen, one of the bouncers, opened the door slowly, his eyes closed tight. "You decent?"

"I am. Stacey is debatable," said Brooke with a hard look in the woman's direction.

They'd been at odds since Brooke had started at the club nearly a year ago. Stacey liked to break the rules to make bigger tips. Brooke couldn't stomach the idea of being touched by any of the men who frequented the establishment. She also wasn't about to get naked for any of them.

She had certain needs that went above and beyond carnal pleasures and ran more along the lines of survival, which was why she'd even sought out a job at a club like this. She fed from the sexual lust in the air. She'd never dare give in to her darker side and engage in sex with the men from the club. No. If she needed to sate the need fully, she'd call Gram. He'd come and do what needed done.

She'd dance and pour their champagne but

nothing more, no matter how much Stacey tried to push the envelope.

Brooke wasn't proud of her job, but it paid the bills and kept food on the table. Plus, the establishment had rather loose hiring practices and didn't require a background check or anything in the way of real references or identification. It wasn't as if she could work in cyber security like she'd planned. No. She'd be too easy to possibly find, even with her skill set, if she worked for a legit company. She did odd jobs on the side that were computer related and far from legal, and she did utilized her skills to try to stay a few steps ahead of the madmen hunting her. She did whatever it took to stay hidden from The Corporation.

She had done the impossible. She'd gotten away from them and lived to tell the tale. So had Edee. The two had been close before but the ordeal they'd lived through had left them inseparable. They stayed on the move together, staying off the grid, always worried they'd be located again. It had been a year since their last run-in with The Corporation, but that didn't mean they were home free.

She headed to the door and Glen held it open for her. Stacey followed behind. They followed Glen to the VIP room. As they entered, music that made her think of Egypt came on. To the left of the door was a large bucket of ice with champagne bottles in it. Not just any ones. The most expensive the club had to offer.

There were grapes, cut-up fruits, and cheeses on small wood trays. Stacey took one tray and Brooke grabbed the other.

Glen stood at the entrance, putting his back to the room. He'd only intervene if one of the women shouted for help. Other than that, they were alone with the big spenders.

You can do this.

She nodded as if that would help keep her spirits up and her confidence level high. As she began to walk in the direction of the seating area, she caught sight of two men there, each wearing masks that covered their faces fully. Whoever the clients were, they certainly had a hard-on for Egyptian history and flare.

Stacey began to sway her hips. At five-four Stacey was five inches shorter than Brooke, but the woman had curves aplenty. Something the men who came to the club always seemed to like.

Brooke rarely bothered to dance. She tended to offer seductive smiles, food, and drink.

Nothing more. She didn't need to. What she carried inside her would make the men think they were having the time of their lives. She'd get the energy she needed and a good-size tip. Everyone got what they wanted.

One of the men had long brown hair and was in a deep blue designer shirt. It matched his eyes. The man to his right had on an off-white shirt that looked expensive. His ink-black hair hung just past his shoulders. Instantly, she thought of Malik.

Brooke faltered in her step as her gaze traced its way over the man's neck and upper chest. She could see hints of tattoos peeking through the open portion of his shirt. Instantly she thought of her time in Egypt. Of her night with Malik.

Her heart ached for him. Ached knowing he'd died at the hands of the sick bastards who took her.

He'd died because of her.

She had to force thoughts of him from her head and focused on the man with the dark hair. Instantly her body responded just as it had five years ago. The man with the black hair stared out from behind the mask, his dark gaze locking

Act of Passion

on her. For a split second, it felt as if they were the only two people in the club.

She nearly tore her mask off, but resisted.

It wasn't until Stacey nudged her that Brooke realized she'd stopped moving in the direction of the men. She swallowed back a lump in her throat and walked towards the men. She couldn't tear her gaze from the man with the black hair.

He sat up in the chair, his dark gaze never leaving her. When he made a move to stand, the man next to him pulled on his shoulder, keeping him seated.

Brooke's body tingled with awareness, as it had done five years ago with Malik. This would normally be when she'd put the food on the table before the men and then keep her distance while managing to look interested in them. She didn't stop where she normally did. No. Boldly, she went right up to the man with the black hair.

Instantly his hand found her hip. Brooke had never before allowed any of the men to touch her, but she made no move to stop this man.

Stacey glanced at her and did a double take. She smiled mischievously and then shook her chest, leaning in front of the man with the long brown hair. The man looked pleased, but not very surprised. As if women always threw themselves at him.

They probably did.

Brooke bent slowly before the man with the black hair and held the tray of fruit and cheese out for him.

He took it but set it to the side, on a small table there, his gaze never leaving her. His other hand found her hip. Brooke found herself beginning to move in a seductive manner, her pulse racing with excitement at the man's hot touch.

She gasped.

"Old friend," said the man with long brown hair. "There is a no-touching rule, and you are most certainly touching. I take it my surprise is now just what the doctor ordered."

The man ignored his friend and shocked Brooke by grabbing her and setting her on his lap. She tensed as burning need slammed through her. Again, she thought of Malik, though she wasn't sure why. He was gone. Dwelling on the past would gain her nothing but more tears, and she'd cried a river already.

She wanted the man's hands roaming over

her body as much as she'd wanted Malik's touch all those years ago. She wanted to know what the mystery man looked like under the mask.

His thumb found its way to her lower lip. Brooke bit his thumb lightly, drawing it into her mouth. The man growled and thrust his hips up, his long, thick erection evident through his designer pants. He ground against her and she closed her eyes, tipping her head back, loving the feel of him under her.

He ran his hand over her exposed throat and then skimmed it down, heading between her breasts. She made no move to stop him. It was as if she craved his touch. Like she'd been waiting for it.

Her power flared and she was powerless to stop it. It latched on to the man, drawing energy from his arousal. His eyes widened as he drew one of the straps of her barely there top down, almost revealing a nipple. She made no move to stop him. If anything, she wanted him to do more. To touch her everywhere.

Brooke moved on his lap, the feel of his long, hard erection under her making her want more. She dipped her head, going for his neck, although she wanted to remove his mask and go for his mouth. She held back. Whatever was driving her, making her act out of the ordinary, pushed her onward.

As her mouth ran over his neck, he stiffened, jerking under her, increasing his movements. She licked a line down his neck, even his taste reminding her of Malik. The pain of learning of his passing years ago again hit her hard, and she found herself wrapping her arms around the stranger's neck as she fought back tears.

He returned the embrace, holding her to his body as if he needed comfort as well. They remained that way for a bit, simply holding one another. Brooke then returned to kissing his neck. She kissed her way down to his collarbone. She eased open his shirt, her hands roaming over the hard planes of his torso. She rubbed against him, wanting desperately to chase away thoughts of Malik.

Her power flared more, latching on to the mutual attraction between them. The man grabbed her hips and began to control her movements on his lap.

"Tut," said the man with the French accent. "I take it this one is more your type. More to your liking."

Tut? That was a strange name.

"Yes," the dark-haired man growled, his

voice so deep that she felt it reverberate through her.

"Happy birthday, non-birthday, Tut," returned the Frenchman with a slight laugh. "Though, you should know that you're dangerously close to putting on a show here. I get the feeling that sharing this one wouldn't go so well for me."

"Auberi," said the man under her, his voice even making her think of Malik. "No."

Auberi snorted as Stacey tried to mirror Brooke's actions on him. He didn't pay her any mind as he looked over at Brooke. He smiled and winked.

Brooke eased backwards on the man's lap, wanting to look her fill of the hot specimen below her. He had a body that could turn any head. She pushed open his shirt more—and froze.

The very same tattoos that Malik had were on the man, though there were considerably more tattoos around them than she recalled Malik having. Still, thoughts of Malik crashed into her.

The man under her couldn't be Malik. He was dead. Haneez had been very clear that they'd spared Malik no torture before giving him the death he'd begged for. He'd even shown her pictures of the scene of the murder. It had been pure gore.

And it had been her fault.

Haneez had made sure she understood as much. And there hadn't been a day that had gone by that she didn't remember that horrible fact. She'd cost a man his life. A man who had given her the most incredible gift ever.

Even though reason said the man she was with now couldn't be Malik, she found herself desperate to verify as much. She tugged at his shirt in an almost crazed state. He didn't try to stop her. When she saw another of the tattoos she remembered, everything around her seemed to slow.

"Son of the god king," she said softly, tears welling as her hands began to tremble.

The man caught her wrists and tipped his head. "What?"

"Listen, asshole, either you tell me if this girl works here or I snap your neck," a man with a deep voice said from outside the VIP room. "Look at the picture. Tall, knockout, brown hair. Trust me, you'd remember her. There might be a hot redhead with her."

Gasping, Brooke pushed off the man under

her as the hair on the back of her neck rose. She didn't need to be told she was the one the man was looking for. And she knew who he was with.

The Corporation.

Brooke grabbed Stacey, who was trying very hard to excite Auberi, who seemed almost bored with her.

Stacey tried to shrug off Brooke but it didn't work. "What the hell?"

"Get out of here. Go out the back way. Don't stop for any reason." Brooke stared down at the woman she didn't particularly like. "The men coming can and will kill you. Go!"

Stacey backed up, fear and confusion showing on her face.

"You need to go too," she said to the men in the chairs. Neither made a move to get up. "Follow Stacey. She'll get you to safety."

Brooke could run as well but she knew the men coming were far more than human. They'd catch her quickly, and she couldn't have that. After just over four years of running from The Corporation, she'd learned a thing or two about being prepared. She hurried to the other side of the VIP private section and grabbed a chair, pulling it over and standing on it. She pushed open one of the vents and pulled out a bag she'd stuffed there months ago.

Brooke grabbed the burner phone from her bag and pressed the button for Edee. Edee answered on the second ring. "They found me. Get to safety. If I'm not there by morning, they have me or I'm dead. Take her and run. Just like we talked about. Get her to one of the boys. It doesn't matter which. They'll find one another. And be safe."

"Ohmygod," said Edee. "I'll keep her safe. Be careful. I forbid you from dying or being caught. Do you hear me?"

Her throat tightened. "If I don't make it, make sure she knows how much she was loved." Brooke hung up and put the phone back into the bag.

In seconds, she was yanking out clothing from the bag. She jumped off the chair and put her back to the high rollers who either didn't understand what she'd said or were incredibly stupid, because they still hadn't moved.

Hot and stupid.

Figures.

Brooke tossed the mask aside, still keeping her back to the men. She put on the black workout pants in record time, ripping off the stupid skirt she'd been forced to wear. It was pointless and the last thing she wanted to be in while dealing with the men coming. She yanked off the barely there costume top and yanked on an exercise cami.

"What are you doing?" asked Stacey, touching Brooke's arm.

She grabbed the running shoes from the bag and put them on, knowing she couldn't run in the heels she worked in. "Get out of here, Stacey! These guys don't screw around."

The blond's eyes widened. "What's going on? Who are you talking about?"

"The men in the outer area of the VIP section. They have Glen and are demanding he tell them if I'm here." Brooke glanced in the direction of the door. "We don't have much time."

"Wait, are you saying you can hear what is happening in the other room?" asked Stacey, disbelief resonating in her voice. "No way. What the hell are you doing? I could really use the extra tips tonight. It's not the night to flip out."

"Listen, stay if you want, but they *will* kill you. They won't believe that you don't know how to find me," stated Brooke clearly. "I don't much like you but I don't want you dead either."

"Ouch, fuck, man, let me go," cried Glen from just outside of the room. "She's in the VIP room giving a lap dance to a rich guy. You broke my arm!"

"Tut, relax," said Auberi. "Let us see how this plays out."

Brooke reached into her bag again and yanked out several throwing knives. She tucked them into the back of her waistband and put the cami over them.

"Shit!" shouted Stacey. "You have weapons in here? What's happening? Do you know how to use those?"

"Get the hell out of here!" yelled Joe a second before a shot went off.

Stacey began to scream as a group of men in suits flooded into the room, all armed, and none seeming too worried about getting caught. The front one locked gazes with Brooke and his lips curved upwards. She knew him well, though only by his last name, which was what everyone called him.

Johnson.

"You're a hard bitch to track down," Johnson said, pointing a gun at her. "Come quietly or I splatter the brains of everyone in this room. Want that on your conscience, 53?"

She tensed at the shorted version of the label she'd worn for nearly eight months. Test Subject53B.

Brooke didn't want anyone hurt because of her. Not again. She needed to get the high rollers and Stacey to safety.

She put her hands up slowly.

Johnson's grin widened, looking even more sinister. "Good girl. Now, walk slowly over here."

A low growl sounded from behind her, but she didn't dare take her gaze from the men who had entered the room. She did, however, throw her power at the high-rollers, keeping them in place and coated in protective energy.

Johnson looked towards the high rollers. "Playing the hero will get you a bullet between the eyes. The bitch is coming with us."

"Don't hurt anyone," said Brooke as she took a step in Johnson's direction.

He glanced at a big guy to his left that Brooke didn't remember from her time being held. "Grab the girl. Be careful, she's a wily one."

The guy didn't look convinced. "She's

smoking hot. Doesn't look like she could put up much of a fight though."

"Do not touch her."

Brooke tensed, her entire body tingling at the sound of a voice that matched Malik's. She knew it was the man she'd been giving a lap dance to, but that didn't mean she could shake the thought of Malik from her head.

Johnson looked past her. "Willing to die for a whore?"

The sound that came from Tut was identical to the noise Malik had made when Haneez, whom she'd used to think of as Mr. Rings, had called her a whore at the resort five years back.

Brooke couldn't stop herself as she turned to face the high rollers fully. There were simply too many similarities for her to ignore or rationalize away. As she locked gazes with Tut, who was still in his mask, he gasped.

She looked back at Johnson.

"Please don't do anything," she said, tearing up. "I don't want anyone else's blood on my hands. I have enough as it is. Let them all go and I'll let you take me without a fight."

"No!" yelled the man in the mask.

Johnson laughed. "I'll consider letting them live. And we know all about the blood on your hands. They tell me they had a lot of fun torturing your boyfriend before granting him death."

Brooke flinched. "He wasn't my boyfriend."

"Right. I forgot," said Johnson snidely. "The guy you gave it to right before they took you. They tell me he cried like a little bitch before they slit his throat."

Unable to stop the tears from falling, Brooke surrendered to them. She closed her eyes and kept her hands up. "Stop. Please. I don't need to be told about it again. Haneez told me about it in detail enough."

Johnson snorted. "Haneez has it bad for you. So does the boss. I wouldn't be surprised if he gives us fat bonus checks and then takes you away somewhere private and keeps you all for himself. Tell me, how many times have you handed it out to him?"

Tut growled louder this time.

Brooke stared at him and Auberi. "Please. Stop. They'll kill you."

Someone grabbed hold of her by the back of the neck, jerking her hard, making Tut growl more.

Auberi spoke. "Patience, Tut."

The man holding Brooke laughed, sounding

young. He pressed his face to her neck, inhaling deeply. "Have you smelled her, Johnson? She smells good enough to eat."

Johnson snorted. "Yeah. They did something to her that has that effect on a lot of us. Careful, she's more than just a pretty face."

The guy pushed his face into her neck. "What are you?"

Growling, Johnson looked at the man next to her. "Bring her and kill the witnesses."

The very idea that the man in the mask would be hurt left Brooke reacting. She threw her elbow into the man near her, kneed him, and then grabbed for his sidearm. She yanked him in front of her to use as a shield as Johnson fired at her, hitting the guy instead.

Stacey wailed like a banshee.

Johnson and the men with him came at her in force. Brooke blocked out everything, including the man in the mask as he yelled. She dropped the man they'd shot and turned quickly, kicking one of the men before pointing the weapon at him and pulling the trigger as she aimed at his heart.

She sensed something coming at her from the side and ducked, just as a clawed hand went past her head. She came up fast, shooting the man who had just tried to take her head clean off. She scored a direct hit between his eyes. She shot another just as the gun was knocked from her hand, skating across the floor next to the man in the mask.

Two men tackled her and one did a partial shift. He lifted his clawed hand and rammed it through her shoulder. Brooke didn't make a sound, but she did thrust magik at them, knocking them off her. She hissed as pain radiated through her shoulder. She ran and slid across the floor, nearly running into the wall of power holding the man in the mask and his friend. She snatched the weapon with her good arm and turned onto her back, firing at more of the men.

The pain grew to unbearable levels. She thumped her head on the floor and dropped the weapon to rub the area that was hurt. A fair amount of blood was running free from her. "I am really fucking sick to death of getting clawed."

She hissed again and knew her eyes were going from olive green to a bright, vibrant emerald green. In an instant, her shoulder healed over fully.

Gasps sounded behind her, and she looked

at the high rollers, who were within touching distance of her. The men looked stunned. She grinned even though the situation wasn't amusing. "So, my day blows. Yours?"

"Behind you!" shouted the French one.

Brooke spun, kicking out wide. She grabbed the man's head and twisted fast, snapping his neck, grabbing his weapon and lifting it straight out. She shot at Johnson, who dodged the head shot but ended up taking the bullet in his stomach.

The remaining four men watched her carefully.

"Kill her!" Johnson yelled.

The other men gulped.

Brooke grinned and kept aiming at them. "Willing to die for that asshole?"

"What is she?" one asked. "She smells like a mix. Did they make her that?"

Johnson made a move to come at her and she shot him in the upper thigh, causing him to fall to one knee. She shot his other upper thigh, making him cry out. "I am going to enjoy ending you, bitch!"

She blinked, her eyes returning to normal. "Yeah, I'm shaking here. Really."

The men behind Johnson radiated fear.

Johnson snarled. "If she gets away, Elm will kill us all."

Fear rushed over her at the mention of Elm. The man was even worse than Haneez. As far as she could tell, he was one of the higher-ups from the facility she'd been held at. And he was anything but human.

She'd not seen him since she'd escaped and prayed she'd never see him again.

As the temperature began to drop in the room, she knew her prayers weren't being answered. Elm had arrived.

Johnson bit his lower lip. "Smells like the boss is here. Someone is going to pay for running out on him. And you can't possibly stand against him. He's as old as time, bitch!"

A tall, sinewy man with long white-blond hair entered the room. He was dressed in a fitted high-end suit and from all appearances, he looked a lot like a sexy rich guy. He was, but his heart made him hideous.

He came to a stop next to Johnson and touched the wolf-shifter's shoulder. "Now, Johnson, is that any way to speak to my future wife?"

The guy in the mask growled again.

"Tut, not smart," said Auberi. "Can't you smell that?"

Brooke tensed. Did Auberi know Elm wasn't human? Could he sense the power that Elm held?

Elm's green gaze locked on her. "Now, Brooke, are dangerous toys really necessary?"

He lifted a hand and the weapon was torn from her grip.

Elm looked to her and smiled, licking his lips. "You are even more beautiful than I remember. And a great deal smaller."

She stiffened.

"Tell me, did *it* survive?" he asked, and Brooke knew exactly who he was talking about. His lip curled. "Wrong that I hope it didn't? But, I can't give you one so it will have to do. That is, if those higher than me don't already have great plans for it."

Johnson laughed, pushing to his feet, grunting as he did. "Can I have the redhead when we find her?"

Elm nodded. "I don't see why not. But don't break her. This one obeys better when those she loves are at risk. Isn't that right, Brooke?"

Stacey began to scream again, and Elm looked in her direction, lifted a hand, and Stacey's body was propelled across the room.

She struck the wall so hard that there was no way she could have survived.

Brooke made a move to go for her but Elm walked towards her. "Leave it. It's dead."

"You don't have to hurt anyone else," she said, digging deep to find the courage she'd worked so hard to obtain since she last saw him.

"I didn't have to. I wanted to," said Elm, glancing past her at the high rollers. He looked at the injured and dead men that he'd sent for her. "Is this your handiwork or did you have help? Was it the were-shark? He's always been so protective of you."

Brooke found her resolve and narrowed her gaze on him.

He was staring past her again, at the high rollers.

"What do we have here?" he asked.

Brooke put her body in the path of the men and shook her head. "No one. They're no one. Just clients here."

He glanced around, a look of disgust on his face. "This is where you work? What you've been reduced to?"

"A whore is as a whore does," said Johnson, wetting his lips with his tongue.

Elm went eerily still before turning his head

slowly in Johnson's direction. "What have I told you?"

Johnson gulped and sweat appeared on his brow. "Not to call her a whore."

Elm smiled but it never reached his eyes. "Now, Brooke, this charade has gone on long enough. You've had plenty of time to come to terms with your future. Come with me now, and I will let the rest of the people in this establishment live. Resist, and I will have my men kill each one slowly."

One of the men she hadn't killed yet leaned over. "Boss, what is that smell on her?"

Elm squared his shoulders. "Fae."

"No other Fae chick I've smelled was this good," said the man.

"She's from my line," said Elm. "Women among our line are rare. Probably why her father tried so hard to hide her with a human as a child. He was smart to suppress her gifts, leaving her smelling human for so long."

The man in the mask sounded strained.

"The redhead smells the same," said Johnson.

Elm nodded. "Because she too is from my line. Not surprising the two found one another. Like seeks like."

"So you want to bang your sister?" asked another of the men.

Elm centered his icy gaze on the man. "Of my line does not mean related to me. You are a wolf, yes? Are you related to everyone in your pack?"

"No," the guy said.

Brooke closed her eyes, trying desperately to keep her mind from going back to the time she was held prisoner by Elm and others like him. Back to the worst months of her life. The time when she learned monsters were real and she was one of them.

Pull it together, she said to herself. *If you let him win, he'll destroy everyone you love.*

She took a deep breath and opened her eyes. "I'm not going back with you. I'll never go back to that place."

Elm grinned. "Brooke, you misunderstand. I have no intention of returning you to the holding cells. I've bargained with them to keep you for myself."

Tut growled so loudly that there was no way to ignore it.

"You can't win this, Tut," said Auberi. "Trying will be your end."

"Smart man," said Elm, narrowing his gaze

on the men. He threw power at them and Brooke looked to them, fearing they'd be dead.

They weren't. Her magik had somehow managed to block Elm's.

"I'm never going to be some fucked-up version of a wife to you, sicko. I hate you," said Brooke, wanting to keep Elm's attention on her and off the men behind her.

Elm grinned. "Now Brooke, is that any way to speak to your future husband?"

She flipped him off.

He snorted. "While you are gifted, you are no match for me. Do not force me to harm you. I will," he said, looking hopeful that he'd get to do it.

She narrowed her gaze on him, knowing how he liked to mentally torture others in addition to physically torturing them. And she knew how he didn't like being questioned or challenged. "Aww, Elm, I'm disappointed. You talk a big game but really, you need a bunch of punk-ass flunkies to do your dirty work. If I'm so limited in my skill set, why not just come and get me yourself?"

"Boss, want us to shut the bitch up?" asked Johnson, making a move to come at Brooke.

Elm threw magik at Johnson and all the rest

of the men, thrusting them back against the walls of the room, pinning them in place. He set his sights on Brooke and removed his jacket, casting it aside before he rolled up his sleeves, his gaze never leaving her.

He moved to her in four long strides and began to circle her slowly, licking his lips as he stared at her. "You are so beautiful, Brooke. I dislike knowing I will have to beat you into submission. But I will be quick about it."

She stayed aware of where he was at all times. "Pfft, bet a lot of women already know just how quick you can be."

He came at her from behind and she ducked and twisted around, avoiding being hit.

He looked gleeful. "Interesting. You are faster than you were when last we met."

Because I'm not eight months pregnant, jerkoff.

He came at her again, with skill and precision, making a move to strike her in the face. She leaned back out of his reach and came up, punching him in the jaw.

The men in the room gasped.

Elm smiled more, wiping blood from his lip. "You have more fire than I thought. That means fucking you will be that much more fun. I was holding back, worried I'd harm you too much, but Brooke…I will hold back no more."

"Do you like to hear the sound of your own voice? Because I gotta tell you, it grates on my last nerve," she said.

His gaze darkened. When he lunged for her, he did it at an incredible speed.

She spun and extended her leg, kicking him in the chest, knocking him back from her. She ran at him and leapt in the air, spinning in motion, kicking him again, knocking him back more. She didn't stop. Rage for what he'd put her through led her actions.

He caught her with a backhand, hitting her jaw, knocking her off her feet.

He lifted his hands and balls of blue flames appeared in them. She rolled as he threw one at her. Brooke kept rolling, just missing the strikes.

"You cannot stand against me and win, Brooke. I am thousands of years old. You are not. And no one has ever taught you how to wield the gifts you were born with," he said.

She let her power build and grabbed a knife from the back of her pants, throwing it at him. It embedded in his arm.

He hissed and then laughed. "You *do* have a lot of fight in you."

He formed a bigger blue ball of fire and threw it at her.

Brooke tossed her hands up and white light came out of her palms, going to the blue ball of fire, making it dissipate.

He gasped. "How?"

She sprang to her feet and they began to circle one another.

He threw a hand up and wind hit her, but she held her ground, refusing to budge. She, in turn, hit him with a blast of wind as well, and he slid back on the floor.

He ripped up and off the floor as if pulled by strings, his skin shimmering, his hair lifting slightly as though he were standing in a breeze. His eyes began to glow. "Brooke, continue and I will be your end. I am not your average Fae. I am so very much more."

Lowering her head, she let her powers rise fully. Her eyes tingled and she knew they were now a vibrant green. And she knew the second her skin began to shimmer as his did, from the round of gasps that went through the room.

When she lifted her head, she found Elm staring wide-eyed at her. "Neither am I."

"Brooke?" he asked, his voice a whisper. "How?"

Her jaw set as her powers moved out and over the room, lifting chairs and tables. She thrust them at Elm and the others with him. Johnson and the other men were all struck hard, falling to the floor.

Elm lifted a hand and parted the objects flying at him, as if parting the Red Sea. He then sent a table flying at her. He stared at her and sniffed the air. His eyes lit with excitement. "I recognize the smell of that power."

She dropped the items she was making fly. He was right, she'd not been taught from birth to use her powers and was burning through them too fast. Her skin stopped shimmering and her eyes returned to normal.

"This changes everything," he said. "A female royal has not been in our line since your mother died. And even before that, she had been the only one for centuries." He stiffened. "Had she not run off with that dirty shifter she called a mate, she would have been *mine*. I'm willing to accept the fact you have animal blood in you because you are of royal lineage."

He came at her again and she leapt up and onto a chair, balancing on it before leaping and throwing it into the air. She caught it and then struck him in the side of the head. He went to one knee. He then grabbed her leg and yanked it out from under her. She landed on her back and he was on her in a heartbeat, pinning her to the floor with his body. He inhaled deeply. "Princess, you have no idea how good you smell."

"Do not pet-name me, jerkoff." She glared at him.

He laughed. "Brooke, have you any idea who your mother was?"

She didn't reply.

"She was a queen."

Brooke stared at him. "You expect me to believe my mother was a queen? Try another one. She cut cute shapes out of my peanut butter and jelly sandwiches and she baked cookies with me. You got the wrong info on me."

He ground against her, his erection pressing to her stomach.

Brooke saw the way he looked at her with nothing short of rapture on his face.

"I cannot believe she had a child," he said. "I see it now. You have her classic beauty and her body. But your skin coloring is more like your father's. As is your hair coloring. How did I not sense this on you years ago?"

She glared at him. "Get off me!"

"Get the fuck off her," Tut ground out.

Elm started to look in Tut's direction and Brooke panicked, knowing the monster could and would kill the men.

She grabbed Elm's cheek, directing his attention back to her before letting her power rise slightly, knowing she was tapping into the side of herself that exuded and demanded sexual lust.

He licked his lips. She felt his power drawing upon hers, trying to feed his need for sex.

She stared up at him. "Well, are you going to do this or not?"

He tipped his head, appearing confused. "Brooke."

She let more of her power up to greet his, and he instantly began to grind against her. She nipped at his jaw without actually making contact with him.

He gasped, loosening his hold on her.

She flipped him over and straddled him, lowering her body, coming just shy of kissing him, her power riding high. He looked enraptured. So much so that he didn't notice her going for the last of the knives she had on her.

She drew them out and bit his lower lip, making him moan.

Brooke sat up quickly and plunged the knives into his chest. She rolled off him fast, and thrust power at him, sending him sliding across the floor and into his men.

She knew it wouldn't kill him, but it would hurt him for a moment. Enough time to possibly slow his responses. Putting out her hands, she drew upon the energy around her and her hair lifted as wind circled. And she swayed, burning through her power at too high a rate. She spun around and thrust it at the men behind her, breaking her hold on them. She nearly tipped over from exhaustion.

Suddenly the man in the mask was in front of her, grabbing and holding her to his powerful frame. He lifted her and ran with her in the direction of the back exit. Auberi followed close behind them, tossing his mask along the way. They made it to the fire escape, but instead of going down the stairs, the man holding her went up and over the railing.

Brooke held tight to him, expecting pain to come. None did. The man landed almost catlike before standing tall with her still over his shoulder. Auberi landed next to them without so much as a hint of pain.

Somehow, she managed to squirm free of the masked man's grasp. She fell out of his hold and came up fast, bursting into a run, knowing she had to get to Edee.

She made it to the end of the alley and bolted out and into the street. Dark vehicles were parked at all angles in it. She knew what that meant. More men from The Corporation. She made a move to run in the other direction but the side door of the van nearest her opened and large arms yanked her off her feet and into the van.

Chapter Fourteen

MALIK TRIED to run after Brooke, only to find his friend ripping him back. "No!"

"Asshole," snapped Auberi from the right, drawing Malik's attention before grabbing him. "We have men shooting at us from above and more coming from the front and you want to chase a stripper? Granted, she's a powerful stripper, but a stripper all the same. Admit it. The stripper kicked ass."

"Never call her that again," he returned before thinking too hard on it. He inhaled deeply as the words fell from his mouth.

He could barely think straight. Brooke was not only alive but she was a supernatural? That couldn't be. Could it? His irrational behavior all those years ago had been caused by the medication PSI had been testing, hadn't it?

He'd never had another dose of the meds, yet he still reacted the same way to the woman. And it was more than obvious that she wasn't human after all. That could only mean one thing.

She really was his mate, and he'd not only chased her away all those years ago, he'd done so again the minute they were together again. And now The Corporation was after her.

Auberi pointed to the end of the alley, which was filling with more bad guys. "Oh look, the evening just got more interesting. Happy birthday, non-birthday, Tut."

Malik's lion pushed up fast, wanting to be free. It took all of him to stay in control enough to think. He charged at the men and felt Auberi there, close at his heels.

Two men in partially shifted form rushed at him. He could smell the mix of supernatural on them. They were functioning hybrids, unlike the ones who smelled like death and were basically rotting from the inside out. Apparently, the enemy was getting better at perfecting their creations.

Malik collided with the men, roaring, the

fierce need to get to Brooke all-consuming. The men lifted him off the ground, a true testament to their strength. He flipped, rotating his arms, breaking their hold on him. The second his feet touched the ground, he struck out at the man nearest him, connecting. The man's head snapped back but he kept coming. So did the other.

Auberi's curses in French reached Malik, and he knew his friend was figuring out they were up against super powered supernaturals. The knowledge that something as lethal as the hybrids were after his woman did something to Malik, giving him the added boost he needed to strike with a vengeance. Claws emerged from his fingertips and he slashed out, catching one of the men by the throat. Malik pushed hard, cutting through the man's neck fully. He then set his sights on the other male. He made short work of the man and raced down the alley to the street.

He was just in time to see a dark van speeding away, its tires squealing, the scent of honey and lotus coming from it. They had Brooke. They had his woman.

Auberi rushed up next to him. "We really need to see about the vitamin regimen Dr.

Franken-Krauss has those assholes on. I want some. Do you think it would be like the little blue pill? Best invention ever."

Malik's mouth burned with the need to change at the thought of Brooke with the men. He took off running after the van as if he had a chance of catching up with them. He was fast, but even he couldn't run at the speed they were going. The knowledge that he'd never catch them on foot did nothing to deter him. He had to get to her. He had to protect her.

As the red taillights drew farther away, a profound sense of loss hit Malik. If they got away, the chances of him ever finding Brooke again were nearly zero. That simply was not an option.

"No!" he roared.

Auberi caught him by the shoulders and spun Malik to face him fully. "Tut! Focus. Take a deep breath."

He did but it didn't help. "Auberi, I have to find Brooke."

Auberi stiffened. "As in the same Brooke you mentioned spending time with several years back? The one you lost control of your beast with and bit, trying to claim? The human?"

Malik nodded, still trying to home in on his

senses to figure out what direction the enemy had taken Brooke. "It was her. The girl from the club. They have her."

"It's clear she's anything but human." Auberi sighed. "We'll call for backup and request satellite footage of the area. We will find out where they went with her."

Malik knew that wasn't likely. The Corporation had moles and traitors working for them within PSI. They also had their own technology that was leaps and bounds above that of humans.

Knowing it was hopeless, Malik fell to his knees, his entire body aching. He wanted to scream, to shout, to kill, anything to get the hurt out of his system. He knew it wouldn't help, but still it was what he wanted to do. He lowered his head, emotions welling in him. He wasn't the type of man who cried. His mother had been fierce, as had his father. Crying was something that simply was not tolerated.

Auberi pulled out his cell phone and put a hand to Malik's shoulder. "James, by chance is your mate still a hacking genius? Can she reposition a satellite for us and grab any imagery it has? The Corporation has struck again and they've taken a young woman."

Auberi gave their coordinates and stayed on the line with James. The man had only just been freed from nearly a year of being a prisoner in one of The Corporation's facilities. James knew better than anyone what horrors the place could and would inflict on those it took.

Malik fought to keep from shedding tears that desperately wanted to come. He'd been so close to her again. He'd touched her, caressed her, inhaled her glorious scent, had her lips on his skin, all to have her ripped away at the last second. Fate couldn't be that cruel, could it?

Unable to contain his emotions any longer, Malik growled loudly and punched the concrete as if that would solve anything. All it did was hurt his hand.

"Yes, that is just three blocks from here if memory serves," said Auberi, surprise in his voice.

Malik perked. "What? Laney got the satellite repositioned already?" Even for Laney, an expert hacktivist, that was impressive. "Where are they taking Brooke?"

Auberi had the nerve to shush him. "If they had her, they would not be tearing up the area looking for her. Call me back if anything changes. We're headed in that direction. Send backup. Only the most trusted. And equip them with tranquilizers. I believe my furry friend here may have a repeat plaza performance if this ends poorly."

Malik didn't even bother to object. It was true. He would lose control if he didn't find her or if she was hurt. There would be no way he could keep it together.

Auberi yanked him off the ground and then brushed Malik's open shirt, trying to smooth out the wrinkles. It was such an Auberi thing to do that it actually helped Malik to gather his wits about him. His friend disconnected the call.

"James and Laney are patched into the police frequencies. Reports of armed men in black SUVs are coming in three blocks from here. They wouldn't stop for takeout if they had what they wanted—your woman."

Auberi cupped Malik's cheek in a manly way. "I believe she lives, and she has managed to escape them, at least for now."

Chapter Fifteen

BROOKE RAN DOWN A SIDE STREET, trying to lose the men who were after her. While she'd managed to break free from the van, she was far from out of the woods. Elm and his men from the club wouldn't be out of commission for long. She'd basically stunned them and it would wear off. And Elm would heal his wounds quickly.

And most of them could track her scent. She'd learned that years ago. Being held by sick bastards had taught her a lot about things she'd never dreamed were real. She'd gotten a crash course in the paranormal and supernatural. And she'd had to learn the rest on her own.

She went up and over a set of trash cans by a backdoor to what smelled like a restaurant.

Clearing them with room to spare, Brooke landed on her feet and looked back, needing to know if she'd lost them yet.

As men poured in from around the end of the building, each wearing earpieces and openly carrying weapons, her entire body tensed as cold began to form in her hands. She couldn't lose it now. Not yet. She needed to get away, and if she couldn't avoid capture, she needed to be sure she didn't live to be able to give them any information.

There was simply too much at stake.

Brooke turned and started to run again. The side street was a dead end, but she wouldn't let that stop her. In seconds, she'd already soaked in her surroundings, knowing the best route to take —it went up.

She leapt up and seized hold of a metal fire escape ladder and swung herself up and onto it, drawing on the speed and strength the very people chasing her had ensured she had.

A bullet whizzed by her, going through her hair, narrowly missing her neck. The sounds of sirens grew nearer and she knew local law enforcement wouldn't help. The people chasing her were widely connected. The odds of the police being diverted by The Corporation and its affiliates were great. That was also something she'd learned long ago.

Trust no one.

She climbed higher and dodged another bullet.

"Aim for the torso!" shouted one of the men. "Elm wants her alive. No fatal shots!"

Brooke kept going higher and higher. One of the men fired at her again and this one ricocheted off the metal railing, near her hand.

There was snarling and then more gunfire, but no bullets came near her. She'd been hunted for too long by The Corporation to think for a minute the men had missed that wide. No. They were trained killers who were more than human.

She slowed enough to look down. The entire end of the street was blocked off by SUVs now. Something was happening down there. The men who had been after her had turned and were converging on something or someone else.

Her head told her to keep running. To put as much distance between herself and the bad guys as she could. Her body refused to move. It was as if she were frozen in place, the overwhelming urge to see who or what had caught the men's attention was great. Whatever it was, it was pissed.

Her jaw dropped as she watched one of the men in the suits get tossed in the air like a ragdoll. He fell back into the mass of men. Blood splattered onto the building across the street in such an amount that there was no doubt the owner was dead.

"Move," she said out loud, hoping her body would obey. It didn't. Her hand tightened around the railing as she remained locked in place.

Half the men splintered off, their attention coming back to her. Two lifted their weapons and aimed. Even with the threat of being shot, she couldn't get her body to respond.

Another man in a suit flew into the air and then landed with a thud that echoed loudly. A man with shoulder-length black, wavy hair emerged from the crowd of men, his back to her. This one wasn't in a suit. He was wearing exactly what the man in the Egyptian mask had been wearing at the club.

He had a handgun held up like he more than knew his way around one. He popped off a shot and one of the men who were aiming at her went down fast. The man shot another in a fraction of a second. He stepped partially under one of the lights from the building and turned around.

She saw his face and thought for sure her mind was playing tricks on her.

"Malik?" she whispered, and his gaze snapped up to her.

He was dead. That was what she'd been told. What she'd believed for years.

It was him, but his hair was shorter than it had been five years back.

He'd been the man she'd rubbed all over at the club? The man she'd wanted to give herself to the same way she'd given herself to him all those years ago?

Another shot rang out, this one coming from above. Brooke glanced up to find men in suits descending from the roof on the very same fire escape she was on. They opened fire on her and she jolted back fast. Too fast. The railing gave out behind her and she reached out, trying to catch hold of anything to keep her up, but she missed.

Vaguely, she heard Malik shouting her name, sounding frantic. She shut off, focusing on twisting in preparation for landing on her feet. Shots came from above and one hit her in the arm and another hit her in the upper leg, the pain and impact throwing her off. The ground met her, and it wasn't with open arms.

Pain raced through her and she lay there on her stomach, the wind knocked out of her. There was a huge roar not far from her and then an explosion of gunfire around her. She waited, expecting to be shot again. The Corporation was very aware of her healing abilities. After all, they'd given them to her. They'd have no issue filling her with bullet wounds they knew would heal if it meant they got their clutches on her again.

No bullets struck her.

Confused and disoriented from the fall, she lifted her head slightly. It took a second for her vision to clear.

When it did, she found Malik there, not far from her, his upper body seeming even larger than before. Tan fur coated his arms and long claws tipped his fingertips. His normally dark eyes were a vibrant amber as he spun and slashed open the neck of one of the men in a suit.

Pain radiated throughout her as she began to put the pieces together. Malik was a shifter? Everything began to make sense then.

Someone touched her shoulder lightly, and she gasped as pain went through her again.

"How hurt are you?" asked a familiar voice. One she'd heard at the club and knew belonged to the man called Auberi. "You require medical attention. First, I have to try to cage the lion before he goes on a killing spree that extends beyond these assholes. Do me a favor and try not to die. I'll *never* get him settled down if you die. Plus, I really hate doing reports."

Brooke lay there and closed her eyes a moment as her body began doing what it did—healing. Her arm and leg began to burn and she knew the bullets were starting to dislodge as her body expelled them. The act always hurt as much as getting shot. And she'd know, she'd been shot enough over the years. Hissing, Brooke managed to turn over onto her back as the bullets pushed all the way out of her.

Her gaze went up and she saw that the men from the roof were nearly to the base of the fire escape. The men aimed their weapons past her, onto Malik.

A burst of adrenaline moved through her and she thrust up and off the ground, snatching a discarded weapon on her way up. She stood, swayed, and began firing. She was no stranger to guns anymore. Gone was the naïve girl of five years ago. The Corporation had killed her, leaving the new Brooke in her place.

She hit four of the men in suits before stumbling to the right and nearly falling.

Auberi grabbed her around the waist with one arm before taking the weapon from her and firing at the remaining men. They fell like flies onto the ground. "That won't keep them down long. We need to get you out of here. Of course, we need to get Malik to calm down enough not to attack us first."

She leaned against him as her upper leg began trying to heal the damage from the bullet wound fully. It burned as if someone was pouring acid on her. She cried out and clung to Auberi, who held her, rocking her in place.

"Tut, she lives and she's in great pain. Cage the lion or you will *really* lose her," said Auberi, his French accent going from slight to intense.

Malik kept cutting through the men in suits as if he'd never even heard Auberi speak to him.

"Brooke, the bloodlust has taken him. Soon he'll fully shift and could possibly be stuck in that form for good."

She shook. "He's really a shifter?"

Auberi nodded.

"W-what are you?" she asked. "A shifter too?"

"Hardly!" he shouted, clearly offended at the suggestion. "Don't be afraid, but I'm a vampire."

She calmed slightly, her attention going back to Malik. He looked feral. "What's wrong with him?"

"It's the bloodlust I mentioned. It means his beast has too strong a hold on him. Talk to him," he said, still holding her. "He'll listen to you."

She doubted Malik would listen to anything in the state he was in. He looked like a one-man killing machine. As he took down the last of the men near them, he stared around, his amber gaze rimmed with red.

"Malik, stop. Please," she said softly. "Think with your head, not your fists."

He tipped his head in an unnatural way that screamed animal, not human. Blood dripped from his clawed hands. He looked savage. Nothing like the man she remembered. The Malik before her was lethal. That should have terrified her. It didn't.

She pushed out of Auberi's embrace and tried to take a step in Malik's direction. Her leg gave out on her and she started going down.

Strong arms caught her, lifting and holding her close. At first, she thought it was Auberi—until she glanced over to see him standing there, grinning. Brooke sucked in a big breath as she realized Malik was the one who had her.

He stared down at her, and she saw the red and amber receding from his eyes. The fur on his arms vanished as well. He looked confused. "I saw you fall off the side of the building. I thought you were dead."

"I thought you were dead too," she said, barely able to get the words out.

"She's not dead?" asked Malik, his gaze moving to Auberi.

The vampire snorted. "No, though if you squeeze her any tighter you might be the death of her."

Malik eased his ironclad grip and she wiggled to get down. He set her on her feet but kept her close. "Brooke? How? When? You're not human?"

Tears broke free from her as she stared up at him. With a tentative hand, she reached out and touched his cheek. "They told me they killed you."

His hand moved over hers. "They lied."

She cried harder.

He hugged her to him. "My sweet. No tears please. I don't think I can handle them."

She shook as she cried harder, pressing herself to him. A small laugh came from her as she eased back. "You're not human either."

"No, I'm not." He stared down at her with desire in his eyes. "It's part of what I couldn't tell you. Why didn't you tell me that you're Fae?"

She wiped her cheeks and stepped back more. "Because I didn't know then."

He grabbed her and yanked her to him again before pressing his lips to her forehead, his body shaking slightly as he kept a tight hold on her. "I couldn't find you. I looked for so long."

He'd looked for her?

"Why?"

A long breath came from him. "For reasons you still aren't ready to hear."

She held onto his forearms. "Malik, we have to get out of here. What I did won't keep Elm and his men down for long."

"What exactly did you do to them?" asked Auberi. "And how do you even know them?

"It's a really long story. Malik, I have to get

to Edee. If they find her first…I can't even think about it. They'll take them both."

"Take both of who, my sweet?" he asked, tilting her chin up, his dark gaze raking over her.

"Och, we missed all the fun," said a familiar Scottish voice from the other end of the alley. "Did you leave any of them for us to kill, Tut?"

Brooke spotted Striker stepping over dead bodies. He had a full, long beard now.

Boomer was next around the corner. He looked at Brooke and closed his eyes slightly. "You're okay? What about Edee and the child?"

"Child?" asked Malik.

Brooke stared at Boomer. "How do you know about her?"

Boomer kept walking towards them. "Information found its way to us tonight."

"Are you all supernaturals?" she asked.

"Yes," he said, his jaw tense.

She sank against Malik again, the weight of the last five years hitting her hard. "We have to get to them both before Elm or the rest of them do. Please! Help me."

Malik nodded. "Of course. We'll help Edee and her child."

She was about to tell him everything when

Garth came around the corner, with Rurik close to him.

She jerked back from Malik. "You're with *them*? Ohmygod, all this time I thought they killed you, and you were in league with them? Were you a warm-up for things to come in Egypt? Why help me tonight if you're part of The Corporation? Why stand against them?"

"W-what?" Malik asked, looking confused. "Part of The Corporation? Brooke?"

Striker tilted his head, his long red hair falling over one shoulder. "Lass, we're nae with that place. When information came up that included photos of you and Edee, Boomer called us all in to aide in finding you both. We came in this direction and Corbin and Duke followed another possible lead."

"Photos?" asked Malik, looking at his friends.

Boomer sighed. "The thing James wanted us to look into was this—Brooke and Edee. I saw their pictures and saw the order The Corporation had put down for them, retrieve at any cost. I knew you couldn't be brought in. Not with how badly you lost your shit over Brooke in Egypt. I didn't want you walking onto the scene to find she was dead."

"You sent me away from the office with Auberi, knowing I've been hunting for Brooke for years?" asked Malik, hurt in his voice.

Boomer sighed. "Don't forget, Duke, Corbin, James, and I are mated. We know what it's like to realize your woman is in danger. We've each felt it. We've each nearly lost ourselves to our beast side because of it. We didn't want that to happen to you. We hoped we could intervene and protect Brooke, Edee, and the child before The Corporation got to them."

Malik twisted away from Brooke and grabbed Auberi by his shirt, snarling. "You fucking took me to party when my mate needed me?"

The men all sucked in big breaths.

"Did he just call the American girl his mate?" asked Rurik.

"Aye," said Striker, eyeing Boomer. "You were right."

Boomer put his hands up. "Malik, stop. Auberi didn't know. We kept him out of this because we know how close you two are. We know you can read each other's tells really well. If he knew what we were doing, you'd figure it out, and if we were too late and Brooke was already taken or dead, we would have never gotten you back from your lion form."

Auberi offered Malik a soft look. "Had I known, old friend, I would have insisted you be brought in. I may not understand why anyone in their right mind would want to tie themselves to one woman for eternity, but I'm not a total dick."

Malik released the man and reached for Brooke, who backed up more, staring around at the men, confused. "Brooke?"

She narrowed her gaze on the men. "I don't understand. Why are you all helping me yet working with a guy who is really well connected in The Corporation? Elm's best friend?"

Striker scratched the back of his head. "She thinks we're in cahoots with a tree's best friend? I do nae understand women in the least."

"What do you mean?" asked Malik. "Who is Elm's best friend?"

She pointed to Garth. "He's one of the men who tortured Edee."

"Wait, you were actually taken by The Corporation?" asked Boomer, his gaze hardening. "Our intel only said you were recently targeted by them. We knew you went missing in Egypt but we didn't know who was responsible."

"Och, lass, you must be mistaken about Garth. He's nae working with them. He hates them as much as we do," said Striker. "And I do nae think he's friends with a tree, but Vikings are nae the smartest lot so anything is possible."

She shook her head and then paused, really looking at Garth. "Where's the scar? The one above your right eye?"

Garth gasped. "She's talking about Grid."

Malik tipped his head. "Grid, the brother you haven't seen in centuries?"

"Yes," said Garth, his expression hardening. "Rumors reached me that he was running with unsavory people, but I didn't want to believe it." He looked to her. "I'm sorry he hurt you. Please know I had nothing to do with it. No one here did. We dedicate our lives to protecting innocents."

Boomer touched his earpiece and then spoke. "We're with Brooke now, so are Malik and Auberi. From the number of dead bodies littering the area, I'd say one hell of a retrieval team was sent for her."

Brooke's pulse raced as she realized Boomer was right. They had sent a large team after her and this wasn't even all of them. The ones from the club would be coming soon as well.

Boomer locked gazes with Brooke, his expression grim. "Corbin says they're at your house. There are signs of a big-time struggle and blood all over the place. They haven't found any bodies. Is there somewhere else Edee might go? Somewhere she'd take the child?"

His words sank in and she felt her knees getting weak. "They found them?"

Boomer touched his earpiece. "She's in shock. I'll try to get the information from her." He paused a second. "Yeah. I know."

"What?" demanded Striker. "Did they find Edee and her babe?"

"No. But they did find two bags that looked to have been packed for a woman and child. The bags were on the street."

Brooke's legs went out from under her. She fell to the ground.

Malik was to her in an instant. He went to his knees next to her and hugged her from the side, rocking her gently as she cried. "Shhh, my sweet, we'll find Edee and her child."

Boomer made his way to her and bent. "Brooke, I saw the pictures of the little girl. She's not Edee's, is she?"

"No," whispered Brooke. "She's my daughter. She's so tiny…and they have her."

"Daughter?" asked Malik, shock in his voice. He released his hold on her and stood fast. "You had a child with another man?"

"Take a calm breath, Tut," said Auberi. "It's been years since you last saw her. You explained to me that suppression drugs were in play then. Your wires probably got crossed. It would explain how she could have a child with another. Clearly, she found her mate."

Malik stormed away from her. He punched the side of the brick building and roared. Garth, Rurik, and Striker all went at him, pulling him back from the building.

Boomer stayed close to her. "Brooke, how old is she?"

"Just over four," replied Brooke through her tears. "She has to be terrified. I have to find her. I have to find them both!"

"Calm down, Tut," said Striker.

Malik shoved Striker. "Don't tell me to calm down! My mate found a way to have a child with another man! I claimed her. I thought she was human and I claimed her! She's anything but human. She shouldn't have been able to have children with anyone but me. I'm going to find the guy who touched her and kill him!"

Boomer helped Brooke to her feet. "Auberi, can you help her?"

Auberi was suddenly there, holding Brooke to his powerful frame. She flinched as Malik shouted more. He stepped out of the circle of men and pointed at her. "I spent five years hunting for you, and you were what? Shacking up with some guy, popping out babies?"

Stunned, she jerked and stepped back, out of Auberi's embrace. It took her a moment to stop crying long enough to speak. When she did, she didn't bother being nice. "Let's recap, shall we? I spent a night with you almost five years ago, and you kicked me out of your room and your life. Remember that? That doesn't give you the right to judge me, and you certainly don't own me."

He snarled and the men all grabbed him, keeping him in place.

Brooke narrowed her gaze on him. "And to answer your question about how I spent my five years, I spent the first eight months after you chased me away from your room being held in a secret facility owned and operated by The Corporation. Want to know when I found out I was pregnant? Day *two* of being there, Malik. The guy in the cell next to mine said he could smell the change in my body. He told me I was expecting."

Malik stilled.

She kept glaring at him. "Since I'd only been with you, that really narrowed the field on who the baby's father was. So, to answer your question, I spent the first eight months that I was pregnant with *your* daughter being tested on and tortured—mentally and physically. It was all I could do to keep her safe from them. When we were freed, the fight to protect her didn't end." She jabbed herself in the chest with her pointer finger. "I was hunted like a fox by a pack of wild dogs. Edee and I had to stay on the run. I delivered your daughter in a gas station bathroom. And when I held her for the first time, I knew she was worth every bit of the pain and torture I'd gone through. She was worth the heartache and grief I suffered when they told me they'd killed you. She was worth the testing they put me through."

The men all lowered their gazes and released their hold on Malik.

He stared at her. "I…? We? You? She's…?"

Striker lifted his head. "Och, Tut, that may be the worst apology I've ever heard, and I've botched more than my fair share."

Boomer reached for Brooke. "We'll help find her. We won't let her or Edee be hurt. If Edee happened to get away, where would she go? We can check there first."

Malik averted his gaze and Brooke snorted.

"You know what, *Tut*," she said, her tone mocking and full of rage. "I don't want or need your help finding Edee and Bethany."

Boomer grabbed her shoulders. "Brooke, ignore him. He's not a factor in this right now. You can trust me. I want to find them. Tell me where to look. Let me help you. Let *us* help."

"I'll take you to the set meeting location. What if she's not there? What if they have her and my daughter?"

"Then we will move heaven and hell to get them back," said Boomer.

Garth stepped forward. "We won't rest until they're safe."

Rurik nodded.

Striker lifted his chin. "And we'll make the bastards pay for ever thinkin' they could dare to take them."

Nodding, she lost her battle with tears again. "Thank you."

Chapter Sixteen

BROOKE STAYED PRESSED against the door of the large SUV she'd been placed in. Boomer was driving, Striker was in the passenger seat, and Malik was in the second row with her. Auberi, Rurik, and Garth were behind them in another SUV. And Corbin and Duke were supposed to meet them at the safe house.

Since they'd gotten in the vehicle, Malik hadn't spoken a word. He'd not even looked at her.

"We'll find them, Brooke," said Boomer, glancing up at the rearview mirror to look at her. "I promise you that."

"Aye," said Striker. "No one hurts a child on my watch. No one."

"Thank you for your help," Brooke said softly, her hands shaking. "Does anyone have a phone I can use?"

Malik withdrew his phone and handed it to her, never saying a word.

She stiffened. "Does anyone *else* have a phone I can use?"

"Aye," said Striker, handing her his phone.

She started to dial a number she'd memorized, only to find it pulling up on its own in Striker's phone. Brooke blinked. "Why do you have Gram Campbell's number in your phone?"

Striker twisted around in the seat. "The better question would be, how is it *you* know Gram?"

She could feel Malik's heated gaze on her but didn't bother looking at him.

"Please tell me why you have his number in your phone."

Striker nodded. "He works for the same place we do."

"Wait, you're all with PSI?" she asked.

"Aye," said Striker.

Boomer glanced in the mirror again. "Did Gram tell you about PSI?"

"Yes," she replied.

"Brooke, how do you know him?" asked Boomer evenly.

"He saved my life," she confessed. "At first I thought he was a guard at the facility I was being held at. A new one they'd only just hired. But it was quickly apparent he wasn't like the rest. He wasn't evil. He and another man who started there about the same time got Edee, Cody, and me out of there."

"Cody?" asked Boomer.

"The guy who was held in the cell next to mine. The one who told me I was pregnant. And the one who tried so hard to protect me and the baby from harm." Her hands continued to shake.

"Lass, you still have contact with Gram and this Cody?" asked Striker.

She nodded. "It's been months since I've seen either of them. The last time Gram and I saw each other, it ended poorly."

Striker narrowed his eyes on her. "He hurt you?"

"Oh gods, no," said Brooke. "Gram would never hurt me. We had a falling-out because I told him I wouldn't marry him."

Boomer cleared his throat, glancing

nervously in the mirror at Malik. "So, you and Gram were a couple then?"

"Yes. For three years. He's listed on the birth certificate as Bethany's father. He insisted. He loves her like she was his. It was hard to refuse his offer, but I didn't want him hurt again because of me."

"Again?" asked Striker, also watching Malik closely.

"Johnson and a team of men found us. Gram took me and Bethany on a mission with him. He said it wasn't a dangerous one, but that he didn't want to be gone that long from us. Edee thought it was a great idea so she pushed me to go too. Everything was really good for the first two months. It felt right. Like a real family. And then one night we were asleep in bed and suddenly there was so much noise that it stunned me. Gram responded faster than me. He already knew the sound was people breaking into the house, heavily armed. He shouted for me to get in the closet but I couldn't. Not without my baby."

Brooke rubbed the palms of her hands on her pant legs. "I didn't listen to him. I ran for Bethany's room. She was screaming and scared. I didn't realize Gram intended to get to her and get her to safety. I ran out into the hall without thinking and Gram shouted my name a second before men opened fire on me. He put himself in the path of the bullets. Had his handler not been close, Bethany and I would have been taken and Gram would have died. They filled him with so many silver bullets that it nearly killed him."

Striker's jaw tightened. "Aye, I remember a report coming in about Gram being hurt in the line of duty, but it dinnae say how seriously or what mission he was on."

"It was bad. Really bad. I thought I was going to lose him too," she said. "That he'd be dead just like I thought Malik was."

"He dinnae die," said Striker. "Sounds like he dinnae blame you in the least for what happened. Am I right?"

She nodded. "The first thing he said when he opened his eyes at the special hospital they had him at was, 'will you marry me *now?*" I almost said yes. I should have said yes." She looked up, blinking back her emotions. "He was so hurt when I told him we were going. That I refused to put him in danger by staying with him. And he was extra angry when he found out what I was doing to make a living."

Striker eyed her. "And what was that?"

"I work at a strip club, for lack of a better word."

Striker pursed his lips. "I'm normally all for strippers, but I can see Gram's issue with it. I do nae think it's sitting well with Tut either."

Brooke looked over to find Malik's face was stone-like as he stared ahead.

A snort broke free from her. "He doesn't care. He couldn't get rid of me fast enough after we were together. And the second he heard I had a child, he said what he thought of me. So I don't really give a rat's ass what he thinks of how I supported *my* daughter."

Malik's gaze whipped to her. "You think I don't care?"

"Yes."

"Well, in her defense, Tut, you did act like an arse when you found out she had a wee one. And you've nae said a word about the child being yers. If I was the lass, I'd think you dinnae care too. And I'd probably kick you in the balls. I'm actually considering kicking yer arse *for* her."

Brooke leaned forward and patted Striker's shoulders. "I really like you."

"Most women do," he said with a wink.

Pointing, Brooke slid up in the seat more and touched Boomer's shoulder. "There. Turn right. It's the first house on the left. That is one of the safe houses Edee and I agreed to meet at first if something happened."

"You've more than one?" asked Striker.

"Yes. Gram, Cody, Armand—Gram's handler—always insist we have more than one. Their motto is we can never be too prepared."

"Gram still in the picture then?" asked Boomer.

"He's never been out of it. Hurt by me saying no to marrying him, yes. Upset at the job I picked and that I didn't let him take care of us, yes. Out of the picture, no. We haven't seen each other because I asked him for time. He calls me twice a day and I know he moved closer to where we are. I know he watches the house a lot, afraid for us," she said, her gaze sliding to Malik.

He didn't look at her.

"Lass, stay in the vehicle while we check on that," said Striker, motioning to two large, matching SUVs parked in front of the safe house.

She nearly panicked—until she caught sight of a small pink plastic butterfly hanging from the rearview mirror in one of the vehicles. She twisted in her seat fast and grabbed Malik's thigh. "She's safe! Bethany made him that butterfly on his mirror."

Malik's gaze locked on her hand.

She squeezed his leg. "Our baby is safe."

She touched Boomer quickly. "Can you make sure Garth stays back a bit until we explain to Edee that he's not the same man who hurt her?"

He nodded, his expression sympathetic. "Will do."

"Thank you!" Brooke was out of the car before it came to a full stop. She ran in the direction of the porch, only to have a large dark blur intercept her, catching her gently.

As she stared into the face of the tall, black-haired, muscular man with royal blue eyes, she found herself unable to speak.

Gram Campbell yanked her against his body and held her there, everything on him tight. He then tilted her face upwards and dropped his lips onto hers. His kiss was hot and branding. When he ended it, she saw the worry in his face. "When Edee called, I thought…I thought I'd never see you again."

Act of Passion

"Were they hurt?" she asked, still in his arms.

"No," he returned softly. "I got there just as everything was going down. Edee kept Bethany hidden and we dinnae let her see the aftermath."

Brooke threw her arms around Gram's neck. "Thank you. Thank you so much."

Gram kissed the top of her head. "Brooke, it's nae safe for you to live on yer own."

"I know," she said, loosening her hold on him. "I thought we could do it. I thought they maybe gave up on hunting us."

"Och, lass, Elm has convinced himself that yer the closest thing to a mate he'll ever have. That he can force a life with you. He's sick and twisted and has no grasp on reality. He'll nae stop hunting you so long as he lives," said Gram, emotions choking him up. "He already tried to force himself on you when you were expecting Bethany. Had Cody nae been there, I do nae even want to think of what would have happened. We were lucky tonight. He dinnae come himself. He sent his henchmen."

Brooke stepped back from him and bit her lower lip. "He came to the club."

"W-what?" he asked, his voice so low it was barely audible.

She knew he'd react badly to the news that Elm had found her, but she couldn't lie to him. "Johnson led the team that came and then shortly after, Elm arrived."

Gram's blue eyes swirled to a deep brown as a huge growl sounded from him.

Brooke grabbed his hands. "No. Don't give in to the change. I'm okay."

It was clear that Gram was fighting his wolf. "Brooke, he's nae a normal supernatural male. He's unlike anything any of us have ever gone up against. From what Armand and I have found, he's thousands of years old. And he has powers the likes of which I've never seen a Fae have. How did you manage to get away from him? I know we spent a long time teaching you to protect yerself, but that willnae stop a man like Elm."

Brooke started to tell him everything that happened but he gasped and grabbed her, sniffing her.

"I smell him on you—and I smell shifter and vampire on you."

"Campbell, I do nae like you much. If you do nae take yer hands off the lass while yer angry, I willnae stop Malik from tearing you to bits," said Striker.

It was then Brooke noticed Boomer and Striker holding Malik back as Malik's eyes burned with amber.

Gram's brows drew together. "What's going on? Why are you all with her?"

"Malik protected me. So did his friend Auberi," said Brooke, doing her best to diffuse the situation. "And then a bunch of their friends came."

"And *then* they came?" asked Gram, eyeing her. "As in Malik and Auberi were with you to start with?"

"You've no idea just how much one of them beat you to the punch," said Striker, earning him a grunt from Boomer. He shrugged. "Let's be honest here. Malik is the one with a right to be angry. Nae Campbell."

Gram growled. "Tut was at the club, wasn't he? It's nae enough he beds a different woman nightly. He has to pay for the pleasure of their company too?"

Brooke felt as if someone had hit her in the chest with a bat. "I know what type of man he is. For a brief moment, I thought I'd judged him wrong. I didn't. I was young and naïve. I believed in happily ever after then. I believed in love at first sight."

Gram tipped his head, confusion coating his face.

She stayed close to him. "Don't be mad at him for being who he is. He's a womanizer. It's his thing. As much as that killed me inside, it is what it is. And yes, he was at the club tonight. Does it matter why? In the end, he kept them from taking me. I'd used too much power to stop Elm and the others with him. And then when I was shot and fell, I had too much damage that needed to be healed to be able to run or protect myself. Because Malik was there, I didn't have to."

Gram paled. "You used enough magik to stop Elm and you were shot?"

She gave a small nod.

He narrowed his gaze. "How are you upright? I know you, Brooke. I know how yer gifts work and what they need when tapped into." He took a step back and ran his hands over his face. "You did it. You finally gave in to that short chick's requests for you to do more than just pour drinks for men. You slept with one, didn't you? Malik? It was him, wasn't it?"

"Gram, stop," she said, keeping her voice even. "It's not like that. I met him years ago."

Gram sucked in a big breath. "He's the one, isn't he? He's Bethany's father. I knew her shifter side smelled familiar to me. I couldnae place it. It's him, right?"

"Yes."

Snarling, Gram pointed at Malik, and Brooke threw herself in front of the wolf-shifter as he began to shout. "Yer nae coming in here and taking the family I built! You left a young woman pregnant with yer babe and you dinnae come for her when she needed you most. Yer a shite mate, Nasser!"

"Stop!" she said, pushing on Gram's chest. "It's not like that!"

"So he dinnae plant his seed in you and do nothing when you were taken by sick bastards?" asked Gram, his neck muscles popping.

"Aye, 'tis as you said," added Striker.

"Not helping here," pressed Boomer.

"I know, but Tut did as Gram said, and he's nae said a word about his wee one. Speak up dumbarse or yer going to lose her, Tut. You've got to be the one to tell her the truth. It means nothing coming from us."

Brooke teared up and pressed a partial smile

to her face as she stared at Striker. "I shouldn't have said what I did to him. I was hurt and angry but it wasn't his fault I was taken. And it's okay that he didn't want me. I've accepted that. Bethany doesn't know anything about him, and when she's older and asks, I'll tell her something that paints Malik in a good light. There's no need for her to know he didn't want her either." She did her best to remain calm. "Gram is here now. We'll go with him and we'll all be fine. Thank you for everything."

Boomer gave Malik a shove. "She can't hear your thoughts, Tut. If you don't open your mouth and say it all, even if she rejects it, then you have no one to blame when she goes away and you never see her again and you never even get to meet your daughter."

Read his thoughts?

Brooke was about to ask about the statement when the front door of the safe house opened. Edee stepped out, holding Bethany in her arms. The four-year-old looked exhausted and was clutching her stuffed lion that she never slept without. She rubbed her large dark brown eyes, her long black, curly hair hanging to her mid-back.

"See, sweetie, I told you Mommy was fine.

The bad men didn't get her. Look, she's safe and with Uncle Gram." Edee nodded to Brooke.

Bethany perked slightly and dropped her stuffed lion on the porch. "Mommy?"

Brooke hesitated, afraid Gram might attack Malik in his current state. She didn't want her daughter seeing that. "Gram, are you okay?"

"No," he said. "But I willnae do what yer thinking. I'd never scare the child. Unlike some, I love her."

Brooke stepped away from Gram and went in the direction of the porch. She hurried up the stairs and put her arms out wide. Bethany leapt into them and hugged her tight. Brooke kissed the top of her head. Reaching out towards Edee, Brooke mouthed the words "thank you".

Her best friend took her hand and stepped in, hugging them both. She then rubbed Bethany's back. "Mommy's fine, sweetie. And you're so tired. How about I take you up and lay with you tonight? I'm guessing Mommy will come in and sleep with us too."

Bethany clung to Brooke and began to cry softly. "Mommy, I'm scared. Aunt Edee put me in the secret space in my room and then I heard shouting. I peeked out and saw a man hit Aunt

Edee. He was a bad man, Mommy. Aunt Edee threw him out the window!"

Edee sucked in a big breath. "I didn't know she saw that, Brooke."

Brooke lifted Bethany's head and kissed the tears from her cheeks. "Sweetie, it's okay now."

"Is Aunt Edee a superhero?" Bethany asked.

Brooke laughed softly. "No. But she is special. Just like you are. You know how your eyes change colors sometimes? And how sometimes when you're really angry your nails get long?"

She nodded. "Like Uncle Gram can do. He says we're special. He says it's a big gift I have that I can do that. He said most little girls like me can't do that." Her eyes widened. "Did you know he can turn into a dog?"

"Och, lass, 'tis nae a dog," said Gram with a slight laugh. "A wolf. Nae a dog. We've been over this."

Bethany smiled wide. "Mommy, can I turn into a dog?"

"No, precious," said Brooke, happy to see her daughter could still find happiness even with the night she'd had. "From what I'm told, the very fact you can do what you can do is something very big for girls like you. Not many can make their nails long or have their eyes change colors. Let alone do both."

Bethany put her hand up by her mouth and leaned in to her mother, whispering in her ear. "Mommy, would you be mad at me if I told you something bad I did tonight?"

"Sweetie?" asked Brooke.

Bethany eased back in her arms as her bottom lip jutted out. "I know it was bad, Mommy. But when the other man was choking Aunt Edee, it just happened."

Brooke tensed. "What happened?"

Edee rubbed her throat. "Brooke, I don't know. I blacked out for a second. When I came to, Gram was there and had Bethany in his arms. Armand was there too."

Bethany wiggled to get down and Brooke let her. When her tiny feet touched the porch, she rocked back and forth, playing with her curls with one hand. "You're gonna make me take a really long time-out because you said it's bad to hit and be mean. You said I have to not give in and be mean when I want to be."

Brooke bent and touched her daughter's round cheek. "Sweetie, what happened?"

"I didn't stop the mean inside. And it did not like seeing Aunt Edee be hurt," said

Bethany. She bent her head and when she lifted it again, her eyes were amber, her nails were long, and when she opened her mouth, Brooke saw that her incisors had lengthened. She shook her head and it all went away. "I ran out and bit the bad man's leg. He tried to get me off his leg but I held on, Mommy, and I bit him again. Then I scratched him. Then he tried to scratch me back but he was slow, Mommy. Really slow. He couldn't get me. Then I got so mad at him for being a big bully that I pointed at him." She took a deep breath. "And the room got real cold. Then he just flew out the window! I tell you, Mommy, that window had a lot of bad guys go out it. But I didn't break it. Aunt Edee broke it first. Not me."

Edee bent too. "Brooke, she can do what you can do? Did you see her teeth? That's new."

Brooke touched her daughter's stomach, hating that she'd been put through that. "Sweetie, you didn't let anyone hurt Aunt Edee or you. I'd never make you take a time-out for that."

Bethany touched her teeth. "But I let the mean out, Mommy. You told me that isn't nice to do."

Brooke kissed Bethany's cheeks again.

"Sometimes, you have to let the mean out. But not all the time."

"Boy oh boy, are the rules hard to follow. Don't be mean, Bethany. Okay, be mean, Bethany." She tossed her hands in the air. "What's a girl to do?"

A large hand fell upon Brooke's shoulder and she stood, expecting to find Gram there. When she realized it was Malik, she stiffened.

He went to one knee before Bethany. "Hello there."

Bethany eyed him cautiously. "Hello."

"Can I show you something?" he asked.

She nodded.

"Don't be scared, okay? I just want to show you so you know that we're alike."

"We are?" she asked, her eyes widening. "You make people fall out of windows too?"

"Sometimes." Malik chuckled softly and lifted a finger, letting a claw emerge from the tip of it. He then closed his eyes and opened them again, showing the amber in them. He opened his mouth and Brooke saw his teeth do what Bethany's had done. He then closed his eyes and when he opened them again, they were back to dark brown. His teeth returned to normal and the claw receded into his finger.

Bethany sniffed the air and then squealed. "Mommy, he's just like me! Smell him? He smells like me! Not like a dog."

Brooke bent as well, unsure what Malik might do or say. "Yes, sweetie. That's neat, huh? Someone else is just like you."

Malik picked up the stuffed toy lion from the porch and smiled at it. "And who might this be?"

Bethany grinned. "Nas. He's my best friend."

"Nas?" asked Malik. "Interesting name. And he's your best friend? Doesn't seem like he'd be much fun in a conversation."

Bethany giggled. "He doesn't talk, silly. He's not real."

"Oh," said Malik, holding the lion out to her.

"And his whole name is Nasser," said Bethany, taking the lion and holding it close to her. "He makes me feel safe at night."

Brooke felt faint when she heard Bethany's full name for the lion. A name she'd never heard her daughter say before, but a name she'd heard said tonight more than once. It was Malik's last name. She swayed and Malik reached out, catching her.

"Nasser?" asked Malik, his voice tight. He glanced at Brooke. "You said you didn't tell her about me."

"I didn't," said Brooke, shaking her head. "And I didn't know your last name until tonight."

"How come you smell like me?" asked Bethany.

"I think that is enough excitement for one night. Let's get some sleep and we can talk more in the morning. Sound good?" Brooke lifted Bethany, and Malik stood as well.

Bethany twisted and looked at Edee. "She wants me to go to sleep so she can talk to you and figure out what to tell me. I'm a big girl and she doesn't need to worry about me. I can handle a lot. We women always can."

Edee laughed. "Yes, we women can handle quite a bit. And you're right. I think Mommy needs to talk with the men here. Then Mommy has to tell me every single word that was said because I'm dying to know how she ended up bringing *this* group home with her. And why Uncle Gram looks less than pleased. Better yet, she should just have me in the room with her. Saves time later if I know it all firsthand."

Bethany yawned. "I'm not tired."

"Sweetie, you were woken up from a dead sleep tonight and had quite a scare. It's very late and I know you're very tired. Come on with me and we'll get some sleep." Edee reached for her.

Bethany dodged her grasp and looked over at Striker and Boomer. Her eyes widened. "Mommy, you brought home more giants. One of them has makeup on!"

Boomer laughed. "You are a trip, kid."

"Uncle Cody says that to me too," she returned, smiling.

Striker walked up to the porch, his focus on Edee to start. "Lass, yer even hotter than I remember you being."

Edee gave him a droll look. "You're like a bad penny."

He grinned. "Thanks." He then reached for Bethany. "Wee one, yer exhausted. Come on. I'll stand outside yer bedroom door and make sure no one comes in that shouldnae be there. I'll stay out there the rest of the night so you can sleep without worry."

She giggled. "You sound like Uncle Gram. He's very hard to understand when he's upset."

Boomer laughed. "So is Striker."

"Your name is Striker?" she asked. "That's a terrible name."

Striker laughed. ""Tis better than my given name, lass. Come. You and Aunt Edee both look like you could use some sleep. I'll nae let anyone near either of you."

"Promise?" asked Bethany.

Striker crossed his heart. "Promise."

Brooke glanced at her best friend. "Edee, I need to talk to you about something. Someone really. But not with everyone around. Okay?"

Edee nodded.

Bethany kissed Brooke and then went to Striker before twisting in his arms and grabbing Malik around the neck. She kissed his cheek too and he grabbed her, wrapping his arms around her, sliding her gently out of Striker's hold. He closed his eyes and held Bethany tenderly. She yawned again and put her head against his chest, her eyelids fluttering shut.

Malik rocked her gently. "You're safe now, princess."

Brooke didn't dare move. She simply stood there, dumbfounded to see Malik being so incredibly good with Bethany.

Striker surprised Brooke next by pulling her into a hug and squeezing tight. "I'm sorry Tut was a moron. You've a precious family, Brooke.

I'll take the wee one up to get some sleep. And I'll make sure Edee rests too."

She hugged him back. "Thank you."

He made a move to take Bethany, who was now fast asleep on Malik.

A low growl came from Malik.

Bethany stirred slightly but didn't open her eyes. She patted Malik's cheek, her stuffed lion smashed between them. "Don't let the mean out, Daddy."

Everyone froze.

Edee stared at Brooke. "Did she just call him what I think she called him?"

"Aye," said Striker. "The wee one's shifter side knows who Malik is to her. It understands his scent and the bond they share. And it's clear the wee one's gifts sensed who her father was long before tonight. It would explain the lion bein' named after Tut."

Brooke cupped her mouth.

Malik kissed Bethany's forehead. "I'm sorry, princess. I won't let the mean out."

Striker nodded and then took Bethany from Malik, holding her as if he'd held a hundred children before. He looked like a pro. He then ushered Edee through the door and into the house.

"Brooke," said Malik, reaching for her.

She stepped out of reach and pushed her hair behind her ears. "Thank you for your help tonight. You can go now."

"What?" he asked.

"Gram knows how to reach you, right?" she asked.

"You want me to leave?" he asked.

Boomer huffed. "Can you really blame her? You were a giant tool to her."

Chapter Seventeen

MALIK WAS unable to believe his ears. Brooke wanted him to go?

He ran his hands through his hair, shaking his head. "I spent five years hunting for you. Five years fearing the worst. Boomer is right, I *was* a tool. I just…dammit, Brooke, you get my head all screwed up. I've never loved anyone before and I know I'm not doing a very good job of it, but that doesn't change the fact that I *do* love you. And I may have just met my daughter but nothing could drag me away from her now."

Brooke put more distance between them. "Love me? You don't love me. You barely know me."

"Do you understand mating?" he asked, searching for a way to explain that he'd claimed her as his wife. That in the eyes of the supernatural world, she was his forever. That nothing could change that. There was no such thing as divorce for them. He would forever be bound to her.

She eyed him. "A little."

Gram hopped up and over the porch railing, landing next to Brooke. He put his hand on the small of her back and Malik had to control his beast. It wanted to rip the man's arm off, but he knew that would only push Brooke away from him more. He'd already done enough damage to their relationship as it was.

Gram kept rubbing her back. "Brooke, he's trying to find a way to tell you what he did."

Malik really wanted to punch the man.

"What did he do?" she asked, looking between the men.

"Five years ago," said Gram, staring at Malik.

"What? Are you talking about me getting pregnant with him? He doesn't have to tell me that. I figured it out for myself," said Brooke.

Gram sighed and rubbed her back gently. "No. I'm nae talking about that. Malik is trying to find a way to explain to you that five years ago, he claimed you."

Brooke snorted as if the idea was the most amusing thing she'd ever heard of. "But you said you can only claim your natural mate. That you can't just claim anyone. That only true mates can do that. It's why you asked me to marry you in a church, like normal people, because you said we weren't true mates."

"Aye," said Gram, staying close to her.

In a heartbeat, Brooke was in front of Malik. She hauled off and slapped him across the face. "You bastard! We're true mates and you threw me out of your room? Tool!"

He caught her wrist and held her close to him. "Brooke, I won't apologize for claiming you. It's not something I could have stopped. And even if I could have, I *wouldn't* have stopped it. I will say I'm sorry that I thought I did it because of the suppression drugs I took. And I'm sorry that I thought you were human—that the claim didn't work because of that. But I'm not sorry I marked you as mine. And I'm not sorry that you're my wife."

"Wife? What do you mean by wife? I can't be your wife," she said adamantly.

Gram turned Brooke to face him.

"Remember what I asked you when I first met you?"

She was quiet a second. "You asked me if my husband was still alive and when you got me out of there, could I reach him. But you just assumed I was married because I was far along in the pregnancy. I told you then I didn't have a husband and that the baby's father died."

Malik's self-loathing only deepened at her words. He should have been there all along. He was foolish to send her away because he thought he'd hurt her. It was impossible for him to hurt his mate. He'd sent her away and directly into the arms of The Corporation. She'd suffered at their hands, all while expecting his daughter. And then she'd spent nearly four years keeping his daughter out of the hands of the enemy. From the second he'd heard he was a father, he'd hated himself. Hated how much he'd failed both Brooke and Bethany. And the entire car ride to the safe house he'd tried to think of a way to tell her everything he felt for her and to apologize, but the words just wouldn't come.

Gram touched Brooke's cheek. "When I realized that you'd had no idea you were more than human before being taken by them, I stopped pushing you. I saw it as a blessing. You'd told me the baby's father was dead. There was no point in me making the already tragic situation worse by explaining I could smell a claim on you. I thought you'd found your way to having feelings for me because he was dead. That maybe nature saw fit to release you from the hold it has on mates." Gram sighed. "I do nae know how it's gone down the way it has, with Malik being alive. And had I known Malik was yer mate, I'd have taken you to him the minute I got you freed from that wretched place. I'd have made sure you and Bethany were safe and with him."

Boomer came up the steps to the porch. "Question."

Malik nodded.

"I know Malik claimed you, Brooke, but did you return the claim?" he asked tentatively. "You're not a shifter. The way you'd return a claim would be different from how we'd do it."

She stepped closer to Gram, managing to shatter Malik's heart more. "I don't know. I didn't even realize he'd claimed me. How would I know if I'd returned it?"

"You'd know," said Gram and Boomer together.

"Does that mean I'm not his wife?" she asked.

Malik didn't miss the hopeful tone in her voice.

Boomer shook his head. "No. You're his wife, but he's not your husband, if that makes sense. Until you return the claim, he's bound to *you*, but you're not bound to him. I'm guessing that's why you were able to have feelings for Gram."

Brooke's shoulders slumped. "I'm tired and I need a shower. I can't handle all of this right now."

Gram caught her wrist. "Brooke, you need to tell Malik everything that happened to you. He needs to know what you require after tapping in to your gifts. He can't help you if he doesn't know everything."

She lurched back. "I don't want his help! You can help me. You've always helped before."

Gram's jaw jutted out. "The only reason I was able to help at all is because of the Fae blood I carry. And let's be honest. He could help you in less time. Nature gave you to him for a reason, and the verra fact yer upright after going head to head with someone as powerful as Elm is because Malik was close to you. I love you enough to know when I have to step back."

Brooke hugged herself. "You don't want me either? Okay. That's fine."

"Woman, I've asked you to marry me at least ten times. I want you, and I cannae stand Malik. But that does nae change the fact he's yer mate. I may nae like him but it does nae take away the fact yer his wife. You cannae honestly think I want to have you and Bethany taken from me. And trust me, Malik willnae want me around you or his daughter."

"Malik doesn't get a say in my life," she said, still hugging herself. "He lost that right when he told me he regretted being with me. When he threw me out of his life."

Malik squared his shoulders. "I was trying to tell you that I regretted biting you and that I was losing control. I honestly thought you were human, and I was horrified at my lack of control. I was shifting. I didn't want you *gone*. I wanted to protect you from me."

Boomer stepped in. "Malik, why don't you go in with Brooke and stay close to her so she can get some sleep. Gram and I can talk with Corbin and the others when they get here. We'll plan our next move then." He touched Brooke lightly. "I know your first reaction is to push him away. You're hurt and angry with him. You've had a lot thrown at you tonight. But, Brooke, whether or not you *ever* return the claim, Malik will forever love you. He'll forever worry about you, and trust me when I say, you're it for him. I'm guessing he's spent the last five years lying to us to keep us from realizing he's not really been with another woman since you."

"Yes," said Malik, putting up his hand, staring at Brooke. "I'll go in with you and I'll keep my distance. I'll just be here in case Elm and the others come. You don't have to even look at me."

Gram surprised Malik. "Let him do what he was born to do. Let him be yer mate. Let him love you and the wee one."

"I didn't know," she said softly. "I'm sorry. I hate that this is hurting you."

"Aye, I know, lass," he returned. "I love you enough to let you go. I'll figure out something to tell the wee one as to why I willnae be in her life anymore."

Malik went up to Gram and extended his hand. Gram looked at him for a moment before taking it. Malik drew the Scot into a manly embrace. When he stepped back, he nodded.

"Thank you for everything you've done. And while I don't like you, I'm forever in your debt. You did what I should have. You protected my family. You loved them and kept them safe. I'll get used to you being around. It's not fair to Bethany to rip you from her life—and I saw Brooke in ass-kicking mode. If you think I'm crossing her, you're wrong."

"Smart guy." Boomer laughed.

Brooke lowered her head and continued to hug herself.

Gram locked gazes with Malik. "Since she's nae going to tell you, you need to know that using her Fae gifts comes at a great price to her. Usually it's instantaneous. It drains her to the point she collapses. I do nae know how she's managed to stay upright this long, but I do know that it will hit her hard soon. The only way to assist her is by handling her as you would a succubus who needs to feed. Her line of Fae is rumored to be the cousins to the succubi lines." Gram gave him a knowing look. "Because yer her mate, it may nae work the same way. You might be able to feed that need by simply being near her."

Boomer let out a low whistle. "You're telling us that you've had to shag her every time she's gotten drained over the last few years?"

Tensing, Malik exhaled slowly through his mouth, doing all he had in order to drive the images of Gram taking Brooke from his head. It was hard. Very hard.

Gram snorted. "Was nae a hardship by any means."

Brooke shoved him, but laughed softly.

He grinned. "Lass, it would be a lie if I said anything else. Now, go in with yer mate and let him watch over you. I'll be down here with Boomer. I'll be fine. I give you my word."

Chapter Eighteen

MALIK SAT on a folding chair next to Striker in the upstairs hallway of the safe house. Striker was leaned back, his feet propped up on the wall, with his hands in his lap as he lay there with his eyes closed.

Malik knew the man wasn't asleep. "Striker, go to one of the extra rooms and get some sleep. I've got this."

Striker kept his eyes closed. "I made the wee one a promise. I'll be here when she wakes. You should go check on yer mate. I'll let none harm yer daughter, Tut."

Malik put his elbows on his knees and leaned forward, focusing on the floor. "I'm having a hard time wrapping my mind around the fact that I have a daughter."

"Aye, I suspect that is a lot to absorb. 'Tis also making me wonder if a woman from my past is goin' to show up with a love child."

Grinning, Malik kept looking down. "Turns out your fears may be warranted."

"Yer nae upset about Bethany or learning you have a true mate," said Striker, keeping his head back and his eyes closed still. "Yer pissed at yerself for nae being there for them both all this time."

Malik tensed. "Honestly, I hate myself for it. The reason I didn't say anything at first after Brooke told me I was a father was because I was processing it all, hating myself for how I'd spoken to Brooke, and for not being there for her or my daughter. And I was trying to find the right words to say to her. My brain blanked."

"Aye. But the lass dinnae see it that way," added Striker, folding his hands on his lap and continuing to lounge against the wall. "In her eyes, you used her to get yer rocks off, threw her out of yer life, left her pregnant with yer babe, and left her alone to raise Bethany."

"I know." Malik sighed. "You know how

long I've been searching for her. Hell, you've helped me the entire way."

"Aye," said Striker. "She was nae there to see the look of horror on yer face in that hotel room when you finally were able to cage yer beast. She dinnae see you have to be tranqed by Boomer in the front entrance to the resort, when you'd learned she and Edee had been taken against their wills. She was nae there to witness you refusing to eat, to even shower and shave, when we first got back to the States, because yer only focus was finding her. And she could nae read yer mind when you learned you were a father."

"Want to tell me how you became such a fountain of wisdom when it comes to relationships, women, and handling children?" asked Malik halfheartedly.

Striker peeked out of one eye at him. "Och, Tut, I'm nae an expert at women. They confuse me too. But I've spent centuries fucking up when it comes to them. So I am an expert at how to fuck it up. I just took that expertise and reversed it."

With a snort, Malik sat up and stretched. "The guys and I tend to forget that under all the bravado, all the joking, and all the focus on hot chicks, you're just like the rest of us. You want something more but admitting it goes against your manly code. Makes you feel vulnerable."

"Speaking from experience there, Tut?"

Malik stretched his legs out. "Yes. I spent my life bedding endless women. Without them, my lion would have been too on edge, too volatile. My father was the one who told me when I was in my teens that I needed to spend time in the harem room at least several times a week or risk losing myself to my beast."

"Malik," said Striker slightly. "I know you do nae like the man who fathered you. I've been yer friend long enough to pick up on that fact. And I do nae think you were particularly fond of yer mother either."

"No," replied Malik with a snort before he stiffened. "I turned into my father. He used to bed everything he could. He was, uh, different from most shifters. Even though he mated my mother, he wasn't bound by the same rules of mating as the rest of us are. He would fuck random women all through our home, in the bath while my mother was there, having to watch him do it. It was as if he wanted to punish her for being his mate. Punish her for not being Egyptian and for the fact his sons weren't fully Egyptian then either."

Striker grunted.

"I don't think he ever saw her as a worthy mate. Like he wanted her to pay for him being stuck with her if he wanted sons," Malik said, his chest tightening. "I know he forced them on her. And I know she resented my brothers and me because of her hatred for my father."

Striker touched his shoulder. "Tut, no offense but yer father sounds like he was a bag of dicks, and yer mother does nae sound like a winner either. While you may have been like yer father to a point with all the women over the years, yer nae him. When Brooke told me you asked her to marry you and live with you, I knew you'd fallen for her. We all thought she was just a human. Not one of us smelled supernatural on her. I smell it now. But then, there was nothing."

Malik closed his eyes. "I should have sensed she was more. When I was with her, buried deep, fighting my beast, I swore I felt Fae power around us. It vanished almost instantly. How did I not see it for what it was? Brooke."

"Because yer a cat-shifter and yer slow and dim-witted," said Striker evenly. "You cannae be faulted for yer deficiencies. Look at it this way: in the end, you got a super-sexy wife, and a daughter who is precious."

Malik nodded. "Bethany is so beautiful, smart, and funny."

"Thankfully, she looks like her mother but with yer hair and eyes. Yer an ugly sod," Striker said, keeping his head back. "I wouldnae want you as a father, but I'm nae a four-year-old little girl. She may verra well think yer great. Plus, in case yer a dick, she'll have me, Uncle Striker."

Malik laughed softly. "Thanks. I think. Want to tell me how it is you're so good with kids and why I never noticed it before?"

His friend jerked slightly, as if the question pained him. "Aye, I'm so guid with them because I'm a giant child. I can relate to them."

Malik highly doubted that was the actual reason.

"I know you've been fighting the urge to go into that room and hold yer daughter," said the wolf-shifter.

"All I want to do is pack her and Brooke up and take them home with me. I want to give them everything they've ever wanted, and I want to be the father I should have been all these years. But how do I tell Bethany who I am to her? It's one thing for her cat to recognize me, but she wasn't awake when she did that. How do I look at her and explain that I wasn't there for her or her mommy when they needed me most? How do I explain missing the first four years of her life? And how do I make Brooke see how much I love her? How much I want to be with her forever? And how sorry I am?"

Striker shrugged. "Tell Brooke that you love her and let her sort out her feelings for you on her own. And you could just look at Bethany and say, *lass, I'm yer father*, and be done with it. Seems simple enough to me. You cat-shifters complicate everything."

A tiny gasp came from the other side of the door to the bedroom Edee and Bethany were in. Bethany opened the door enough to peek out with one eye. She stared at Malik like she wasn't sure she believed what she'd just heard.

Striker sat up fast. "Shite."

Bethany's eyes widened more. "That's a bad word."

Malik stood and swallowed hard. "Princess, what are you doing up?"

"I had a bad dream." She opened the door more, narrowing her gaze on Malik. She walked out of the room and moved close to Striker, watching Malik closely. Bethany climbed onto Striker's lap and touched his wild beard. "Give it to me straight, Uncle Striker. Is that guy my dad?"

Striker looked at Malik, and Bethany pushed his other cheek, making him focus on her. "You tell me straight or I'm waking up Aunt Edee, who told me she always wants to kick you in the shins when she sees you."

Striker's lips twitched. "You've a lot of yer father in you. He's stubborn too."

She gave him the stink eye. "Spill it, bucko."

Striker laughed and tried to hide his amusement with the child. "I think you should ask him. That's nae for me to tell you."

"Chicken," she said.

Striker put his hand on her back. "Aye."

Bethany looked at Malik. "Well?"

He took a deep breath, unsure how to handle the situation. He didn't want Brooke even madder at him, but he desperately wanted to tell Bethany the truth.

"Yes, sweetie. He's your father," said Brooke from behind him.

He gasped and spun around in the chair to find Brooke standing there, wearing a thin, short nightgown. There were dark circles under her eyes.

Striker grunted. "Och, the two of you are like ninjas. I dinnae hear either of you up and about."

Malik stood fast. "I'm sorry. I didn't think she was awake. I'll go."

Brooke touched his chest as she walked past him. "Bethany, do you have any questions for Malik or me?"

She nodded. "Is Daddy going to live with us now? Are we going to be a real family?"

Malik found himself rubbing Brooke's back, moving even closer to her. "Princess, I did some things that I have to make up for. You're too young to understand what I'm saying, but one day you will. I'll be in your life as much as I can be. As much as Mommy says is okay."

Brooke bent and touched Bethany's cheek. "Daddy and I will discuss what will happen from here."

Bethany glanced at Striker. "That didn't sound like a yes to me."

Striker pursed his lips. "Was nae a no either."

Bethany smiled and tugged on Striker's

beard. "Can I keep you? I've always wanted a dog."

Striker's eyed widened. "I'm nae a dog."

"I know," said Bethany, giggling and leaning against his chest. "Mommy, Uncle Striker is gonna tell me a bedtime story and then he's gonna come in the room and sleep in the big chair there. Aunt Edee will feel better. She'll know she's safe too. You go talk to Daddy."

"Bethany." Brooke tried to lift Bethany, but she clung to Striker.

"You told me that when you're upset or sad it's important to talk about your feelings," said Bethany. "And that hugs make everything better. Hug her, Daddy, quick. I'll get to keep you and get a dog."

Malik laughed softly. "I'll see what I can do, princess. How about I tuck you in and I watch over you tonight?"

Bethany gave him a look that said he was talking crazy. "How are you gonna get Mommy to stop being mad at you if you're with me? Oh boy, you're gonna take a lot of work. Aunt Edee says all men need trained like a puppy. I get it now."

Brooke laughed. "There are days I really

worry about her influence on you. Why don't you come sleep in my bed with me?"

A calculated look came over Bethany's face. "Okay, but only if Daddy gets to come too. And only if Uncle Striker will sleep in the big chair in the other room to watch over Aunt Edee so she can sleep and not be afraid."

Striker beamed. "She's got a future in politics."

"I don't know what that means, but if it means I get a dog and a dad, I'm okay with that," said Bethany.

Brooke met Malik's gaze. "If you want to stay in there with us, you can."

"Yes," he said quickly, when he really wanted to jump for joy.

Bethany touched Striker's cheek. "Promise you'll watch over Aunt Edee. She's not as tough as she looks. She cries a lot in her sleep."

Malik went to Bethany and lifted her into his arms. "You don't have to worry, princess. Striker will make sure she's safe."

"Aye. Though I do nae want to be gelded so I'll stay right here."

Brooke smiled at Striker. "There are two queen beds in there. I know you're taller than a queen bed is long, but it's better than trying to sleep out here. And Edee will pretend she's mad at you come morning, but she'll be very grateful to know someone she trusts was there to make sure she was safe. Armand sometimes holds her at night so she can sleep."

Striker stood and stretched. "Okay, but if I'm missing vital parts come morning, I'm blaming you."

"What does that mean?" asked Bethany.

Malik grunted at Striker. "Nothing, princess. Let's go get some sleep."

Brooke took Malik's hand in hers, and he recognized the act as the olive branch it was. He squeezed her hand gently as she led him towards the bedroom. He went in expecting two queen beds, but found just a king there. He paused in the doorway. "Brooke?"

Her hand went to his chest. "I'm trying."

He lowered his gaze. "Thank you."

She ran her hand up his chest to his neck, as she teared up.

Bethany put her lips near Malik's ear and whispered, "This is where you kiss her, Daddy."

"Princess, I don't think Mommy would like it if I did that."

His mate eased up against him and then did a group hug.

Bethany kissed Malik's cheek and then leaned and kissed her mother's. "See, we're a family."

Malik couldn't help but squeeze his girls tighter to him, desperate to make it a reality. To be a real family. The next he knew, he was staring into his mate's eyes. He wanted to kiss her, but he understood she wasn't ready for that yet.

Brooke nodded to the bathroom. "You've got dried blood on you. Go on in and shower."

He touched her chin. "Brooke."

She bit her lower lip and stepped away. "I'll get you something to put on. Don't take this wrong, but I think you and Gram are the same size. He and Armand make sure all the safe houses have clothing in them for all of us."

Malik sat Bethany on the bed and she stood, hugging him more. "Mommy is right. You smell like old blood. It's kind of gross."

Malik chuckled and tapped the tip of her nose. "Then by all means, let me clean that off."

"Good call," said Bethany, climbing under the covers in the center of the large bed.

Brooke went to the dresser and found Malik a pair of pajama bottoms. She handed them to him, her hands lingering over his.

He hurried into the bathroom and took the fastest shower of his life, fearful Brooke would change her mind about permitting him to be close to them. When he came out, he found Bethany was sound asleep but she was no longer in the middle of the bed. She was all the way over on the left with Brooke in the middle, curled around her, sleeping as well.

Malik couldn't look away from them. His girls. His chest began to burn with the idea that he'd missed so much time with them. He walked around to the other side of the bed and climbed in behind Brooke. He didn't intend to touch her, but he couldn't stop himself. He put an arm around her, his hand coming to a rest on Bethany's arm. He gave a tiny squeeze and buried his face in Brooke's hair, feeling totally and completely whole.

He lay there thinking of all the ways he wanted to try to make things up to Brooke. And how he wanted to make sure Bethany knew how important she was to him. How he didn't plan to miss a day with her again, let alone years.

Brooke moved slightly and put her hand over Malik's. "I'm glad you're not dead."

He kissed her shoulder. The very one he bit five years ago. He spoke softly, in his native language, telling her how she was his everything. And thanking her for such a beautiful, precious daughter.

As he drifted off, he held his girls to him tighter, afraid they'd vanish if he dared let go.

Chapter Nineteen

STRIKER KICKED AWAKE, his wolf agitated and alerting him to danger. He moved off the bed in record time and checked on Edee. She was still asleep. Unable to shake the feeling that something was wrong, he made his way to the window and looked out. It was still dark.

At first, nothing seemed out of the ordinary. Still, he remained. He saw it then, men moving around the house next door, all armed, all headed towards the safe house.

We've got company, he pushed out with his mind to his teammates, knowing they'd all hear him.

He went to Edee and bent, touching her shoulder lightly. "Lass."

She came awake with a start, fright in her eyes. When she looked up at Striker, she calmed, but looked confused. He put a finger to his lips and she grabbed his hand, hurrying out of the bed.

The door to the room opened and Duke was standing there with extra weapons in his hands. He tossed one to Striker, who caught it with ease with one hand.

Striker looked to his friend. "Get her out of here."

Edee squeezed his hand tighter. "I can't go. If Elm is with them, you guys won't stand a chance."

"Lass, this is nae up for discussion. Go with Duke. Now," said Striker, looking around for her shoes and something warmer to put her in. He found a pair of slip-on shoes and bent, letting go of her hand long enough to grab them.

The redheaded she-devil took off and pushed past a stunned-looking Duke.

"Brooke!" she yelled.

Striker cursed and ran after her. She made it to the door of the bedroom Brooke was in just as it opened. Malik was there, holding his daughter and ushering his mate into the hallway.

Brooke and Edee grabbed each other, hugging before they looked at the men. It was Brooke who stepped forward. "Go. Get Bethany to safety. We'll hold them off."

The men all shared a look that said what they were thinking.

Like fucking hell!

Gram and Auberi were up the stairs in seconds. Striker had heard Auberi, Duke, Corbin, Garth, and Rurik arrive before he'd drifted off. They had more than enough men to take a stand and protect the women.

"Does she listen to you?" asked Striker, pointing to Gram, but motioning to Edee.

Gram grunted. "Och, she does nae listen to anyone."

Malik held Bethany to him with one arm and touched Brooke's cheek. "My sweet, go with Gram and Auberi. They'll get you all somewhere safe."

Bethany began to cry and Malik kissed her cheek. "No tears, princess. I won't let anything bad happen to any of you."

She clung to Malik, crying harder.

The sight broke Striker's heart. "Tut, take yer family and the she-devil there with you. The rest of us will—"

A huge explosion rocked the house.

Bethany practically scaled Malik while Duke and Striker threw themselves over Edee and Brooke. It was instinctive, protect the women at all cost.

Gunfire erupted from below.

Brooke eased out of Duke's hold, but kept her hand on his arm. "Go! Edee and I will slow them down."

Auberi twisted and shot at someone coming up the stairs.

Smoke began to filter up the stairs, and Striker knew the house was on fire. It wouldn't be safe for anyone soon. There wasn't time to argue with the women. "Och, we're wasting time. Women, you will listen to me on this!"

Brooke and Edee leveled gazes on him that made his manhood tuck and run. He grabbed Duke by the shoulder and shoved him in front of him. "I mean you two will listen to *him*."

Auberi shot someone else. "Whatever we're doing needs done now."

Malik locked gazes with Gram. "Princess, will you let Uncle Gram hold you?"

Bethany shimmed out of Malik's hold and ran to Gram. He lifted her, holding her close to him, nodding at Malik. "I'll keep her safe. You'll get Brooke out?"

"Yes," said Malik.

Striker eyed the two men. "Och, can I trade one of you? The redhead is nae safe to be near."

Gram touched Auberi's shoulder and Duke pushed in front of them all, taking point. Gram was next with Bethany and Auberi pulled up the rear.

"I'll lead," said Duke. "Auberi?"

"Right behind you," said Auberi.

Striker made a move to grab Edee just as something crashed in both of the rooms near him. Instantly, he smelled vampire, mixed with something else. Twisting, he slammed into a vampire and tackled him to the ground as another came at him from above. Just his luck they'd be multiplying.

The one under him bit his arm and Striker punched the man in the face. The other one grabbed his head, attempting to snap his neck. He reached up to knock it away when all of a sudden a lamp hit it. Edee threw herself at the vampire trying to break Striker's neck.

Much to his shock, she managed to knock the vampire off him.

Worried for her safety, Striker let claws emerge from his fingertips and then slashed open the neck of the vampire below him. It gurgled and twitched. Pushing off the vampire, Striker ran at Edee and lifted her off the vampire as she kicked and hit it. He set her aside and the damn woman spun around and kicked him in the shin.

"Och! I'm on yer side," he said, stiff-arming the remaining vampire, never taking his gaze off Edee.

She gave him a hard look. "I know."

"But you kicked me anyways?" he asked, hitting the vampire again.

Edee nodded. "Yes. Be warned, I want to do it again."

The vampire came at him again and Striker let his claws out again. He slashed and took the vampire's head off with one swipe.

Edee did a double take and then put two thumbs up, smiling wide. "Badass, Scot, totally badass."

"Yer nae right in the head, are you?" he asked as another vampire came through the window. "I'm getting really tired of this."

Garth was suddenly there, helping as yet another vampire used the window as a point of entrance. Garth let his hand partially shift and rammed it into the vampire's chest, killing it at once.

Striker went to grab Edee to get her to safety when he saw her staring wide-eyed at Garth, before paling and dropping to the floor. She huddled there, shaking and crying. When he realized it was because she no doubt thought Garth was the man who'd tortured her, his chest tightened. He wanted to find Grid and kill the bastard himself.

Garth put his hands up as they returned to human form. He met Striker's gaze and connected on their mental path. *I don't want to move and scare her.*

Aye, said Striker.

He moved to the redhead quickly and then tentatively touched her shoulder.

She lowered her arm slightly, peeking out at him, red rimming her eyes. When she saw Striker, she launched herself at him, hugging him around the neck, clinging to him.

"Lass, yer safe. That's nae the same man who hurt you. Garth has a twin brother with a scar by his eye. He's nae a guid man. Garth is. He's worried that he's goin' to scare you more, so he's nae moving a muscle right now."

He eased Edee to her feet.

She stared up at him, her gaze searching his face. "Really?"

"Aye," returned Striker.

She sank against him and put her face to his chest, relief going through her. She stepped out of his grasp, but didn't go far. Wiping her cheeks, she looked at Garth.

Garth eased closer, keeping his hands up. "Edee, I'm so sorry for what Grid did to you. Know that when I find him, I will kill him, brother or not."

She took a deep, calming breath, her fear lessening enough that Striker could sense it. She offered a soft smile to Garth. "I'm sorry about the freak-out. It's just, well, he…he more than just hurt me. He and another man spent eight months terrorizing me."

Smoke built around them in the room. Striker knew they had to get out of the house, but he also knew Edee needed this moment. So he resisted the urge to make her go.

Garth eased a little closer. "Can I hug you?"

She sighed and looked down. "I understand now that you're not him, but, Garth, I don't know if I can let you touch me in any way yet."

Garth nodded. "I understand."

"It's not you," Edee said quickly. "It's just, you look exactly like him…and I spent too many nights pinned under him."

Striker's wolf tried its hardest to surface. It wanted to save Garth the time and kill his brother—slowly.

Garth drew in a sharp breath. "Edee, I'm so very sorry. Please know that."

She looked up at him, and inched towards him. She touched his arm lightly—then gasped, moving closer to him. "I understand now! Garth, you need to go—*now*. You have to get to your wife. He'd laugh when he was hurting me, telling me that he planned to do what he did to me to your mate. He said his brother was a do-gooder, and he couldn't wait for you to walk in and find your mate with him right before he kills her. I didn't know he had a twin."

Garth's brow crinkled and he slowly put his hand on Edee's shoulder. "Edee, I'm not mated. I've no wife."

"Wait, do you have another brother?" she asked.

He shook his head.

She cupped her mouth. "Then, yes, you do. He told me he's been watching her for years. Since she was a child even. Watching her grow into a beauty that you didn't deserve. You *do* have a mate—and he's got her in his sights."

Garth stiffened. "W-what? I have a mate?"

She nodded and surprised Striker as she patted Garth's chest. "Yes."

The smoke thickened. "We've got to go, now."

Garth looked to Striker. "I don't want to scare her more. You take point. Edee, stay close to him. I'll be right behind you."

Edee blinked at them both. "I'm not leaving. If Elm comes here for Brooke I have to help her."

Striker rubbed the bridge of his nose. "I'm going to regret this."

He went at her fast, throwing her over his shoulder.

Chapter Twenty

MALIK GRABBED his wife and put his body between hers and the hybrid rushing at them from the master bedroom. He took a fighting stance and waited for the hybrid to reach him before striking out with full force. That one went down and another dove in through the window. He made sure Brooke was still behind him.

He smelled another hybrid coming, this one from the direction of the stairs. He went low and then came up with his claws extended. Malik snarled as he ripped out a hybrid's throat. The one on the floor sprang up and he spun around, slicing open the thing's face and neck. The hybrid dropped instantly.

When he turned to go for Brooke, he found

her delivering a series of wicked kicks to a hybrid in the hallway. She then punched the hybrid in the face, knocking him down the steps in the process. When she looked over her shoulder at him, it was with the face of a warrior. A woman who wouldn't back down.

A fierce mate.

"Bethany," she said, her breathing heavy.

Malik ran past Brooke, grabbing her hand in the process. They took the stairs quickly. What used to be the front door was totally engulfed in flames. When he reached the bottom of the stairs, he bent and tore out the throat of the hybrid Brooke had kicked the crap out of. He helped Brooke over the body, keeping her away from the flames, and then looked up to see Armand there. A man he'd not seen in at least a decade, since Armand had left the Crimson Ops division of PSI and moved over to the Shadow Agent side of things.

Armand had a hybrid lifted off the ground with one hand. He glanced at Malik and nodded.

Brooke slowed. "Armand, where is Bethany?"

Armand tipped his head in the direction of the kitchen area. "He's taking her out the back."

Auberi came through the front window, looking as if he'd been in one hell of a fight.

Malik made a move to head to the kitchen when another explosion came from that direction. He spun and used his body to protect Brooke. Something cut into his back but he ignored the bite of pain as thoughts of Bethany being injured hit him. Instinctually, he turned and raced in the direction the explosion had come from. The area filled quickly with smoke.

Bethany screamed and he followed the sound of her cries, unable to see clearly with all the smoke. Malik shut off, his lion pushing up, helping to guide him through the black smoke. Bethany screamed again, her cries sounding farther away. Flames rolled at him, nearly hitting him. He bent and tried to see through the thick smoke.

"Gram!" he yelled, coughing as he inhaled a large amount of smoke.

No response.

He didn't care if he burned alive, he wasn't about to leave his child. With a roar, he ran headfirst into the burning kitchen, ignoring the bite of the flames. He tripped over something massive on the floor. As he hit the floor, he twisted and realized the mass was Gram.

He wasn't moving and no heartbeat could be heard.

Armand appeared. "I've got him. Go after the little one! Auberi is with Brooke."

Malik pushed to his feet and ran deeper into the burning room to find the back end of the house was missing. He jumped over the flames and landed in the backyard. It took his senses a moment to work properly from all the smoke. The second they did, he heard a child's cries and shot off, running full force in the direction they were coming from.

He more than cleared a six-foot privacy fence in one jump, landing in someone's backyard before repeating the steps three times. When he landed again, he looked up to find two hybrids running. One was trying to keep hold of Bethany, who was scratching at the man's face and neck, her eyes glowing amber.

Malik charged the men and snapped the neck of one, before corralling the other who held Bethany. "Give her to me," he said, his lion so close to the surface that his voice was deep.

The man knew he was screwed. He backed up a bit, putting a clawed hand up to Bethany's face. "Stay back or I kill the kid. I don't care how much the bosses want her."

"My daddy is gonna teach you a lesson about being mean," said Bethany, looking over at Malik and smiling wide. "Let your mean out, Daddy."

The man gasped, staring from Malik to Bethany. "You're her father?"

"Unhand my daughter or I will rip you to shreds," he said, pacing back and forth, never taking his eyes from the man. His beast wanted to be let out to sink its teeth into the man's neck.

The guy gulped, sweat beading on his brow. "S-Stay back."

Snarling, Bethany lifted her hand and raked her nails down the man's face so deeply that she drew blood. She then bit him—hard. The man dropped her and she landed on her feet and did a back tuck, rolling away and covering her head and face so she couldn't see what was happening. "Do it now, Daddy!"

Malik charged the man and when he was done with him, the man was dead. Malik twisted around to find Bethany still tucked in a tiny ball. He covered the distance to her quickly and scooped her up in his arms, holding her close. He covered her small face in kisses.

She kept her hands over her eyes as Malik ran with her, going over the fences again. He held his daughter to him as if she were precious cargo.

Because she was.

He cleared another fence and when he landed, it was in a side street. Tires squealed as headlights lit the area. He held his daughter to him.

The SUV peeled to a stop. Duke rushed out of the driver's side. "Tut! They have Brooke and Auberi is hurt pretty bad."

Bethany uncovered her eyes and stared up at Malik. "Daddy, they have Mommy?"

Malik didn't want to put his daughter down but he had to get to his mate. He locked gazes with Duke. "I need you to get her back to headquarters. Can you do that?"

"Of course," said Duke.

Corbin rushed out from a side yard, his eyes wide. "You have the child!"

Duke reached for Bethany but she clung to Malik.

She kissed his cheek. "You let your mean out big time, Daddy. Get Mommy back."

"I will, princess," he said, handing her to Duke. "Go with Duke. Listen to him."

Duke took Bethany into his arms.

Malik grabbed Corbin's arm. "Go with him. Protect my daughter."

Corbin nodded. "Yes, of course."

Striker came up and over the fence with Edee in his arms. He landed and bent, trying to hold on to a very pissed-off redhead.

She grabbed his beard and yanked.

He cringed. "She-devil!"

"Go back! They have Brooke!" she said, jerking free from Striker and standing.

"Aunt Edee!" yelled Bethany, halting the redhead before she inflicted more pain on Striker.

Edee spun around and yanked open the back door of the SUV, hugging Bethany to her.

Malik looked at her. "Go with them. We'll get Brooke."

Edee nodded.

Striker threw his hands in the air. "Sure, listen to him!"

Malik turned and ran down the side street, heading in the direction of the burning house. He hoped to catch Brooke's scent and track her. He made it to the main street and Garth sped up in one of the enemy's vehicles. "Get in! You'll never get to her in time on foot."

"Auberi?" he asked.

"Rurik has him. He's getting him to PSI."

He listened and before he even had the door closed, Garth had the pedal to the floor. The Viking zipped around the abandoned vehicles and drove over a number of bad guys. He turned down another street and floored it again. Garth maneuvered around a car that was turning right.

Suddenly, he slammed on the brakes just as Brooke ran out into the center of the street, bleeding heavily, the bottom of her short nightgown torn.

Garth managed to avoid hitting her as Malik jumped out and ran to Brooke, catching her and holding her against his body.

She was bleeding but he didn't know where the blood was coming from.

He felt around and nearly threw up when he realized she'd been clawed multiple times. She collapsed in his arms and he swept her up, loading her into the SUV. He moved onto the backseat next to her, as he tried to stop the bleeding.

Garth wasted no time as he sped away from the area, glancing back in the rearview mirror. "Malik?"

"Drive!"

Chapter Twenty-One

BROOKE CAME AWAKE, unsure where she was. Looking around, she found herself in a giant bedroom. It was quite possibly the biggest one she'd ever seen. The walls were a golden yellow and the bed she was on was bigger than a king-size one. It had red sheets and bedding. A white canopy was above her.

She stared around the room, still unsure where she was.

As she concentrated on the last thing she remembered, she tensed. Elm and a team of around fifteen hybrids had come at Brooke and Auberi. Auberi had killed three of the hybrids before Elm threw enough power at him to send him flying into a huge tree. The man had gotten up and tried to go at Elm again, only to find himself being hit with a bolt of power so strong that he gone down hard.

Brooke had done her best to fight against the hybrids while Elm watched, but she'd used far too much power at the club. She'd not replenished her system yet. So much so that the men were able to get too many licks in and her body couldn't heal them quickly. She'd thrust what little power she'd had left at the men to hold them back and then she got to Auberi, trying to lift his dead weight.

Rurik had burst through the tree line and grabbed Auberi with ease. He'd demanded she run while yelling at the men who hurt her that they were going to pay for hurting the little American girl.

Brooke had run and found herself on a street as a vehicle sped at her.

Then she'd seen Malik's face a second before darkness overtook her.

The huge walnut door in the bedroom opened slowly and Edee peeked her head in, smiling wide when she saw Brooke was awake. The redhead hurried into the room, wearing a long blue dress that Brooke had never seen her in before.

"Bethany?" asked Brooke.

Edee smiled wider. "She's safe."

"Auberi?"

Edee glanced away. "He's better."

"Where are we?" asked Brooke, looking around. "Did I fall down a rabbit hole and land in the Prince of Persia's bedroom?"

Pursing her lips, Edee sat on the edge of the bed. "In a sense, yes. We're at Malik's house. He insisted on having you transported here once he had you checked over fully by some guy named James. He took care of Gram too."

Brooke grabbed her friend's hand. "Gram was hurt?"

Nodding, Edee glanced downward. "It was pretty bad. Brooke, Gram isn't doing so well. He's at that headquarters place and James is staying close to him. He swears Gram will be fine but that he needs extra time to heal. James says that Gram must have wrapped his body around Bethany's and protected her from the explosion, taking the full force of it. I overheard the guys whispering that it's amazing he lived."

Brooke covered her mouth with her hand as she teared up. Gram had been hurt severely? "I have to see him. I need to be there with him."

"Malik just got back an hour ago. He's

been checking on him daily," said Edee softly. "From what I can gather there was a lot of bad blood between them, but Malik has set all that aside. I guess nearly getting killed protecting Bethany made Malik see the guy in a new light."

Brooke sat up. "Was anyone else hurt?"

"Auberi was pretty banged up, but was too worried about everyone else to stay in bed like a good little vampire. He's healed now. Claims the blood of virgins fixed him," she said with a snort. "He's something else. And can I just say that is one fine-looking dead guy. And Striker was hurt trying to keep me safe, but manly pride kept him from admitting as much. He's fine now."

"I'm so sorry," said Brooke. "I hate that they keep hunting us."

"Me too, but I think things will be different now. These people have sort of closed ranks around us, like we're family to them or something. I swear to you at least fifty different men from PSI have shown up here to check on you, and to let Malik know they were there for anything he needed while his mate healed."

"I still have a hard time understanding the entire mating thing," confessed Brooke.

Edee leaned and hugged her. "Go take a shower. I'll grab you some clothes."

"How long have I been here?" asked Brooke.

Edee stood. "It's been five days since everything happened."

Brooke turned and put her feet on the floor. "Ohmygod, my poor baby! She has to be freaking out. I need her. Where is she?"

Edee laughed softly. "She's currently hosting a tea party. Go shower. She's fine. I promise. Let her have this time with him."

"Him?" asked Brooke.

"Her father," confessed Edee as she walked in the direction of a different door. "He dotes on her. And she's already got him and all the other alphas here wrapped around her little finger. They're kind of hopeless. The kid works them all with ease. Now clean up, you're starting to smell."

"I need to see Gram," said Brooke.

Edee sighed. "Honey, James and Auberi both told me he's going to be fine. He just needs some time. And there isn't anything you can do right now. They're keeping him knocked out. Armand is there a lot. Did you know he's technically a doctor? He's been keeping me updated.

We're trying to notify Cody but he's gone radio silent. Might be an Outcast thing."

Their time with Cody in the facility had taught them a lot about what went on the supernatural world. They learned that some supernaturals were natural born, some were man-made, and many were hunted. Such was the case with Cody and the other Outcasts—considered failed experiments in the eyes of the government.

Brooke nodded and went in the direction of what she hoped was a bathroom. It wasn't. It was a closet that was bigger than her first apartment. She came out of that room and entered another, only to find it was another closet; this one with rows and rows of women's clothing and shoes. Edee walked out from around a corner in the huge closet.

"You're supposed to be in the shower."

Brooke stared around. "I can't find it. His house is like a palace. He lives with a woman?"

Edee lifted a brow. "No. Why do you ask?"

Brooke motioned around the room at all the clothing. "I doubt he cross-dresses."

"No," snorted Edee before pausing. "I did meet a cross-dressing chimpanzee though since hanging out with these guys. Came over with

Boomer and his mate Haven. Bethany and the chimp watched a movie together and were inseparable. They both wore princess crowns and matching pink tutus for it all."

Brooke tipped her head. "I'm sorry but what?"

Edee laughed. "You'll see whenever Boomer brings Lil' Duke back over. And the bathroom is this way. Can I just say your man's house has more bedrooms than I can count? One guy should not live in a place this size alone."

Brooke looked around the closet. "He apparently doesn't."

"Oh, honey, he had all of this brought in for *you*. He asked me to pick things you might like, and he bought some things I think he wants to see you in. Those pieces are in the back…and really bring to light how naughty he is."

Brooke stepped back. "He got all this for me? Why?"

"Because you're his mate—his woman—and before you freak out on me, know that it's a good thing, Brooke. He loves you so much."

"He doesn't really know me…" she said, her voice trailing off as she looked at the endless amount of clothing he'd gotten for her. "This is all too much."

"Honey, you ain't seen nothing yet. He had a wardrobe brought in for me too and has set me up in another wing of the house. Yes, you heard that right, his house has wings. No joke, I had to have him draw me a map for the first few days. I kept getting lost. And you haven't even seen Bethany's room or playroom yet. Good Lord, he's treating her like a princess. I think she might have a different outfit for every day of the year. And her playroom could double as a toy store. I told him he was going overboard, but he ignored me. Paid people obscene amounts of money to make it all happen in less than two days."

Brooke simply stared at her friend. "I don't know what to say."

"Say you'll shower. You smell. Come on, it's this way."

Brooke followed her friend into a bathroom that made the closet look small. She showered and then stepped out to find Edee there with a dress and shoes for her.

When she was done, Edee took her hand and they walked out into a huge hallway. She stared around wildly. "Wow. He *is* the Prince of Persia."

Edee laughed, letting go of her hand. "You haven't seen anything yet."

Brooke followed behind Edee, who stopped outside a set of double doors. Edee pressed a finger to her lips and then pointed into the room. Brooke peeked in the room to find that it was as Edee had described, a toy room for a princess. In the center of the room was a white circular table with chairs all around it. In each chair was a large male, each wearing a variety of items, from clip-on earrings to a feather boa.

Striker had an obscene amount of blush on his cheeks and lipstick that was smeared. He also wore a pair of dangly earrings. Not one of the men looked comfortable on the small chairs, but each had smiles pressed on their faces as Bethany poured them cups of tea from a tea set that looked expensive.

She poured Malik's tea last and then climbed onto his lap, adjusting Malik's tiara that matched her own. "Daddy, want to eat one of the cookies Uncle Striker helped me make?"

Malik's face scrunched a second before he blinked. "I would love to, princess."

Striker coughed as he sipped his tea. "I wouldnae if I was you."

Brooke was torn between laughing and

crying at the sight of the men all spending time with her daughter.

Corbin's hair had a braid in it with a pink bow and he held his pinkie finger up as he sipped the tea.

Duke grunted, wearing a feather hat and a feather boa. "Nice pinkie finger, Captain. Want a crumpet to go with your fading manhood?"

Corbin looked over at Duke and grinned. "Interesting, considering you're wearing a feather boa."

Malik slid Striker a sideways glance. "I cannot believe you bought my four-year-old daughter a boa."

Striker bit his lower lip. "I dinnae buy it so much as the last female I had over at my house left it behind."

Bethany beamed. "You mean you have tea parties at your house too?"

Duke snorted.

Corbin lowered his head, trying not to laugh.

Boomer, who looked entirely too comfortable having a tea party, flashed a wide smile. "Explain this one, Striker."

Rubbing the back of his neck, Striker looked

nervous. "Um, well, erm, aye. I have tea parties at my house too."

Bethany clapped. "Fun!"

Edee rolled her eyes as she glanced at Brooke.

Boomer grabbed a cookie and took a bite. In an instant, he was trying to avoid spitting it out. He failed and grabbed a napkin, spitting the cookie into it.

"Told ya so," said Striker partially under his breath.

"Uncle Striker, want more lipstick on?" asked Bethany.

Striker's eyes widened. "No. I'm, uh, guid. Thank you."

She eyed Duke.

He growled. "No."

She jutted out her lower lip in a pout.

Duke sighed. "Fine, but give me a less red color than you gave him. He looks like he charges by the hour."

Malik nudged Duke hard.

"What does that mean?" asked Bethany.

All the men shook their heads and answered at the same time, "Nothing."

Bethany paid no mind to them as she grabbed a lipstick off the table and hurried off

Malik's lap and climbed onto Duke's. She then proceeded to put lipstick on him poorly.

Boomer laughed. "That is why I did my own."

Edee held up a phone and snapped a picture of the men. She smiled. "This is priceless. I've met their mates. The women are going to love this picture."

"I think you all look beautiful," said Brooke, entering the room with Edee.

Malik stood quickly and pulled the tiara off his head. "Brooke, you're up? I didn't hear. I'm sorry. I wanted to be there."

Bethany jumped off Duke's lap and ran for Brooke. "Mommy!"

Brooke grabbed her and lifted her.

Malik was to them quickly, supporting Bethany's weight as if she was too heavy for Brooke. His dark gaze lingered on her. "How are you feeling?"

"Like I slept for a week," she said with a wink before kissing Bethany's cheek and neck, making the child giggle.

Bethany smiled. "Look, Mommy. Daddy made this room for me to play. And he made me my own bedroom. Want to see? Come on, I'll show you."

She wiggled, squirming down and then tugging on Brooke's hand.

"Does this mean I can stop drinking this tea crap?" asked Duke.

Bethany whipped around and pointed at him. "You said a bad word!"

Corbin laughed. "Shall I put him in a corner, poppet?"

"No. But he shouldn't say that word. Right, Mommy?"

Brooke ran her hand through her daughter's curly hair. "He's a grown-up, sweetie."

"That is totally debatable," said Boomer.

"No comments from the guy who put on his own makeup," snapped Duke.

Brooke teared up as she stared at the men. "Thank you all so much."

They each stood and nodded to her.

Boomer grinned. "Malik is like family to us. That makes you family, Brooke."

"That's very kind to say, but please don't think I'm expecting anything from Malik," she said. "This was all very generous but we can't accept it. We need to go soon."

The men shared a look and then came in her direction.

Corbin looked to Bethany. "I have not seen your bedroom yet. Can I come along?"

She beamed. "You all can!"

She put her hand in Corbin's. "Come on, Brit. Is it true you're a Bloody English Bastard who stole Uncle Striker's country?"

The men all looked at Striker. He in turn shrugged. "It's never too early to teach the lass the fundamentals."

Brooke failed to keep from laughing. She teared up.

Malik wrapped his arms around her and kissed her temple. "I'm really sorry about letting Striker around our daughter."

Brooke leaned in to his embrace as they walked. "Hon, she's had Edee around her all her life. I think you know she's worse than Striker."

Edee laughed.

Striker glanced at them as Bethany continued to lead them to her bedroom. "'Tis true. The she-devil is worse than me."

Bethany came to a stop at a large door. She opened it and dragged Corbin in first.

When Brooke got to it, she stopped in an instant, looking around the room. It was enormous. There was a huge bed that had a castle-style headboard that looked as if it was also a playhouse of sorts. The carpeting looked like it was grass with walking paths on it, a small pond, and rocks. When she realized the entire room was princess themed, she grabbed Malik's hand.

Bethany ran to her. "Mommy! Look at what Daddy did for me."

"I see it, sweetie," she said, bending and drawing her daughter in to her, holding her tight. She kissed Bethany's head. "Do you love it?"

"Yes."

"What do you love most about it?" asked Brooke, running her hands through her daughter's hair.

Bethany smiled at her. "I love that we're with Daddy now. That I get to see him every day and I get to see him watching you sleep. He was worried about you. Me too. He told me you'd be fine but needed lots of sleep."

Brooke choked up. "Your favorite thing is your father?"

She nodded profusely. "This is what I always wanted. I wanted a family. I have you, Daddy, Uncle Gram, Aunt Edee, Uncle Striker, Uncle Duke, Uncle Boomer—who has been helping me learn how to put on makeup—Uncle

Corbin, Uncle Auberi, Uncle Armand, Uncle Garth, Uncle James, and even Uncle Russia… wait, Uncle Rurik. And most of them gots wives. So I got all of them as aunts too. I'm going to get the rest of them married off soon. They need all the help they can get. Especially Uncle Striker."

Brooke couldn't stop the tears that came. She touched her daughter's cheek. "It sounds like we have a very big family now."

She smiled. "Did you know that I'm going to get cousins too? Some of them are having babies. And they told me the babies would all be my cousins. Neat, huh?"

Brooke lost it, crying hard and bear hugging her daughter. "Really neat."

"Mommy, we're gonna stay, right? You're not going to make me leave Daddy and my new big family, are you?"

"Sweetie, Daddy and I need to talk about it."

Her face crinkled. "What's to talk about? You love him and he loves you. Seems pretty simple to me. Why do grown-ups have to make everything so hard?"

Edee laughed softly.

Corbin bent near Bethany. "Your father tells

me you like to bake. What do you say we all go down to the kitchen and make something together?"

Striker groaned. "Again?"

"Okay," said Bethany, a sad note to her voice as she twisted to look up at Brooke. "How come we gotta go, Mommy? Daddy said we were going to live here with him for good. That we're a family now."

Brooke glanced at Malik. "He did, did he?"

Edee came in for the assist. "Let's go bake a pie."

Striker opened his mouth and Edee pointed at him. "Before anything lewd falls out about pies, remember there are little ears here."

"That just rendered him mute for life," said Boomer.

Corbin put his hand out to Bethany. "I think your parents need to talk about some things."

Bethany eyed him. "Well why didn't you just say that to start with? I don't want to eat Uncle Striker's baking either. He better hope the wife I find him can cook."

"Och, it's nae that bad," said Striker. "Never mind. It's that bad. How about we go downstairs and I order pizza for everyone?"

Bethany sighed loudly, sounding relieved.

"Good plan. I didn't know how to tell you that your cookies are terrible."

Corbin laughed as he led Bethany down the hall in the direction of a large staircase. The men all followed after him. Edee stayed behind a second, standing near Malik.

"Brooke," Edee said. "Hear him out. She's his daughter too, and he didn't know about her. I've been with them all week and I can safely say he loves her so much. Keep that in mind when you have your talk with him. And ask him to explain how the mating process works fully. From what Boomer told me, you and Malik have some things to finish up on that end."

She walked off, leaving Brooke alone with Malik.

Chapter Twenty-Two

"THANK YOU FOR THE DRESS. Okay, for everything, but I can't accept all of that," Brooke said.

He took her hand in his and walked back in the direction of the bedroom she'd woken in. He said nothing as he entered, taking her with him and then shutting the door.

"Malik?"

He faced her, still holding her hand. "I love you. And I want to hold you right now so bad it's killing me."

Brooke closed the gap between them and put her arms around his neck.

He lifted her off the ground and spun her in a circle. "I love you so fucking much. I get your trust in me is shaken. I deserve that. I chased you away and then you went through something horrible."

Brooke tried to speak but he kept going.

"I will beg you to stay with me. I can't lose you and Bethany," he said, his hand skimming her cheek tenderly.

She put her hand over his. "Malik."

He stopped talking.

"I did go through something horrible. But I came out the other side with a beautiful baby girl. I would never change her or wish her away. She was worth every second of everything I went through."

"She's perfect. You've done such an amazing job with her," said Malik, lowering his head. "I should have been a part of that. I can't change the past but I can beg for the future. Let me be part of your lives. Let me love you."

She pressed her mouth to his, surprising herself.

He growled and lifted her again, walking her towards the wall, as he'd done five years ago.

She tugged at his shirt, wanting it off him.

He pressed her to the wall and then put his palms to it, grinding his hips against her.

She broke the kiss and Brooke laughed as she wiggled to get down.

He set her on her feet and she put her back to him. "Help me out of the dress."

"Brooke?"

"How long will your friends keep Bethany occupied for?" she asked.

"For as long as we need," he confessed. "They're all mated—except for Striker. But they all know how important this is for us."

"Then take your clothes off, Tut," she said with a wink. "I need to feed the side of me that requires sexual energy and I want you to be the man with me when I do it."

Wasting no time, he tore his shirt off. He then slid his pants off, kicking them aside. He stroked his cock, watching her a moment before unzipping her dress and kissing the shoulder he'd bitten years ago. He put his lips to her ear. "I didn't understand that I'd claimed you fully."

She let the dress fall to a puddle at her feet, keeping her back to him still. "What does that mean, exactly? How did you make me your wife?"

"When I bit you during sex and told you that you were mine," he said, bending and easing her panties off her. He kissed her bare ass cheek as he did.

She remembered it well. "Yes?"

"That is how a shifter male claims his woman. How he marks her and binds himself to her for all eternity," he said, pressing his front to her back. "I knew what I'd done was a claiming, but I thought you were human. I couldn't understand my loss of control with you. I blamed it on suppression drugs I was testing for work. I'm so sorry, my sweet."

She reached back and ran her hand over his thigh. "I thought you used me. That you played a game with me."

"Gods no," he said, pressing his lips to her shoulder again, his cock nudging at the cleft of her ass. "Tell me how to do this, how to give you what your body needs."

A sultry laugh came from her. "Malik, you just have to fuck me."

He moved her hair away from her neck and smiled against her skin before nipping it playfully. "I think I can handle that."

She knew he could.

He took hold of her wrists and lifted her arms above her head, pressing her palms to the wall before her. He rubbed against her and used one hand to stroke himself. Then he pressed the head of his cock to her wetness and lifted one of her legs enough to raise her body off the ground slightly.

Malik pushed his cock into her pussy and Brooke moaned, trying to move her body to counter his move, but the way he had her held and pressed to the wall, she couldn't move. He was in total control of the situation. He pushed in all the way and she gasped.

"Malik," she whispered.

He kissed the spot he'd bitten years ago. "Brooke," he said his voice deep. "Give me this. I need to sate the beast."

"Yes," she returned.

Suddenly, he was moving at an inhuman speed, in and out of her, being far more sexually aggressive than he'd been five years prior. And she loved it. Loved him thrusting into her so hard and fast that her breasts pressed into the wall. She used her hands to keep from being totally flatted against the wall and to push back at Malik, wanting more.

Her toes began to tingle and tiny shockwaves of pleasure began to work their way up her body, heading to her core. The darker side of her that craved sex and sexual energy came out to play, soaking in what Malik was giving her. It too wanted more.

He gasped and fucked her harder, seeming as if he'd drive himself right through her. Or push them both through the wall. Her power built. As it did, Malik's rhythm began to waver.

He lifted her leg higher, and in turn, lifted her higher as well. "W-What is that?"

Sweat slicked her skin lightly as he pummeled her body with his, making her power wrap around him, filling her with what she needed. "Sorry. Can't control it."

Growling, he pushed in deep and held, but she knew he wasn't coming yet. "It feels so fucking good."

"Mm, I know," she murmured with a lazy smile.

He pulled out of her slowly, teasing her, making her whimper before he shoved in deep again with a growl. As he drew out of her painfully slow once more, she hit at the wall, wanting more.

"Please," she begged. "I need this."

He licked her shoulder and then gave it a tiny kiss before he began pounding like a piston into her.

Brooke cried out loudly as pleasure raced

through her. She tried to pull off him, her orgasm that strong. She wasn't sure what was going to happen and her first response was to run from it. Malik didn't let her. He kept going, kept thrusting into her. Her entire body spasmed. She cried out again and he roared, slamming into her, jetting seed into her.

Her body ate up the energy around them. She hadn't felt this good in years.

Malik's body twitched as he remained in her, continuing to come.

"Malik?"

His whole body trembled. "My sweet, it's been a long for me. Sorry."

"Sorry? I want to do that again," she said with total sincerity.

He chuckled, his body starting to calm. He eased out of her with great care and then turned her to face him. He lifted her again and kissed her mouth, making love to it as he carried her to the bed and laid her out on it. He eased up alongside of her, facing her as he pinned her to his frame.

Chapter Twenty-Three

MALIK HELD his mate in his arms, afraid to move for fear that he'd learn it was all a dream. That she wasn't with him, that he didn't have the most beautiful daughter in all the world, and that he was alone once more.

Brooke kissed one of his tattoos. "That was amazing."

"Yes, it was," he said, running his hands into her long hair. "I'm not sure I can stand. My legs are still shaking from it all."

She laughed and bit lightly at his chest. "Bet you say that to all the girls."

He tensed. "Brooke."

"Yes?"

"I've not been with another woman since I

was with you in Egypt," he offered. "When Boomer said as much, he was right. I explained I bound myself to you. That means you're it for me for the rest of my days. You are the only woman I will ever want. You're my wife in the eyes of the supernatural world."

She glanced up at him. "You haven't had sex in five years?"

"No. Well, I've masturbated. That doesn't really count," he said.

She kissed his chest and laughed softly. "You really want us to stay with you here for a bit?" she asked.

He caressed her back. "I want you to stay with me forever."

She slid out of the bed and went into the bathroom, leaving him lying there, unsure if she was staying or if she'd want to go. It wasn't safe for her or Bethany to be out in the world unprotected with Elm and Johnson still unaccounted for. If he had to, he'd shadow them to assure they were safe and well—even if it meant he'd forever have to follow behind her.

He'd do that for her.

For his daughter.

Pride welled in him as he thought of Bethany. Over the course of the week she'd been living with him, he'd gotten to know her. She was funny and so very bright. She was also incredibly intuitive. James wanted to look at her, in an attempt to figure out what The Corporation had done to her in utero, but Malik couldn't stand the idea of her being subjected to any testing, even if it was painless.

The very idea that Brooke might want to take his daughter far from him was like being stabbed in the gut. Already Malik had missed so much time with her. He didn't want to miss another day.

While he'd never imagined himself a father, he now couldn't imagine her gone from his life.

Brooke emerged from the bathroom and walked towards the bed, her naked form making his cock harden instantly. He pulled a pillow over his groin but found he couldn't tear his gaze from his mate. She was even more beautiful than she'd been when he'd first met her. All he wanted to do was get lost in her again. To feel her wrapped around him and to know she wasn't ever going to leave him.

Brooke sat on the edge of the bed. "Can I see Gram?"

The moment the words left her mouth, his

desire was doused. She wanted him to take her to her ex-lover? She was going to leave him.

A slight nod was all he could manage.

"Thank you."

He looked away.

She traced her hand over his leg. "Malik."

He looked at her and knew he was about to do the one thing he hated to do—he was going to cry.

"I need to make sure he's okay and I need to tell him something," she said, still tracing her hand up and down his leg. "He should hear it from me that we're going to be a family. He shouldn't hear that from anyone else."

It took Malik a moment to wrap his mind around what she was saying. "You're not leaving me for him?"

"No," she said, sliding her hand under the pillow and touching his cock. "When you asked me to marry you and move in with you years ago, I wanted that. I wanted to be with you. I didn't know why. I get it now. We're supposed to be together, right?"

"Yes. A mate is the other half that makes a supernatural whole. You make me feel whole," he confessed. "Without you, I'm empty inside."

She moved up and over him, her lips finding

his. Her kiss was hot and branding. He slid his hands through her hair and held her face to him, returning the kiss. He made a move to slide the pillow out from between them and Brooke laughed as she stopped the kiss.

"Malik, we need to go downstairs. Our daughter is currently at an incredibly impressionable age and she's with Striker."

When she put it that way, he cringed.

She laughed more. "And besides, we need to discuss some form of birth control or we'll have another child to add to the mix before you know it."

He thought about how he'd released in her, filling her beyond the brink with his seed. The very idea of planting his seed in her again excited him. He wanted a life with her. A big family. Everything.

She kissed his cheek quickly and then eased off him, leaving him too hard to move with any kind of ease. "If I wanted to return the claim, how would I do it? Would I have to bite you during sex too?"

"Honestly, I don't know. For me, it was instinctual. I did what felt natural. My body took the lead and I simply followed."

"I thought I'd hurt you," she said softly.

"When we were having sex, I felt this overwhelming urge to let go of what I can do. To let it be totally free. I was scared of hurting you so I held tight to it. Was that my body trying to return the claim?"

He sat up slowly, his body stiff, his erection still in full force. "More than likely, yes. But we won't know exactly what you are until James's test results come back."

"Edee can tell you what I am. She memorized our charts while we were being held. All I wanted to know was if what they did hurt my baby. I didn't care about me."

"I'm sorry I wasn't there," he said, meaning every word of it.

She nodded. "I know."

Malik toyed with her breast. "I understand that you don't feel for me what I feel for you, but Brooke, I would like a chance at being a mate to you and a father to Bethany."

She slid up and over him again, licking his thigh on the way up his body. She lifted his cock and licked it as well, making him harden once again in the blink of an eye. "Brooke?"

She caressed his erection lightly. "I can't let you in again and then not be with you for five years. Do you understand that?"

He pushed her hair back from her face. "My sweet, I can't be away from you for a minute. I more than get it."

She slid her mouth over his cock head and Malik's body instantly strained. His lion wanted to peek out. He didn't let it. Brooke moved her mouth down his shaft, taking him to the back of her throat.

He nearly lost it then and there. "My sweet."

Her head bobbed up and down on his cock and she drove him mad with pleasure. The same energy he'd felt five years ago began to emanate from her. He eased in and out of her and all he could think about was being buried to the hilt in her pussy once more.

Surrendering to the pull, Malik grabbed for Brooke and lifted her before lining up with her wet core and driving himself into her while he yanked on her shoulders.

She moaned loudly as she tipped her head back. Her power ran through him more, letting him know it was coming—they were going to fully bond.

Malik took hold of her hips, thrusting into her, grunting like a wild animal. He didn't care how he sounded. He wanted to fully join to her.

He wanted to know he was her husband. That they'd never be apart again.

Brooke's jaw dropped and she met his gaze. "M-Malik, something is happening…deep inside."

"Don't fight it," he said, on the verge of coming.

Brooke's olive-green eyes swirled with icy blue a moment before she dipped her head, putting her lips close to his. "Mine."

His beast rushed up, pushing through the surface, making his mouth change shapes. "Mine," he returned, grabbing her and drawing her down on him before biting her neck.

Suddenly, his body felt as if an electric charge went through it. Everything on him hummed with pleasure and it felt as if hundreds of thousands of webs were being woven between them.

He took hold of her hips and began pumping up and into her with a speed that was far from human. She cried out in his arms and he released his mouth's hold on her neck, licking the spot at once and swallowing down her blood. She came and he followed quickly behind her. The moment he released, the threads between them snapped in place, leaving him no doubt they'd completed the ritual. They were a fully bonded pair.

Husband and wife.

His lion curled up deep within, totally and completely content for the first time in his entire life.

Brooke kissed him tenderly. "Is it done?"

"Yes," he said, unable to stop himself from starting to move in her again. "My sweet, if we don't get out of this bed right this second, we might never get out of it."

"Can we shower fast, spend time with Bethany, and can I please see Gram?" she asked, staying on him. "I have to see him. I need to know how he's doing."

"I know, love," he said, his jealousy over her with Gram lessened now that she was his wife in every sense of the word. He slapped her butt cheek playfully and then growled, barrel rolling her, leaving him on top. "Mmm, woman, I love you so much."

She smiled up at him and he realized she'd yet to tell him she loved him too. While it stung, he understood why. He withdrew from her and kissed the tip of her nose. "I'll shower in the bathroom next to this one. If I don't, I'm not going to be able to stay out of you."

She laughed as he rolled off her and stood, his legs nearly going out from under him. "Woman, you have got to stop making my legs shake after sex. It's going to take away from my manly vibe."

Brooke laughed so hard she was silent.

Malik chuckled as he grabbed his pants, throwing them on quickly for fear he'd step out of the bedroom and his daughter be near. That or Striker would start talking about measuring contests again.

Chapter Twenty-Four

BROOKE HELD Malik's hand as he entered a large gaming room. There was a giant big-screen television playing a family-friendly movie. A sectional that looked custom made because of its enormity was in the center of the room. Striker was on it, along with Edee and Bethany.

Edee was asleep on the large sofa with Bethany tucked against her, while Striker sat with his feet propped on a huge ottoman. The other men were gone, replaced by Armand and Auberi, who were sitting at a bar along the far side of the room.

Brooke went to get Bethany to put her to bed, but Striker shook his head. "Let the wee one sleep. She's nae hurting anything where she is. I'll sit with them both and watch over 'em until morning."

Auberi lifted a drink. "We explained we would, since we're nocturnal and all, but the stubborn Highlander who looks like he spent the night in a French whorehouse thinks vampires aren't sufficient bodyguards."

Armand laughed and eased off a stool. He was dressed as he always was, as if he'd just come from an important board meeting of some Fortune 500 company. His long black hair was down tonight. He stopped just shy of hugging her and sniffed the air.

"You've mated," he said, a smile tugging at his lips. "Good."

"You're not mad?" she asked, afraid he'd be upset because he'd always seemed supportive of the relationship she had with Gram.

"You've mated yourself to a powerful, honorable man I consider a friend. I could ask for nothing more," he said, drawing her into his arms.

"Have you seen Gram?" she asked, worried for her friend.

Armand nodded, his gaze flickering to Auberi.

Auberi neared her. "We have him in a

medically induced coma to speed his healing process. His burns were severe. In addition, he took a great deal of shrapnel, as well as suffered numerous broken bones. From what we've been able to piece together, he basically took the entire force of the exploding back end of the house. It was Bethany who told us as much. She said her Uncle Gram knew there was going to be a big boom and he turned with her, taking her to the floor and covering her with his body."

Brooke teared up. "Will he be okay? Will he heal fully?"

"With time, yes," said Auberi. "For now, he rests. Though, I'm sure he will like hearing your voice. I, like some others, believe he can indeed hear you if you were to talk to him."

She looked towards Bethany's sleeping frame. "I want to see him, but I'm terrified to take my eyes off her. I'm afraid The Corporation will come for her again."

Auberi chuckled. "They would never dream of setting foot upon this property. For one, it has state-of-the-art security. For two, the alpha within is thousands of years old. He can and will kill them with ease. They know as much."

Brooke's jaw dropped. "He's how old?"

Malik groaned. "Uh, about that."

She stared at him and then sucked in a big breath. "Tut is right. Great, my husband is basically a reanimated mummy."

Auberi laughed and then went to Malik, drawing him into a hug. "Congratulations, old friend. May your union be blessed with many more children and a life of love. Now, take her to PSI so she can see her ex-boy toy. Try not to eat anyone while she's doing it."

Malik shoved him lightly. "You'll stay to watch over the girls?"

"Of course, until this Elm is dealt with, we'll keep extra security on your home and your loved ones." Auberi turned to Brooke and shocked her by hugging her tight. He put his lips to her ear. "He has never given his heart to another. Take care of it. And please don't make us cancel poker nights."

She laughed and squeezed him gently. "I'll take care of it, and I'd never dream of canceling poker night. But you should know, tea parties are apparently a thing here and no one is spared. If you're invited in, don't eat the cookies and do your own makeup."

He stiffened. "Noted."

Chapter Twenty-Five

MALIK STOOD JUST outside Gram's hospital room. PSI had a medical facility that was lightyears ahead of what was available to humans. Often, medications and new medical techniques were developed within the walls of PSI and refined for use on humans.

There was a large glass wall between Brooke and Malik. She was in the room, sitting by Gram's bedside, her hand on his. The sight didn't set Malik's lion off. It saddened him to know Brooke hurt and that a man who'd protected his family was injured and suffering.

Brooke's cheeks were stained with tears as she stood and leaned over Gram, kissing one of the few spots on him that wasn't being treated for burns. Areas that should have already healed, but hadn't. "I'm so sorry," she said.

Malik's hearing could easily pick up on her words even though she was talking in a low voice.

"Thank you for what you did for Bethany. I will never be able to thank you enough. And I'll never be able to explain how much you mean to me," she said, crying softly. "I never understood what you meant when you said that we loved one another as much as nature would allow. I get it now, Gram. I get you fully understand how mating works. A part of me wishes I could have loved you the way you deserve to be loved."

Her words cut Malik to the quick.

He looked downwards.

"And another piece of me feels so incredible guilty for feeling that way," she confessed. "I couldn't understand what was missing all these years. You were so good to me, to my daughter, to my best friend. You tried so hard to get me to let you take care of us for good. I know helping us put you at risk at work. And I know that without you, I'd be dead and my daughter would be in the hands of madmen. "

Malik continued to look down, his body tense with emotion.

"Words will never be enough for me to express what that has meant to me, Gram," she said, sounding as if she was crying harder. "Please be okay. Please fight to get better. Edee mentioned bad blood between you and Malik. I don't know what the bad blood is, and I don't care. All that matters to me is that one of my best friends in the world and my husband get along."

Malik looked up to find her standing next to Gram's bedside, touching him lightly, crying. He wanted to go to her and pull her into his arms, but he knew she needed this time with Gram.

"And Gram, I need to hear that you forgive me for doing what felt right, what felt natural. That you forgive me for loving Malik."

Malik swayed at the sound of her admitting she loved him.

Someone cleared their throat behind him and he turned to find James there.

James nodded towards the glass wall. "Hard pill to swallow?"

"How can I be upset with her for caring about him when he was there for her when I wasn't?" Malik asked. "He should be fully healed by now."

James reached into his pocket and withdrew

a syringe that was partially melted. He handed it to Malik to inspect. "This was found on the scene. I analyzed it and I think it's something Donovan Dynamics cooked up to suppress a supernatural's gifts. Gram is testing positive for it in his system. I don't know how long it will last, but I think it's stopping Gram from healing as we would. We're doing our best to quickly reverse engineer it."

Malik tensed. "Will he die?"

"I'm working on something to try to counter it. I wanted to ask your permission to speak with Brooke about drawing more blood from her. She has healing abilities that I've never seen before. I think I can use her gift to help him." James took the syringe from Malik and put it back in his pocket. "And Malik, you should know that I fully believe that dose of suppression drug they gave him was created for Brooke. I think they had every intention of temporarily stopping her in order to subdue her and take her. Knowing them, they realized it was all going sideways, and when they came up against Gram, they panicked and used it on him."

Malik's stomach tightened. "They have a weaponized drug that can hurt Brooke?"

"Yes. It's not a surprise. They held her for

eight months. They had free access to test on her. Stands to reason they've spent the four plus years since working on something to stop her." James put his hand on Malik's shoulder. "She's a blending of more than one type of Fae and something else. Something that took me totally by surprise."

"What?"

"I've run the tests three times and even sent them over to the I-Ops for them to analyze. They came back with the same results," said James. "We have a match on her ancestry. I was able to prove with nearly one hundred percent certainty that her father is one of us."

"Who?" he asked.

"Abasi," said James before taking a deep breath.

Malik hadn't heard the name in almost three decades. Abasi had been a fellow Egyptian like himself, and was nearly as old as Malik. The man had also been from a line of cat-shifters. He had been of noble blood and had been instrumental in the creation of PSI. He, along with others like him, had wanted to make a difference for the better. And he'd walked the walk for centuries before going off the grid without any warning.

James spoke. "I know you were close to Abasi for a long time. And I know you took it hard when he up and vanished. We all laughed that he was living it up in some exotic location, probably bedding endless women. Guess he was having a daughter instead. Your mate to be exact. We should reach out and try to find him. I think he'd want to know she's safe now."

Malik stared in at Brooke. He remembered her telling him of her father and how he'd read books about ancient Egypt to her. He also remembered what she'd told him about how she'd ended up living with her maternal grandmother. "Abasi is dead."

James shook his head. "I'm sorry. He was a great guy. There's something else I want to talk to you about."

"I'm not going to like this, am I?" he asked.

"Probably not," he said, glancing in at Brooke and Gram.

"Just say it." Malik tensed, readying himself for whatever would be thrown at him.

"She has small amounts of vampire and cat-shifter in her. But most of her make up is Fae. From what I've been able to match up from my database, the Fae line she's from is one that feeds off sexual energy. Basically, the Fae cousins to the succubus."

"Gram told me as much."

James swallowed hard. "Malik, I need you to think about what I'm saying to you. I think being with you, and being claimed by you, sort of flipped her supernatural switch. It unlocked what she had in her. Her Fae side. If I had to guess I'd say she had some sort of failsafe there, to keep supernaturals from finding her and from knowing she's more than human."

"Okay. Yes."

James grunted. "I'm telling you that you turned on her supernatural side—the side The Corporation wanted. And she was pregnant with your child. A child who had to be a huge drain on her system even with the testing and manipulations they were doing on her to increase her healing abilities."

Malik still wasn't following.

James put his hands up. "Never mind."

"Tell me."

"Tut, who do you think fed that side of her from the second she delivered that baby?"

"Gram did," said Brooke, standing at the doorway to the room. "He took me from the horrid place and when he did, I couldn't even stand. My body was spending so much time and effort keeping Bethany safe within me that it couldn't heal me any longer. Gram smelled me, and knew I was of the same line of Fae as him—not related or anything, but that the odds I'd heal like his kind do would be high. Since he's also a wolf-shifter, he could smell everything they'd pumped into my system."

Malik stiffened.

"I was so weak that Bethany was at risk," she said, looking away. "Edee was nearly catatonic. Armand never left her side. Gram never left mine. And Cody was with us, worried for Edee and me. We'd formed an unbreakable friendship with him. And he protected us as best he could in there."

She put her hand out to Malik and he went to her at once, drawing her into arms. "Malik, Gram and I didn't instantly fall into bed together. In fact, we both went out of our way to avoid it. I'm not saying this to hurt you. I need you to understand why it came to be." She took a big breath and put her head to his shoulder. "Gram understood fully what I needed—sexual energy. I kept getting weaker and weaker. He was taking me to this underground clinic that he said could be trusted fully. I went into labor."

Malik kissed her temple.

"Edee was with us. She'd not spoken a word in the month that we'd been free. It's not my place to tell you what she lived through, but I will say that it changed her. It took her spark. She's slowly getting it back."

Malik ran his hand into her hair and rocked her body gently, feeling her pain as if it were his own.

"Something was wrong. My contractions weren't normal. And they were instant and way too close together," she said, sniffling. "Gram knew that between what I'd endured at the facility for eight months, and Bethany being incredibly powerful in her own right, that she was putting a huge strain on my system. He knew, deep down, that only one of us would make it. Bethany or me. Because without what my body needed, it couldn't handle the load."

Malik gasped, holding her tightly to him.

"He also knew that time wasn't on our side," she confessed. "He peeled into a gas station, carried me to the bathroom, laid me down gently. I don't remember a ton after that because of the pain and the room fading in and out. I just remember him bending over me, asking me to forgive him before his mouth was suddenly on mine. I didn't understand why he was kissing me and I didn't have the strength to ask or protest. The longer he kissed me, the less pain I was in, the more alert I became."

"He was feeding you the sexual lust you required," said James, easing closer. "It wasn't in him to let you suffer. I've known him a long time, Brooke. He's a good man. I also know him enough to know it probably killed him to do that. He already had a firsthand look at what you'd suffered through while being held, and I'm guessing its far worse than any of us will ever know."

She nodded. "It was."

"Brooke, if you'd like to speak to me in private, Malik will leave us to talk," said James, giving Malik a knowing look.

Malik's entire body tensed when he realized why James offered to make him leave in order to speak to Brooke. He wanted to know the full extent of what she went through—and the man suspected it went far beyond testing and physical abuse. Not that either of those wasn't horrible in their own right.

Brooke clung to Malik. "Haneez tried to

touch me in the van after they'd taken me from the resort. Something happened that I couldn't wrap my mind around. I felt this weird cold feeling and he was suddenly propelled away from me. I also had this huge flash of my mother come to mind. I remembered seeing her do something similar when I was young."

James rubbed the bridge of his nose. "I had a feeling Malik's claiming was what triggered your dormant supernatural abilities."

Malik held his wife tighter, hating knowing she'd suffered.

Brooke's hand came to his chest as she ran her hand over the spot of his "son of the god king" tattoo. "I thought my mind was playing tricks on me. But at the resort when Malik was challenging Haneez, I didn't notice anything out of the ordinary with him, other than every time he was close to me it felt like bugs were crawling on me. Then in the van, he was suddenly in the back of it, grabbing me and telling me that he'd warned me. That I was a whore and it was time I learned my place."

Malik stiffened. "Wait. Haneez is Asshat?"

"Yes," she said. "He tried to...hurt me. Then he was suddenly thrust away from me but I didn't understand how or why. He glared at me and then smiled. He told me that his men were attacking you as he spoke. That they were going to make you suffer and kill you. And if I ever did that to him again, he'd kill me. I didn't understand then what he was saying. I was terrified for myself and Edee and felt like my heart was breaking because I'd sensed at the nightclub that Haneez was going to hurt you in some way that would be devastating to you, Malik."

"Brooke, he never touched me," said Malik, rubbing her back gently.

James cleared his throat. "That's not true, Malik. From what the other men have told me, knowing she'd been taken and that she'd not left of her own free will *did* devastate you. It killed a piece of you, and from what the guys said, you weren't the same man after that."

"I wasn't," he said. "I felt like I was going through the motions of life when all I wanted to do was die. But that wasn't an option because deep down I knew she was still alive, despite everyone else thinking she was dead."

"They tell me that you never stopped looking for her, but as time went by you did it in secret." James stayed close to them. "And they said they couldn't understand your obsession with a human female. That you were acting like she was your mate."

Brooke kissed his neck.

"Brooke," said James softly. "What else happened while you were held?"

Malik rubbed her back more.

"When we got to the place, the men who took us dragged us in. It was then I saw who I thought was Garth. I was too stunned to the point I couldn't speak. How could a man who had been funny and caring hours earlier look so sinister and be so cruel?" She twisted in Malik's arms, facing James. "He took a weird interest in Edee. One I didn't notice him doing at dinner or the club."

"Because he wasn't really Garth," added Malik.

She nodded. "He grabbed Edee with one hand and me with the other as he dragged us into the facility. He threw me at a man with long white-blond hair."

Malik fought the urge to growl, already knowing who that man was. Elm.

Brooked caressed his thigh, as if sensing how on edge he was. "The man, Elm, sucked in a big breath and when I looked up, his eyes were swirling. I screamed and he dragged me against him, licking his lips. Then the same thing that happened with Haneez in the van happened again. I felt cold all around me and then Elm was suddenly thrust away from me. He looked up at me with this hungry look."

"He figured out you were of his line," Malik said, wanting to hunt the man and kill him.

"Yes. Over the next few months, he began to spiral from bad to monstrous. He hated that I was pregnant and that the people in charge wouldn't let him hurt me or the child." She took a deep breath. "But that didn't stop him from trying. He'd hit me with so much power that he'd leave me broken for days. The doctors there changed up the tests they were doing. One day, they came into my cell and strapped me down to the bed. They started injecting me with stuff and hooking me to IVs. Cody, who was in the cell next to mine, went nuts."

James met Malik's gaze.

"He shouted at them, banging the bars like a crazed man. They laughed and told him they'd figured out who I'd come from. Who my parents were. And they informed him they'd see to it I was as powerful as my father and my mother. About an hour or so later, I was still strapped down and Cody was still there, clutching the bars, his gaze never leaving me. His eyes widened and he gasped."

James offered a knowing look to Brooke. "Is that when your healing abilities started?"

"They'd been building from day one, but they went into overdrive that day. And Cody told me I smelled like a cat-shifter all of a sudden. A cat-shifter and old, ancient power." She stood tall, easing out of Malik's hold slightly. "One second I was strapped down and the next, the straps undid themselves—like magik. And I came off the bed in an unnatural way, landing crouched on my feet, staring around feeling like I was seeing the world for the first time. I had a hand on my stomach, this almost feral need to keep them all from my child."

James put his hands in the pocket of his lab coat and continued to watch her. "It makes sense, knowing who your father was. I know very little about your mother. We don't have records on her."

Brooke stared at James. "You know who my father was?"

He inclined his head. "We do. He was one of the founders of PSI. And he was one of the most powerful shifters we've ever known. I suspect Malik may be more so, but he holds a lot back from us about his lineage, and the full extent of what he can do."

Malik tensed.

Brooke's hand found his thigh. "James, tell me about my father. I have memories of him that seem to grow daily. They all started when I was taken. I could only remember small bits about him before my night with Malik."

"I'm guessing that failsafe that Malik tripped when he claimed you was also there to keep a wall up to your memories. James looked to Malik, as if seeking permission to tell Brooke what she wanted to know.

Malik nodded.

His friend took a deep breath. "Abasi was a great man. And he was close friends with your mate."

She gasped, her head whipping around to stare at Malik. "You knew him?"

"I did."

Her gaze focused on his chest. She moved closer to him and undid his shirt more, her fingers skimming the son of the god king tattoo. "Ohmygod, you really are the son of a god king!"

He bit his lower lip and nodded. "Yes."

She lurched back, her eyes wide. "You were in the stories he'd tell me when I was little. The son of the god king—the king who didn't want to be king."

Malik nodded.

She moved closer to James, but kept staring wide-eyed at Malik. "He'd call me his little princess. He'd tell me that when I grew up, I'd marry a king who didn't want to be king. My mother would scold him, telling him he might ruin it if he told me too much. And he'd look up at her with sad eyes," she said, tearing up. "He'd say, 'Gwenhwyfar, if we don't teach her now, it might not come to be when we have to leave her.'"

James and Malik both gasped.

Malik stared at his wife. "Your mother's name was Gwenhwyfar?"

She nodded. "Yes. Did you know her too?"

"Yes," he whispered. "She was a very powerful Fae. One both loved and feared in the Fae community. I met her once years ago. I was, um, well…"

Brooke rolled her eyes. "Let me guess, you were either in bed with a woman, or coming from the bed of a woman."

James coughed, glancing at Malik as if knowing he was screwed.

Cringing, Malik nodded. "The latter."

Brooke took a giant step back from Malik. "Duke said you'd bedded like six thousand women. Is that true?"

James snorted. "My guess is it's much higher."

Malik glared at him.

James stiffened. "Sorry."

Brooke huffed. "And you actually have the nerve to be pissed at me over Gram? Is there any woman you *haven't* had your dick in?"

James shot him a look that more than said he was totally fucked. That his past had caught up with him.

"Brooke, my sweet, I've lived a long time," he said.

She blinked at him. "So manwhoring is okay if you're in your thousands?"

He opened his mouth, only to be at a loss for words.

She gasped. "Ohmygod, did you sleep with my mother?"

"What? No!"

"Are you sure? I mean, how can you actually keep track?"

James snorted.

Malik exhaled loudly. "I swear to you, I didn't sleep with her. I ran into her while sneaking out of a hotel room in the middle of the night. Suddenly I ran right into this tall, beautiful woman who I hadn't noticed in the hall a moment before."

James put his hand on Brooke's shoulder.

Malik put his hands up. "My sweet, she was just there. I collided with her but she didn't budge. I knew in an instant she wasn't human. She looked at me from intensely green eyes and shook her head. She said that she was so disappointed in me. And my life would change in the coming future. That I'd see the error of my ways and that I'd better hope my mate was able to find it in her heart to forgive me.

"I laughed at her. I mean, who was this mysterious woman trying to tell me about my life and talking about a mate I knew I didn't have?"

James rubbed Brooke's shoulder more.

Her shoulders slumped.

"I made a backhanded comment to her and the next thing I knew, I was slammed against the wall and pinned in place by nothing more than her sheer will and power," he admitted. "She walked right up to me and looked me up and down. She told me when she'd pushed me from afar, when I was young, to not take the throne, it was in the hopes I wouldn't end up like my father. A demi-god who was also a cat-shifter, who saw women as objects, something to serve and sate his needs, and a man who waged wars for his own amusement, because as king he could and because he craved power."

James lifted a brow, hearing about Malik's past for the first time.

Malik kept going. "She said she truly thought when I walked away from a kingdom of my own, that I'd be worthy. I didn't understand what she was saying. She said while I'd done well to avoid being power hungry, I'd failed miserably in not seeing women as objects. She told me my past would come back to haunt me. I asked her who she was, and she looked me right in the eyes and told me her name, a name everyone in the supernatural world had heard before, and she then said that if I hurt what had been gifted to me, she'd find a way to return from the other side and make me very sorry I'd crossed her."

Brooke's jaw dropped. "My mother basically

called you a whore and then threatened your life?"

He snorted. "Yes. She did. And just like that, she was gone. Poof."

James eyed him. "She talked to you like she knew she was going to die sooner rather than later."

Brooke cupped her mouth. "I think they both knew. They'd make comments around me about how they wouldn't be with me long, and then they took me to meet a woman I'd never met before. A woman they said was my grandmother but she didn't feel like…like *us*. She felt like nothing. Sweet and caring, but like nothing. Yet, I really did think she was my grandmother right up until my night with Malik. Then memories flooded back to me."

James patted her shoulder. "She was human."

Brooke looked at the floor. "I remember my father starting to cry as he bent to tell me that I needed to learn to trust the woman. That one day he and my mother would go away on a long trip and that I'd stay with the woman, until the son of the god king came for me."

Malik held tight to his emotions. Abasi had

known all along that Brooke was to mate him. Yet he'd never uttered a word to Malik about it.

"Daddy didn't want to let go of me and Mother told him it had to be. That they could no more change their fate than they could prevent the pain and heartache I'd face one day. And that it needed to be done. She said something about the others not being allowed to smell me or they'd know the truth. My dad was huge but in that moment, he looked so small, so broken. He shook his head and begged her not to do it. Not to suppress what I was born with—that it would make me unable to protect myself when the time came."

James gasped. "Your mother blocked the rest of the supernatural world from being able to sense anything other than human on you. Which is why every operative who was around you swore you were human. Even Malik. But Malik's claim on you changed that—unlocking it, for lack of a better word, along with your memories of your parents being more than human."

Brooke started to cry. "I have the image of my father, who was larger than life to me, openly sobbing, clinging to me, trying to convince my mother that they could change fate, and he kept pointing out that my mate wouldn't be able to sense my need of him, or know to claim me because I'd seem human to him. I remember my mom laughing softly through her tears and telling him that Fate would see to it my mate and I came together, and that my father was wrong, my mate would claim me, even thinking I was human. She told him the power she'd put over me would end then. That I'd be what I'd been born to be."

Malik hugged her tight. "She was right. I claimed you thinking you only human."

Brooke cried softly. "I thought when I was being held captive that I was just making it all up in my head. I tried convincing myself that it wasn't real. That everything I was seeing around me was making me believe my parents were something more too. That seeing my father's eyes go from dark to amber wasn't real. That my mother couldn't possibly do all I'd seen her do. I mean how could anyone predict the future or make things move without touching them?"

James swallowed hard. "Brooke, Gwenhwyfar was the queen of Fae for thousands of years. And then suddenly she was gone, abdicating the throne to another. And she was rumored to be able to see the future and the past. To know things long before they happened. She must have seen what would come to be and I'm guessing that was why she paid Malik a visit. She wanted to prepare him for what was to come and meet him face to face to express her dislike of the lifestyle he was living."

Malik swallowed his emotions, knowing how painful this all was to Brooke. "Why didn't Abasi reach out to me and tell me everything?"

James nodded. "Frankly, I'm surprised Abasi didn't kill Malik, knowing his friend would one day be with you between the sheets."

Malik grinned. "Hearing all of this, I'm more surprised Gwenhwyfar didn't take me out when she had the chance."

Laughing, Brooke wiped her cheeks.

James turned her to face him. "Listen, I can't believe I'm about to stick up for Malik and the thousands-of-women bit, but he's right; he's been alive thousands of years. As a supernatural male, you can't go too long between sexual releases or you run the risk of losing control and possibly succumbing to the darkness that always lingers below the surface until you're mated."

Brooke tipped her head.

"And knowing now that Malik is far more

than just a cat-shifter, that he has the blood of the gods in him, I'm guessing he might require a release even more than average males. Brooke, I'm saying this to you because I honestly thought the same of him as you do right now. We all knew he came from money. And we all thought he was in effect a whore. But I get it now. I don't think he had a choice. And you need to understand that after he claimed you, he never touched another woman…but he went out of his way to make us all think he did, because I think he saw it as a weakness. I bet that mentality came from his father."

Brooke stared up at Malik. He touched her face and nodded.

She threw her arms around him.

James didn't walk away, instead he looked directly at Malik. "What happened at the plaza, Tut? What made you lose control of your shifter side and change forms in a crowded area, forcing several clean-up teams to bring in Fae to erase what the humans saw?"

Brooke gasped. "You did that?"

"Yes, my sweet," he said, kissing the tip of her nose. "I was going about my day and then all of a sudden I smelled honey and lotuses, with something else mixed in. One second I was fine, and the next I found myself pinned under a bunch of PSI guys."

Her brow crinkled…and then her eyes widened. "Ohmygod, I took Bethany for ice cream at a plaza not far from here. She'd just finished with hers when she sniffed the air and her eyes turned to amber. She looked right at me and said we had to leave right away, that he couldn't stop the mean and the longer we stayed there, with his mean up, the more he might get stuck like that."

Malik jerked. Brooke and his daughter had been that close to him months ago?

James snorted. "Well, mystery solved, Tut. You weren't a dick. You were sensing your mate and your daughter. I'm guessing she was the something else you smelled with Brooke's scent. And your daughter must have sensed you wouldn't come back from that if their scents were still in the area."

Malik teared up.

Brooke kissed his lips tenderly. "James, I heard you asking Malik about drawing some blood from me to help Gram. Let's do it."

Chapter Twenty-Six

BROOKE SAT in the passenger seat of Malik's luxury SUV. She'd spotted several more vehicles in his garage before they'd left for PSI. She wasn't sure why one man needed so many cars or such a big home, but he seemed to like it all.

"Do you think they'll be able to figure out a way to help Gram?" she asked.

Malik reached over and took her hand in his as he drove. "PSI has access to technology that won't be on the mainstream market for years. And Gram has the greatest minds in medicine at his disposal. He's where he needs to be, and I know that everyone is going to do everything they can to get him on his feet again.

Brooke squeezed his hand. "Thank you for being good about this."

He caressed her hand with his thumb. "He's done so much for my wife and my daughter that I'll never be able to repay him."

She looked at Malik while he drove and took a moment to let it sink in that she was married now. She was someone's wife.

He glanced at her. "You look like you might pass out. You all right?"

"I am. Just adjusting to the fact we're together for good now," she confessed. "It's a little hard to wrap my head around."

He grinned. "Want me to enlist Duke and Rurik to sing a soft rock ballad in commemoration of our first date? Will that help you wrap your mind around it?"

Snorting, Brooke shook her head. "Please don't. I'm still a bit traumatized from their first duet."

Malik laughed softly.

Brooke kept hold of her husband's hand as she looked out the passenger side window. For a few minutes she got lost in her thoughts. One thing nagged at her. "Malik, what about Elm? He won't stop coming for me. And The Corporation wants Bethany."

He snarled.

She took that to mean he wasn't planning on letting anyone near his family.

She leaned in his direction. "Letting your mean out again, *hubby*?"

He brought her hand to his lips and kissed it, still watching the road. "My sweet, I will unleash a hell upon them the likes of which they have never seen if they dare try to harm either of you. They'll see exactly what I'm capable of when fucked with."

"So, you're a god?" she asked, totally unable to get a grasp on that.

He let out a soft breath. "I guess it depends on how you look at it. I like to think I'm just an extra awesome cat-shifter with a great ass."

She snorted. "I will never forget Edee announcing that in Egypt."

He laughed.

"Thank you for making her feel at home at your house. She means the world to me and Bethany."

"Brooke, she's family to you and therefore she's family to me," he said. "And it's our home, not my home."

"Okay, but I'm going to need about a

century to come to grips with this all," she returned jokingly.

"And, Brooke, you will not be returning to the club to work. Ever." Malik gave her a side-eyed look. "I understand why you worked there. The money and it fulfilled your needs, but no more."

"I'm not going to argue with you on that. I hated working there. You're the first man I ever really touched. Before you I'd use my gifts and make the men think they were having a good time. I could have painted my nails or something and they wouldn't have noticed," she supplied. It was the truth. "But, Malik, I want to work. I spent a long time getting my degree. I'd like to be able to use it, if it's ever safe for me to leave the house without a team of men with me, or a cat-shifting god with a great ass."

He grinned. "About you working. Edee already sat me down and had the talk with me when you were healing. She laid down the law. It was adorable, so I let her rant and rave. She made Striker and Auberi sit through it as well. I'm pretty sure they're a little afraid of her now."

Brooke chuckled.

"She told me you'd want to work. That even

though I had a house with wings, you'd want to do something," he said. "Corbin had been in the kitchen, getting Bethany a snack and overheard everything. He stepped in long enough to inform Edee that you and she were both already set up to work within PSI if you wanted. You wouldn't do what I do, but you'd work in the offices and labs there. We always need experts with computers and scientists. The two of you are a perfect fit. Best part is you can work as many or as few hours as you want."

She teared up.

"And," he said, lifting her hand slightly. "Each PSI division headquarters has its own daycare, preschool, and private school that is for supernatural children only and they're all heavily guarded. They're not on-site but they aren't far from each division. Bethany could start preschool and she'd be safe. Very safe. Striker, Edee, and I already toured the local facility and it's great. She'd be able to make friends her own age, learn, and have fun."

Brooke cried silent, happy tears.

"If you say yes, I should warn you that my team have all informed me that they're going to go with her until she feels safe. Otherwise known as, until they feel she's safe and they aren't going to worry about her." He laughed softly. "Striker is the worst one of them all. He's also the last teammate I'd want around her. So far, he's been nothing but good with her."

She squeezed his hand again. "He's like Edee. And Bethany fully trusts Edee. If we can find a way to stop Elm, I'm all for her going to school. Thank you for handling all of that while I was healing."

"I want the best for her," he confessed.

"Speaking of that," Brooke said sighing. "You cannot keep getting her so much. You heard her. You're what makes her happy. She doesn't need material things."

"I understand and I know I got carried away," he returned, taking a right turn onto a two-lane highway that didn't look heavily traveled. "Part of it was guilt for missing out on so much of her life. The other part was out of excitement. I was so fucking excited to be a father and to have her with me that I went overboard. I promise I'll talk with you first before I do anything else."

"Thank you," she said, laughing softly. She relaxed a bit and then looked forward and behind them. "Is this the same road we took to get to PSI?"

"Yes. Why?" he asked.

"Malik, it had a steady stream of traffic on it before. Why is it so empty and why is it darker than it should be out here? I swear I saw streetlights on the way to PSI. Why aren't they lit now?" As the questions fell from her lips, a sinking feeling came over her. "Elm. He's doing this."

Malik squeezed her hand more. "Baby, I'm going to pull off the road and you're going to drive home. Use the navigation to help you find it. Get there and tell Auberi what's happening. I love you."

"What will you be doing while I'm driving home?" she demanded, already knowing the answer.

He licked his lips as he pulled to a stop on the shoulder of the highway. "Brooke, this has to end. He can't be allowed to hunt you any longer. I won't stand for it."

"He's like a gazillion years old! And he's really powerful," she said, nearly yelling that as well.

Malik gave her a knowing look. "My sweet, take the car and go home."

She stared at him like he was nuts. Because he was if he thought he was going to take on

Elm and all his men all alone. "You're going to get yourself killed and then what happens to Bethany and me? Do you think he'll stop hunting us because you're dead? No. He won't. I can help, Malik. I can take him on with magik and slow him down enough for you to possibly kill him. Together we can fight him."

Malik's face remained calm. Too calm. He touched her cheek lightly. "Brooke, you have to go now. You can't be part of this."

"Why not?"

He teared up while gifting her a partial smile. "Because I can smell your scent changing already. Just like Cody did the morning after we were together."

It took her a minute to wrap her mind around what he was saying. She'd have said it was impossible for him to smell the change he was talking about this soon, but she'd already seen a shifter do just that and be dead right. "Malik Nasser, every time you touch me you knock me up!"

"Yes, Brooke Nasser, I do." He laughed softly, his eyes still moist. "Go home, my sweet."

With that, he got out of the SUV and came around to her side. He helped her out and drew her against him, kissing her to the point she was dizzy. "I love you."

"I love you too and I'm not leaving you."

"Brooke, you have to…"

The air around them cooled quickly and Brooke stayed close to Malik, knowing Elm was too close. No one was leaving at this point.

Snarling, Malik turned and pushed Brooke against the open car door, putting his body before hers. "Come out, coward!"

The darkness parted, and Elm stepped out from it, his long white-blond hair pulled back at the nape of his neck. He ran his gaze over Malik and sneered as additional men stepped forth from the darkness as well. As she spotted all the men who had hurt her, she realized he had the band back together again—including Haneez. Elm waved his hand in the air. "Something is different."

Brooke caressed her husband's back lightly. They were together in this no matter what. She'd not have her family hunted any longer.

Elm gasped. "Brooke, you're mated? To a shifter?"

Malik snarled low and deep, putting his hands out to his sides as fur coated them and claws emerged from his fingertips.

Elm curled his lip, disgust evident. "Like mother, like daughter. It would appear you wish for the same fate as her."

"You're not going to fucking touch her, asshole," said Malik, his voice deeper than normal.

Elm tossed his head back and laughed, doing his part to really drive home the evil villain vibe he was so good at. "And you think to stop me? You're a mere shifter. Nothing more. It's like child's play to me. Do yourself a favor and run away kitty. This is out of your league."

The second the words left Elm's mouth, Malik rotated his head and seemed to get even bigger before her. He roared as his skin began to shimmer, much like hers could do when tapping deeper into her gifts. Malik shimmered a bright gold as his shoulders heaved from his deep breathing.

Elm actually took a small step back, concern washing over his face. "W-what are you?"

Feeling empowered, Brooke moved to Malik's side and drew upon her own gifts. Her skin shimmered as well. Her eyes tingled, indicating they were glowing. "He's the son of the god king and he's my husband. Looks like he's really fucking letting his mean out now. I almost feel sorry for you." She glared at him. "Never mind. I don't feel the least bit sorry for you. I hope he bites your heads off."

Elm backed up more and Brooke knew he'd flee in an attempt to fight another day. She was sick of running. Sick of hiding and being afraid. She threw her power around the area, keeping everyone within the confines of it.

Elm froze and glanced around. "Little Fae, I will let my full power out to counter this spell and it will cause you great harm."

Malik didn't wait any longer. He charged Elm and the others. The other men with Elm converged on Malik in an attempt to protect Elm. Malik cut through them like butter.

Several pulled out weapons, aiming at her husband. Brooke threw power at them, lifting them in the air and slowly squeezing the life from them with no more than a thought. She felt empowered.

She felt like the daughter of a queen and a powerful shifter male.

Haneez aimed a rifle at her and before she could even think to throw power at him, Malik was there, slicing the man in half with one blow.

She'd never seen anything so horrifically awesome in her life. She nearly clapped and threw up all at once. If Edee would have been there, she'd have totally clapped and probably whistled too before slapping Malik's ass to let him know it was a great move.

Brooke found herself frozen in place, captivated by the sight of her husband, the king who didn't want to be king, as he continued mowing down the enemy. When he was done, only Elm was left standing.

The Fae put his hand out in Brooke's direction. "Come any closer and I will hit her with enough power to end that abomination I sense taking root in her."

Anger coursed through her so fast and furiously that her power took the lead. Wind swirled around her and the next thing she knew, her magik was lifting her off the ground and suspending her in the air. She glared at the man who had spent eight months torturing her and five years terrorizing her. Her power slammed into him and she felt it clawing at him from the inside out. Pulling on his power, stripping him of it little by little.

He gasped. "No!"

Malik snatched hold of Elm and lifted him up and over his head. With eyes of red and amber, and gold, shimmering skin, her husband looked up at Elm. "You will never again hurt my mate!"

With that, Malik ripped the man in two and then threw the two halves. Brooke blinked several times, needing a moment to register what happened and then to comprehend that the boogieman himself was now dead. He'd never be able to hurt her again. When it fully sank in, she lowered herself to the ground, clapping and whistling loudly, her power drawing back into her quickly.

Malik lowered his head, returning to normal in the blink of an eye. He had been covered in blood before, but there wasn't a drop of blood on him now. Looking up, he met her gaze. "It is done."

Brooke ran at him and threw herself into his arms.

He spun her around holding her tight. When he set her down, he kissed her lips and smiled sheepishly. "Can we maybe not mention to the guys that I did all that? They'll mock me endlessly for sparkling. Boomer will have T-shirts made. The Fang Gang will try to recruit me. And someone there will erect a gold statue lookalike of me with a Tut mask to pin up on the Asshole of the Week wall."

A choked sob came from her as she hugged him again. "Malik! You did it. You ended it."

He held her tight. "I plan to send his body to The Corporation gift wrapped as a warning to stay away from my family. I feel like they'll understand the message even if I don't include a card."

She smothered his face in kisses and he laughed, keeping her close to him. "I love you so much."

"Mmm, my sweet, I love you too." He exhaled and then lifted a brow. "While you're happy with me, I should probably tell you that what I just did more than likely sent up a giant flare that my brothers and cousins will sense. I know them. It doesn't matter how many centuries we put between seeing each other, they'll all come. And when they do, we're going to have a house full of ancient Egyptian cat-shifters."

Brooke grinned. "Hey, Edee might very well get her Egyptian prince after all."

Malik laughed and kissed her again. "Now. Let's head home, tell everyone *the tree* is dead, and prepare for house guests. Oh, and get Bethany into preschool. And get you back over for James or Auberi to take a look at you to start monitoring the pregnancy."

Brooke groaned. "Relax, Tut. It will all work out."

He grinned. "I normally hate that nickname, but when you say it, it makes me horny."

"Everything makes you horny," she said, rolling her eyes and laughing.

"No, my sweet. Only you do. So, everything about you makes me that way," he corrected.

THE END

About the Author

Dear Reader

Did you enjoy this title and want to know more about Mandy M. Roth, her pen names and all the titles she has available for purchase (over 100)?

About Mandy:

New York Times & *USA TODAY* Bestselling Author Mandy M. Roth is a self-proclaimed Goonie, loves 80s music and movies and wishes leg warmers would come back into fashion. She also thinks the movie The Breakfast Club should be mandatory viewing for...okay, everyone. When she's not dancing around her office to the sounds of the 80s or writing books, she can be found designing book covers for New York publishers, small presses, and indie authors.

Learn More:

To learn more about Mandy and her pen names, please visit http://www.mandyroth.com

For latest news about Mandy's newest releases and sales subscribe to her newsletter

http://www.mandyroth.com/newsletter/

To join Mandy's Facebook Reader Group: The Roth Heads, please visit

https://www.facebook.com/groups/MandyRothReader

Review this title:

Please let others know if you enjoyed this title. Consider leaving an honest review on the vendor site in which you purchased this title. Reviews help to spread the word and boost overall sales. This means more books in the series you love.

Thank you!

Printed in Great Britain
by Amazon